DRAGONS GONE WILD

**BAEN BOOKS
by DAN KOBOLDT**

THE BUILD-A-DRAGON SEQUENCE
Domesticating Dragons
Deploying Dragons
Dragons Gone Wild

To purchase any of these titles in e-book form, please go to www.baen.com.

DRAGONS GONE WILD

DAN KOBOLDT

DRAGONS GONE WILD

This is a work of fiction. All the characters and events portrayed in this book are fictional, and any resemblance to real people or incidents is purely coincidental.

Copyright © 2025 by Dan Koboldt

All rights reserved, including the right to reproduce this book or portions thereof in any form.

A Baen Books Original

Baen Publishing Enterprises
P.O. Box 1403
Riverdale, NY 10471
www.baen.com

ISBN: 978-1-6680-7303-2

Cover art by Dave Seeley

First printing, December 2025

Distributed by Simon & Schuster
1230 Avenue of the Americas
New York, NY 10020

Library of Congress Cataloging-in-Publication Data

Names: Koboldt, Dan (Daniel C.) author
Title: Dragons gone wild / Dan Koboldt.
Description: Riverdale, NY : Baen Publishing Enterprises, 2025. | Series: Build-a-dragon sequence ; book 3
Identifiers: LCCN 2025030428 (print) | LCCN 2025030429 (ebook) | ISBN 9781668073032 trade paperback | ISBN 9781964856445 ebook
Subjects: BISAC: FICTION / Science Fiction / Genetic Engineering | FICTION / Science Fiction / Action & Adventure | LCGFT: Science fiction | Novels | Fiction
Classification: LCC PS3611.O333 D73 2025 (print) | LCC PS3611.O333 (ebook)
LC record available at https://lccn.loc.gov/2025030428
LC ebook record available at https://lccn.loc.gov/2025030429

Printed in the United States of America

10 9 8 7 6 5 4 3 2 1

Dedication:
For Ray Miller, my first scientific mentor.

PROLOGUE

Lisa Hashimoto had spent thirty-six straight hours in the Mojave Desert and she'd be damned if she'd let it get to thirty-seven. Her shift had been over for some time now, but there was always more work to do in the bio trove. Eighty different species of plants thrived here. Most of them were non-native plants that needed arid climates to grow, having lost their own. For some, these were the last living examples. There were seed banks, of course, but even those carried risks. Buildings could lose power. Governments could topple. Hell, the Cairo Repository—one of the foremost seed banks in Northern Africa—had been robbed two years ago by criminals in search of new varieties of marijuana. No place offered complete safety for the last of a plant species.

Besides, even if you had them, seeds didn't always germinate. Countless varieties of now-extinct plants whose seeds were found in Mediterranean shipwrecks or thawed out of glaciers offered proof of that. Every seed wanted its perfect set of conditions. That's what had fascinated Lisa about horticulture, what had drawn her to a lifetime of roots, soils, and seasons.

She finished tucking the last of the Moroccan wandering cactus back into its designated area, and then shook her hands free of the heavy work gloves. It was hot here, desert hot, but that didn't bother her so much as the green tinge to the westward sky. In the last three days, it had grown from a narrow band of fuzz to a thick smudge above the horizon. It looked like a day-old bruise. A storm might look like this, except it was advancing too slowly. Yet still advancing. And the barometric pressure had held steady.

"Dr. Hashimoto?" Kenny Bruce, her research assistant, stood at the door of the tiny metal-frame trailer that served as their base of operations. He was watching the horizon, too.

"Any change to the barometer?" She'd assigned him to watch it, and Kenny knew to tell her the second it dropped. She already knew the answer.

"No, still holding steady."

That meant it wasn't a storm, but it was still something. "Send the drone."

Kenny, of course, already had it charged and on the roof. He started the launch sequence as Lisa came inside and began shedding her desert gear. Everything but the boots went straight into the recycler. She washed her hands at the water reclaimer and then hurried over to the comm center on the far side of the trailer. Rocky desert terrain scrolled past on three viewscreens, one for each of the drone's camera feeds.

"What's your altitude?" she asked.

"Fifty meters."

"Better make it eighty."

Kenny complied without comment. Altitude and speed were the only user inputs required; other than these, the drone flew itself. Kenny sensed the urgency and had set the speed to three quarters of maximum. The drone slowed itself as it neared rougher terrain to the northwest. The burnt sienna landscape became a jumble of rocky crags and boulders, scoured by centuries of sandstorms. Once it was clear, the drone leveled out.

The cameras, too, self-adjusted to maintain focus and capture as much imagery as possible. The video feed snapped back to the horizon, now obscured by a massive, black-green smudge. It reached hundreds of feet into the air, darkening a wide band of sky.

And it was moving. Waves slid over the band like ripples across a pond. Each successive undulation of shadow and sunlight, shadow and sunlight, followed an eerily familiar rhythm. Certain patterns exist in both nature and mathematics; Lisa knew them well. The fact the dark cloud followed one meant it was alive, that it comprised living things. Not plants, of course, but their age-old biological adversary.

"What the hell do you think that is?" Kenny asked. He'd worked for her for almost eighteen months now and was a devout Presbyterian. *Hell* was the first curse she'd ever heard him use.

"We're in trouble."

"Why? Are they birds?"

"Worse, I'm afraid," Lisa said. "They're locusts."

CHAPTER ONE
On Dragons

Dragons lived in human imagination for centuries before we brought them to life. In cave paintings and stories and other art forms, dragons are fantastical creatures. Powerful, cunning, and most of all, dangerous. I think we created them in part to remind ourselves that humans might not always enjoy our position at the top of the food chain.

I'll be honest. For most of my life, I didn't care much about dragons. I liked them just fine, and I enjoyed the stories and games where dragons featured prominently. But my mild appreciation paled next to my brother Connor's obsession. If there was a book with a dragon, he read it. A movie, he saw it. A game, he played it, especially if the point was to tame or befriend a dragon.

I guess I shouldn't have been surprised that he wanted one of his own. The weird part was that he never told me. I just went over to visit him at Mom's house one day, and there it was.

Me, I was swimming in dragons. Octavius was enough, but I'd had the genius idea to get him some siblings. Now I played host to an entire off-the-books reptilian menagerie. All named for emperors, and it was like they knew it. I never truly appreciated the things required to keep a reptilian pet alive and happy, day in and day out, until I had one of my own. Turns out, they're not zero maintenance.

If I left my dragonets alone too long, they'd tear up my condo. If I forgot to feed them, they'd tear up my condo. Heck, if I refused to let Marcus Aurelius binge-watch Animal Planet, he'd then go around and get the other dragonets fired up about something, and together they'd tear up my condo. At least I understood why we got so many returns. I had a bit more sympathy for the customers who threw in the towel. Not complete sympathy, of course. I'd never give up my dragonets no matter how much inconvenience they caused me.

On the bright side, Build-A-Dragon's new partnership with the U.S. Department of Defense seemed to be progressing smoothly. That was as far as I knew, of course. Shortly after being awarded the contract, the DOD decided that not everyone on Build-A-Dragon's design team needed to keep the security clearance required for a defense contractor. We elected to maintain credentials for just two people—Evelyn Chang and Priti Korrapati. The former was the big boss, and the latter was our most capable design tweaker. Or, as she insisted we call her, *refinement specialist*.

It made sense. Andrew Wong and I were best at new prototypes, at designing dragons we'd never seen before. Maybe that meant we had more chaotic minds. Korrapati, on the other hand, took a rigorous and detailed approach with everything she did. Her code, unlike my own, looked like something out of a programming textbook.

That left me and Wong to tackle new design prototypes for a changing world. Dogs had come back to a joyous global welcome. Dragons still had their uses, of course—our contract with the DOD certainly kept the incubators humming—but the business had changed. Dogs resumed many of the roles that dragons had filled during their absence. Not all of them, of course. Dragons were better suited for some tasks, like providing security. Yet the return of dogs at the expense of dragons seemed inevitable, so we had to find new niche markets.

The day we got the call started just like any other. I rolled into the parking garage at 7:43. Traffic had been mercifully light, and I looked forward to getting a decent jump on the day. Korrapati would arrive at 8:30 sharp and I had a briefing with Evelyn at nine. That gave me half an hour of uninterrupted dragon-design time if I was lucky. I parked in my assigned spot, set the alarm on my Tesla, and hurried to the door of Build-A-Dragon's headquarters.

Wong ambushed me in my own office. The thing was, the automatic lights had been shut off, which told me that he'd either kept perfectly still after entering, or more likely was dozing in the guest chair waiting for me. I walked in, the lights flickered on, and I jumped. "Wong! Jesus!"

"Good morning, Noah Parker."

"You scared the crap out of me."

"Sorry. Just excited to get to work."

"Oh yeah? On what?"

He shrugged. "Whatever we have."

"Are there any customs in the queue?" I asked, already feeling I knew the answer.

"All finished yesterday."

"Do you think any of the DOD models need help?"

Wong shrugged. "No clearance."

"Oh, right." I'd already forgotten about that. To be fair, Korrapati would most likely be offended if I assigned Wong to her project. "You could start working on a new prototype."

He gave me a flat look. "If I do, does it print?"

I wanted to say that it would be printed, that we were still in the business of rolling out new dragon models. But that probably wasn't true. Given the sudden new competition from canines in every corner of the business, Evelyn seemed to be advocating caution. Rolling out prototypes into new product lines required a not-insignificant investment of resources. Currently the DOD was taxing a lot of those systems. Evelyn had told me more than once that she wanted to see what would happen with the consumer market as dogs returned before we made big strategic decisions. So we could certainly propose new models, but getting them into production might be a tough sell. "I can't promise that."

He made an unhappy sound.

"Tell you what. If you come up with something good, we'll print a prototype." One of the few true perks of the DDD—Director of Dragon Design—title was the ability to print dragon eggs without higher approval. I'd spent most of my work capital hanging on to those privileges in spite of the financial headwinds. I figured I might as well use them.

"Really?"

"Absolutely." I might take some heat from Evelyn for this, but I felt like the team needed it. "You need to stay sharp, right?"

"Wong means 'sharp' in Chinese," he said.

Yeah, right. I'd been teaching myself Chinese and thus knew that it was one of the most common surnames in mainland China. Wong was always trying to tell me it meant certain things.

He left in a hurry, and I knew he'd dive into a prototype without delay. I remembered those days when I was the one pitching new designs to the director. Knowing you'd get it printed, even as a prototype, brought a certain thrill.

I sighed, and not for the first time, questioned some of my life choices. My girlfriend, Summer, had even asked me, not long ago, if I was sure about taking the job.

"Why do you even want this?" she'd asked.

We were talking about my going back to work at Build-A-Dragon. This was right after everything had gone down with Robert Greaves and the dogs in the desert. When Evelyn had asked us to lunch and dangled the prospect of becoming the triple-D to lure me back.

"She's offering me the most coveted job in biotech," I told her.

"So what?"

"It's a big step up. Director-level privileges."

"Director-level *responsibilities*," she said.

"I'm sure that's part of it."

"Didn't you tell me that you were glad you didn't have her job? You were happy to just do the science."

Man, she'd have made a great lawyer. Anything I said was filed away for future use against me. "It's the natural progression for me. The next step."

"That doesn't mean you have to take it."

"Why shouldn't I?" I asked, aware that I was sounding defensive.

"If it's going to make you unhappy, you shouldn't do it."

"Someone has to."

"Then let someone else."

But there was no one else. At least, there was no one else with the right combination of experience and ability. Wong was an excellent designer, but not leadership material. Korrapati could have taken the job, but she hadn't wanted it. In fact, it had taken a lot of persuasion to get her to come back to the company in the first place. So I stepped up, for better or worse, and now the lack of design work was my problem.

My office phone rang, which startled Wong and me both.

"Is that your phone?" he asked.

"I didn't realize I even had a phone," I said. Telecom was fully integrated with our systems, so when the phone rang a huge, shaking telephone icon in bright green took over my large projection monitor. Honestly, it was a little terrifying.

"Who is it?"

"I have no idea." The caller's number glared at me from the top of my projection screen, but I didn't recognize it. *It's probably spam.* Maybe I'd won the Egyptian lottery again, or had been approved for a small business loan. Scammers were nothing if not persistent. Even so, it was the first call I'd gotten in the office and it piqued my curiosity. I looked at Wong. "I'd better take this."

Wong gave a thumbs-up and shuffled out of the office.

It took me a minute to figure out how to answer the call, which involved making a swiping motion on my touch panel. Hell, even the computer system seemed surprised that someone was calling, or that I'd want to answer. "Hello?"

There was a moment of static, and then a woman's voice came through. "Hello?"

"This is Noah Parker."

"You're Build-A-Dragon, right?"

"Yes." A moment of inspiration came. "This is the dragon design department."

"Good, you're..." she trailed off.

"I'm sorry?"

"I said you're just what I need." She mumbled something unintelligible. "Sorry, our connection here is crap."

"It's all right." I'd just figured out how to adjust the speaker volume, so I punched it up a few notches. "I can hear you fine."

"I'm Lisa Hashimoto, a botanist at Arizona State University."

Yeah, sure you are. She was a scientist I couldn't see on video, and she just happened to work at my alma mater. Which was a matter of public record. I nearly called her on it, but I didn't want to confirm any of the scammer information. "Hey, Go, Sun Devils!"

"Right. Go, Sun Devils," she said in the least-convincing show of spirit ever.

I decided to test her. "What can I do for you, Dr. Hatamoto?"

"It's *Hashimoto*. Lisa Hashimoto."

"Right, my mistake." *Spammer 1, Noah 0.* But I was just getting warmed up.

"I got your name from Dr. Sato."

Crap. I sat up so quickly I nearly fell out of my chair. This was either the most informed scam artist in the history of time, or she was legit. And here I was being a jerk. "Oh. I'm sorry."

"Why? He's a good guy."

"The best," I said. "I . . . sort of thought you were a scammer."

"Have I asked for your social security number?"

Touché. "All right, I thought you were a *very good* scammer."

"This isn't a scam. You design custom dragons, right?"

"Yes, absolutely."

"I'm responsible for two hundred acres of experimental and exotic crops at a bio trove in the Mojave Desert."

"All right." I really didn't see what dragons had to do with experimental botany. Maybe she thought they were tiny, like honeybees.

"There's a horde of locusts growing by the day. Our current projections show it's headed right for our bio trove."

"I'm sorry, did you say *horde of locusts*, like in the Bible?"

"If that helps you," she said.

"Did you do something to offend a higher power?" I couldn't resist asking.

"Who hasn't?"

I laughed. "Good point."

"Locust swarms happen all the time in third-world countries, but that rarely gets in the news. It can happen here, too. Especially when there are severe drought conditions."

"Well, we've got those." Arizona deserts were always dry, but the current rainless streak was setting all kinds of records. Even the cacti were looking a little wilted. "How bad is it?"

"Enough to destroy years of experiments and probably end my career."

Yikes. Now I understood why Dr. Sato had sent her my way. My career had been on the verge of ending a few times. I knew all the feels. Panic. Desperation. Helplessness. "I'm sorry. That really sucks."

"I don't intend to let that happen," she said. "I spoke to my program officer today about diverting some major funds. We want to place a large order for custom dragons that we can set loose against the locust swarms."

It was a crazy idea and I didn't think it would work, but I didn't want to tell her that. "Our customers aren't really supposed to release their dragons into the wild. They can't survive out there, and there are these rules we have to follow..."

She scoffed. "That's a load of crap and we both know it."

"What?"

"Give me your email address," she said.

"Why?"

"I'm going to send you some of the *many* trail-camera photos we have of dragons wandering into our bio trove."

"Pets run away sometimes," I said, rather unconvincingly.

"That's your explanation?"

"Uh, sure."

"Well, I'd better send them to the EPA along with this environmental impact study I've put together."

Oh, hell no. The last thing we wanted was the government poking around, asking awkward questions about dragons appearing where they shouldn't. "All right, all right, you made your point." Besides, she'd already used some of the magic words, *major funds* and *large order*. "Give me the specs."

CHAPTER TWO
The Fail-Safe

"So I had an interesting call today," I told Summer later. We'd driven her jeep up to the Apache Wash Trailhead in the Sonoran Preserve north of Glendale. The trailhead served three major trails of varying difficulty, but if you hung a right at the big saguaro fork you took the most ambitious one, the Apache Vista Trail. It was a relatively smooth rock trail, flanked by scrub grass and prickles on either side but still wide enough for us to walk together. The dragonets circled lazily overhead, chirping to one another and enjoying the late afternoon sun. From a distance, they could probably be mistaken for birds, I supposed. The parking lot wasn't crowded, though, and by unspoken rule the hikers here minded their own business.

"Yeah, me too," she said. "But you go first."

"This botanist who works up in Mojave called to see if we'd make some dragons for pest control."

She wrinkled her brow. "What kind of pests?"

"A plague of locusts," I said, savoring the phrase.

"Shut up." She went to punch my arm, but I caught her fist and laced my fingers with hers together. Maybe it was trite but I liked holding her hand, even when only the dragons were around to see it. I really liked it public, when I could feel the eyes of people watching us, no doubt thinking *wow, that guy's punching above his weight class.* Which was, to be fair, absolutely true. We'd been dating for over a year now; she'd met my mom and brother; I'd met her dad. We still had our

13

separate condos but I was beginning to wonder if that still made a lot of sense. The dragonets were the hardest part of it. We could be together or separate, at my place or hers, but we could never be together at one place *without* the dragonets.

"I'm serious. A plague of locusts."

"I thought that was a biblical disaster from ancient times."

"Yeah, me too. They think it's probably the same species, though. Something called a desert locust. They're from North Africa and the Middle East, but now we have populations in the Southwest."

"So, this is an environmental control thing," she said, with a tone that raised warning hackles on the back of my neck. It had the warning tone of *you shouldn't be doing this because no one should*, which was Summer Bryn's default position when it came to messing with nature. She only granted dragons a pass because they were a synthetic organism, not a natural species.

"Oh no, this is a pro-environment thing," I said quickly. I told her about the bio trove and the plant preserve Dr. Hashimoto hoped to protect.

"So, what do they want the dragons to do?"

"I don't know, eat the locusts or something."

She looked up to where our dragonets were having an airborne fight over the last of the burritos we'd brought for food. Marcus Aurelius, the runt of his litter, had slept for most of the drive and thus decided to join the hike with half a burrito in his mouth. Octavius, my oldest dragon, had clamped around his shoulders and was trying to steal what remained.

"Octavius!" I shouted. "Let him go, that's his."

Octavius snuck one more bite of the burrito and then released the smaller dragon. Part of the burrito fell to the sand, which didn't stop three of their siblings from crash-landing to fight over it.

"They *will* eat anything," Summer said. "But isn't a swarm of locusts, like, a lot?"

"All that means is that if we design the right dragon, we'll get to print a lot of them." I sighed. "It would be good to hear the biological printer running all the time."

"Sure, as long as they don't create a surplus." She gasped and dropped my hand. "Please tell me this isn't a One-way dragon situation."

"We haven't gotten that far yet. Evelyn has to get approvals first, and that might take a while." *Plus, I don't want to get in a drawn-out discussion about the possibility of releasing dragons into the desert.* I knew how that would go. "So that was my call. What was yours?"

"A botanist called me, too, and asked if I could spend my weekends catching grasshoppers with a net. They have a big problem."

I laughed. "Shut up. What was it really?"

"You know our net-positive concept building?"

"Of course." Summer was an architect for a large green-energy firm in Phoenix. They'd designed both of the buildings our condos were in, which were net-zero buildings that basically produced as much renewable energy as their tenants used. A great idea, really, as long as you didn't mind lukewarm showers. She'd been one of the leaders on a new project, a net-positive building, which not only produced its own energy but put some back into the grid. It was a big deal, at least in the green-architecture world. Summer got interviewed by a couple of news outlets and their company won several awards.

"A recruiter reached out after seeing the articles. He has some big corporate client that wants to hire green architects to build their new headquarters."

"Whoa!"

"I know, right?"

"I mean, I'm not surprised. That project is huge, and it's going to save every builder boatloads of money."

She gave me a side-look with eyes narrowed.

"Plus, you know, good for the environment and all that."

She nodded, satisfied. "So, we were talking and he—"

"Wait, you spoke?"

"Yeah, he asked for a call."

Of course he asked for a call. After he'd met her, talked to her, he probably wanted a hundred more calls. "Why did you give him the time of day?"

She shrugged. "He said he had questions about the project."

"Yeah, I know but . . ." The fact of the matter was that I didn't really care for corporate recruiters. They learned about talented people, got their claws into them, and yanked them out to drop into some slightly better paying gig while taking a commission on the new salary that lasted forever. They'd come after my designers once or twice. They were always vague about intentions, usually asking to "set up a call" so they could start their pitch. I guess I saw it as an unnecessary disruption to happy workplaces.

"But what?" she asked.

"Nothing, nothing." I held up my hands, because my opinions were just opinions. Scathing, yes, but only my opinions. "Well, what did he say?"

"He said the market is hot for people with my experience."

"I believe that," I said. "Plus, now you're internet-famous with all of those video interviews, like the hair-flipping one." That was a short video segment where she'd answered several questions and also flipped her hair back a couple of times because it kept falling in her face. The way they edited the final clip, it was like she flipped her hair every six words or so.

She patted my cheek and said sweetly, "Not all of us get known for whistleblowing."

"Ouch." I suppose I deserved that. Unfortunately, it was true: if my name appeared online, it was in the context of yet another article about the now-disgraced former CEO of Build-A-Dragon, Robert Greaves. "Well, are you really looking for another job?"

"I don't know. The net-plus project was my life for two years. Now that it's done, I'm not sure I'll do anything more visible."

"I hate to see you leave, though. The firm has been good to you." Plus, I'd gone to their holiday party and the food was outstanding. Lukewarm, like their showers, but outstanding.

"That's true."

We reached the end of the Apache Vista Trail, which had led us to the top of a large hill. From this lookout point we could see the desert for miles in every direction, or turn back for a spectacular view of Phoenix. The dragonets all settled on a big rock formation near the top of the hill to take it in.

"Do you really think you'll change jobs?" To me, it sounded like a hassle.

"I don't mind talking about possibilities. Besides, it's nice to be wanted."

"You *are* wanted." I grinned.

She rolled her eyes. "Not like that. For my *architecture* skills."

"I like those, too."

"Just shush and enjoy the view."

I did, but I was also thinking about this recruiter. Everything was going so well—her job, my job, us together. If he got his way, things would change. I wanted them to stay the same.

When Build-A-Dragon first produced living, breathing dragons from the genetic sequence alone, it got a lot of attention. This was before my time with the company, but I remembered it well. Some of the attention was good, and some was bad. Arguably the worst came from the United States government, which felt that "synthetic organisms" should be regulated since they did not exist in the natural world. I knew that much from public news feeds. What I hadn't known until Evelyn read me in was the extent of the pitched legal battles that ensued.

Naturally, the government wanted all kinds of regulation. The company, through its expensive lobbying firms, pushed back against any such measures at every level of government.

"What did we want them to do, exactly?" I'd asked her once during a field trial.

"Ideally, no regulations at all."

"Seriously, you wanted them to let us do whatever we wanted, without restrictions?"

She'd looked at me and shrugged. "If there had to be restrictions, do you really want them written by politicians?"

"All right, I take your point."

The U.S. government and the influential lobbyists eventually found a compromise that neither side loved. Build-A-Dragon could produce dragons and sell them under two conditions. First, every dragon we sold had to be registered by the new owner. That was the gimme term—it was in the company's interest to keep records of people who bought its products—but our highly paid intermediaries acted like this was a huge ask. They grudgingly promised to make dragon registration part of the purchasing process. They elected not to mention that the company data-mined far more information about its customers than their current name and address.

Technically speaking, all of my dragonets were unregistered, so I was in pretty serious violation of the rule. In my defense, I hadn't so much bought Octavius as stolen his egg, and he was a prototype rather than a production model. I doubted this would be a sound argument if I were ever caught. Especially if it became apparent that I had several such dragons in my possession. The prototype loophole was all I had, though.

The second condition was more serious: Build-A-Dragon needed approval from the Environmental Protection Agency for any dragon prototypes that would be intentionally released in the wild. They'd gotten it for the Guardian series, of course. Apparently that had been an easier sell, though: the EPA was facing huge pressure to find answers for the feral hog problem, and Reptilian Corporation, as it was called back then, was offering one. Just as the FDA sometimes approved new drugs for Alzheimer's even if there was no evidence that they halted the incurable disease, the EPA was willing to take a chance. With that groundwork laid, I figured the EPA approval thing was more or less a done deal for future models. So when Evelyn pinged me to say she'd heard back from them about the newest prototype, I hurried up to her office to get the good news.

"They said no," she told me flatly.

"What?"

"The EPA sent back the application without approval."

I felt a moment of alarm, but then irritation shoved it aside. "Can they do that?"

She shrugged. "They're the EPA."

I should have expected this. The EPA people could do whatever they wanted, lobbyists or no lobbyists. So we had to play ball. "What are their concerns?"

"Mainly the possibility of a synthetic organism persisting in the wild."

"We have the fail-safe built in." It was a genetically encoded amino acid deficiency that ensured our dragons couldn't survive unless they were under human care. All of our food and supplements provided the missing amino acid. "You told them about that, didn't you?"

"Of course." She tapped her fingernails on the desk and then gave me a side-look. "Apparently they've received a number of reports of dragons living out in the desert."

I schooled my face as best I could, and kept my eyes on the desk. "You don't say."

"You wouldn't know anything about that, would you?"

"I haven't seen anything." I was proud of how sincere I sounded.

"Yes, this is shocking new information to both of us," she said flatly.

Not for the first time, I wondered how much she knew about things I hadn't necessarily told her. Like the fact that some of my Condor models had survived and joined a herd of feral dragons that seemed to turn up whenever Simon Redwood did. Or how the deadly feral attack dragon had nearly killed her predecessor.

"In any event, they would like us to reengineer the fail-safe and add other safeguards to ensure that our dragons do not establish themselves in the wild."

"What kind of safeguards?"

"That's for us to determine, to some extent. But they must be indefatigable. Enough to convince the EPA that there is no risk of our dragons gaining a foothold in these wild environments. It will take some work."

"A lot of work," I grumbled.

"Yes, most likely. But this is important."

I didn't ask, and she didn't say, that our work on any environmental prototypes was on hold until this got done. Without the EPA's rubber stamp, we stood no chance of sending dragon eggs out for hatching in the wild. In other words, this was going to cost us time we really didn't have. "We'll give it the full-court press."

"Thanks, Noah. I knew you would. In the meantime, I'm meeting with our lobbying firm tomorrow."

"Do you think they'll be helpful?"

"Honestly, no. But it's their job to try." She sighed and shook her head. "Sometimes I wish things would go a bit easier for once."

I knew what she meant. It seemed like we jumped from one crisis to the next without any time to breathe between them. All I could do was shrug and give her a rueful grin. "It's always something with us, isn't it?"

I stopped by the break room for coffee and then proceeded to the design lab to get to work. Wong was there, as always, half-hidden by his tower of empty energy drink cans. He was around two thirds through a can-cycle; in about ten days, they'd all disappear and he'd start over.

"Hey, Wong," I said.

He was mumbling to himself in Mandarin, but brightened when he saw me. "Hello, Noah Parker. Are we designing the Wonghoppers?"

"The what?"

"Dragon eats grasshoppers, designed by Wong. Wonghoppers."

I chuckled, because as Wong-inspired names went, this one wasn't bad. "I wish. The Wonghopper has to wait until we redesign the fail-safe."

"We already have that." Wong waved this off, as if unimportant. "Works good enough."

"Not for the EPA."

He wrinkled his nose; that summarized Wong's feelings about government oversight. He came from Shenzen where people could pretty much do what they wanted, at least as far as the science was concerned. China had far more interest in controlling speech. "What do they know?"

"They know some dragons are living in the wild. Specifically, out in the desert."

That chased the casual grin from his face. He remembered what we did out there, and what it was like when the dragons came. He didn't know the whole story, though. I hadn't told him everything about the Condors and the herd of dragons that seemed to show up whenever Simon Redwood needed them.

Or when I needed them. No, it was best not to think about that. "It's not the end of the world. We just need to come up with something that works better."

"Like remembering fail-safe on every design, even prototypes," he said.

"Yes, like that," I said dryly. "Any ideas for how to get started?"

"One-way protocol?"

I grimaced on instinct, remembering our distasteful project creating a courier dragon that expired upon delivery of its message. The science was good; the experience was not. "I'm still trying to forget about that one."

He shrugged. "Have to start somewhere."

That was a fair point, and whether I liked it or not, Evelyn still considered the One-way dragons one of our cleverest designs. The One-ways died happy, at least. That was better than I could say for some of the ferals. "All right, but these prototypes won't be delivering messages. So what's the trigger?"

"Depends on what they're doing."

"Right, and we won't always know that." We wanted as broad of an EPA authorization as possible; I knew that much. Going through this process every time we wanted to design a dragon for a different environment would be brutal to say the least.

"Maybe we do some research on what others do?" Wong asked.

At first I thought he meant designing dragons, and I nearly replied, haughtily, that we were the only ones who did that. But it occurred to me he was talking about the general idea of releasing genetically engineered creatures into the wild. Build-A-Dragon was arguably the most visible and commercially successful endeavor of that type, but it was actually a vibrant field. For example, the state of Florida routinely released millions of genetically altered sterile mosquitoes in an effort to control malaria and other mosquito-borne diseases. "Florida mosquitoes."

"Fast-growing salmon."

"Yes, those things are crazy. Oh, and there's the bacteria that digest plastic."

Wong nodded. "I start making list."

He got out his phone while I brought up another projection monitor to pull up the scientific literature. In addition to mosquitoes, various forms of genetically engineered organisms had been deployed in the field. Some of those were viral and bacterial pathogens, which sounded a little frightening. Apparently it was all the rage to conduct biowarfare on rodents in Europe in the first half of the twentieth century. Until humans started getting sick, at least.

I shook my head. "Biowarfare against rats."

"Crazy," Wong said.

"Those were the days, eh? Doing whatever you wanted to solve a societal problem."

"Spreading poison."

I nudged his shoulder. "No government oversight, though."

He snorted. "Even better, no social media."

"Well, let's focus on the programs that didn't end in PR disasters. Maybe they had good strategies."

We got to work.

CHAPTER THREE
The Biomass

Not long ago, scientists estimated that the combined weight of all insects on the planet—the biomass—was about the same as all humans and our livestock combined. A lot of people thought of insects as pests, but they played vital roles in several ecosystems. They broke down decaying matter, aerated the soil, ate and were eaten. Granted, they also destroyed crops, spread diseases, and stung people occasionally, but the good outweighed the bad. Arguably the most important contribution insects made was to the food chain. That role went back millions of years to the age of pterosaurs—which I liked to think of as ancestors of our dragons. The earliest pterosaurs were small reptiles that fed mainly on insects, and evolved the power of flight to do so.

Granted, Simon Redwood had designed our company's first dragons to pursue a very different type of prey, the feral hog. Our domesticated dragons were supposed to eat the specialized food we sold. Customer feedback and my own experience suggested they'd eat about anything, though. Raw meat. Table scraps. Maybe the occasional house cat. It was almost like they'd absorbed the ravenous appetite of the feral hogs the original dragon model was designed to kill. Come to think of it, we should probably have gotten a lot more complaints about dragons dying if the fail-safe worked as designed. Most customers never read the manual, much less followed the instructions.

Wong hunched over his desk when I returned to the design lab. My office wasn't here but it still drew me in when I wasn't paying attention.

It was like the biological printer—the God Machine—exerted some strange magnetic pull.

"*Nihao, Wong sien-shung,*" I said.

He didn't startle, which told me he'd expected me. "Noah Parker. *Ni Zamaya?*"

That was a casual how's-it-going question, and I answered with one of my favorite phrases. "*Ma ma hou hou.*" It meant *so-so* but literally translated as *horse horse tiger tiger*. Granted, the first few times I'd used it, I'd gotten the tone wrong on the first two words and said something far less polite by accident.

Wong chuckled, probably remembering the same thing. "What did Evelyn say?"

"She said the EPA wants a better demonstration of the biological fail-safes."

He responded with a word in Mandarin that I knew, but hadn't been brave enough to use. "We already have good fail-safe."

"How sure are we?"

He waved the question off. "Amino acid deficiency. Guaranteed."

"I know, but we haven't done any rigorous testing, have we?"

"Not sure."

"I was just thinking, if the fail-safe worked perfectly, wouldn't we have gotten a lot more customer complaints?"

"We don't get complaints," he said.

"That's a good point," He didn't mean that no one complained; he meant that the complaints didn't come directly to us. Build-A-Dragon had a customer service department that handled most of the contact with our customer base. Since I'd become the director of our little group, I'd gotten occasional summaries from them. I made a mental note to ask them about dragons going off the diet. "But let's say you had to start over and make a perfect fail-safe. How would you do it?"

Wong produced an apple from somewhere within the piles of junk atop his workstation. "Have to think." He took an enormous bite, and the next few words were completely unintelligible.

"Um, you have something in your..." I gestured vaguely at his mouth.

Wong pressed on. "Multiple srfschorm."

"What?"

"Multiple strategies of attack."

"Biological redundancy?" It wasn't a bad idea. There were countless examples of pairs of genes that performed similar functions, like breaking down a key metabolite or providing a key protein—kind of like Mother Nature's backup systems for organism survival. They were hard to study with classical genetics techniques because you had to alter both genes to disrupt their usual function. Tough for designing experiments, but good for survival, I supposed. Now we wanted to do the opposite: create multiple pathways to killing the organism. That's what we were talking about, after all. The only true fail-safe was death. "It goes against nature, but I suppose it's necessary."

Wong shrugged. "No approval, no dragons."

That's what I liked about him. He was a realist to a fault.

"All right, you want to work the metabolic angle? You're stronger at it."

"Sure."

"I'll see what I can do with neural pathways." That was my own strength, mood and behavior. When I'd first come to Build-A-Dragon after they licensed my biological simulator, one of the first things I did was add an expansion module that attempted to estimate behavioral characteristics. Most of that came from calculating the rate of neurotransmitter synthesis, release, uptake, and recycling. I loved a good neurotransmitter.

"What neural pathways?" he asked.

That's a good question. "I haven't decided yet."

"Dopamine is good."

"Yes, but I was thinking to try serotonin first."

Wong grunted. "Good luck."

Both of those were so-called monoamine neurotransmitters, a class of brain chemicals found in nearly all vertebrates. Serotonin played a critical role in regulating mood. Once released by a neuron, it could either be repackaged for future use, or degrade into its chemical components. The enzyme that handled such degradation was called monoamine oxidase, or MAO. Several antidepressant drugs worked as inhibitors of that enzyme, abbreviated MAOIs.

Wong had already turned back to his workstation and opened the design for the Rover, which still remained one of our top sellers.

"No, start with the Guardian," I said. That was the original Build-A-Dragon prototype, the one designed to hunt feral hogs.

Wong hesitated and gave me a side-eye. "Not domesticated."

"It's what we got the original approval for, and it's designed for wild environments." Granted, that also meant this dragon wouldn't necessarily bond with humans, but I wasn't sure we wanted that anyway.

He obliged, and I left him to it. On my walk back to my office, I was already thinking about the best way to tackle the neurotransmitter angle. There was another reason I wanted to start with the Guardian. It had far less genetic manipulation than our domesticated models, especially in the neural circuitry. Domesticating the wild animal had required a surprising amount of engineering. Evelyn had held a contest back in the day, one that Wong officially won with some unofficial help from me.

I was glad Wong was redesigning the metabolic form of the failsafe, though that one was pretty simple. All it required was picking an organic compound the dragon needed but couldn't synthesize on its own. Ideally, it would be something easily supplemented in dragon food, like a rare but vital amino acid. Iron and copper offered good avenues of attack, too, because the genes that controlled their absorption and transport were well-studied. Unabsorbed metals tended to collect in dangerous areas, like the brain, and that could be fatal.

Neurotransmitters were a bit more challenging. You couldn't remove a neurotransmitter from the dragon's repertoire. They'd sleep twenty hours a day, refuse to eat, or worse, turn homicidal. The trick was to figure out how to harness the receptors and transporters that kept all of those chemicals balanced. We had designed a neurotransmitter-dragon-destruct sequence once before. Once triggered, it initiated a self-feedback loop that essentially led to the dragon dying of satisfaction. This wild dragon wouldn't be domesticated, and we couldn't rely on a specific event to serve as the off-switch. Quite the opposite.

When Evelyn found me, I was talking to myself. I did that a lot when I was deep into the dragon genetic code. When I worked in the design lab proper, the God Machine's white noise did a good job of drowning it out. Now, alone in my too-quiet office, the self talk was harder to hide.

"Noah Parker, you are doing it again," Evelyn said.

"Oh. Evelyn." I forced myself to blink and look away from my screen. "I know, I'm talking to myself. It helps me think."

"It helps you look like a crazy person."

"Fine, fine." I tapped a hot key that hid all of my projection monitors so I could see her better. "*Ching tsin. Ching tsuah.*" That was an invitation to come in and sit down.

She shook her head. "I only stopped by to see how your work on the new fail-safe is coming."

"Wong and I started today. We're each taking a different line of attack."

"Multiple approaches. I like it." She gave me a sort of side-look. "I'm guessing you gave Wong the metabolic pathway."

"You guess correctly."

"What about you?"

"Guess," I said.

She pursed her lips the way she did when her fantastic mind was at work. "Neurotransmitters."

"God!" I laughed. "How do you do that?"

"Everyone has tendencies." Her smile faded, and then it was back to business. "So, any progress?"

"Hopefully Wong is making some. I'm kind of stuck."

"Your design of the One-way dragon had a neurotransmitter mechanism."

"Yes, I thought of that. But with the One-ways we knew what the trigger would be." They were single-use messenger dragons. Delivery of the message was the end of the line. The little flicker of accomplishment triggered a cascade of ever-increasing neurotransmitters. I told myself it meant the dragon died of pleasure. It was good, clean, and reliable. We had countless videos of One-ways to prove it.

"A wild dragon is unpredictable," Evelyn said.

"Now you see the problem."

"I trust my Director of Dragon Design to take care of it."

Uh-oh. I loved hearing her talk about me that way. But whenever she title-dropped me, it meant she was softening me up for bad news. "So, how are things going in the C-suite?"

"C-suite?"

"Corporate suite." I grinned. "Or in your case, the carnivorous plants suite."

"You are very clever," she said, but her heart wasn't in it. Something was bothering her.

"What's going on?"

"We got an update from the EPA about the wild-dragon program."

"Oh?"

"They put us on the fast-track approval process."

"Hey, that's great!" Anything involving the government immediately became more palatable when the words *fast track* were added.

"Yes, but it moves up our timelines. Also, we won't know for certain when the EPA inspection team is coming. They give us a window."

"How wide of a window?"

"Thirty days. They can show up anytime during that period."

Naturally, I didn't like the sound of that. With stakes this high, we needed to plan and rehearse every moment of the demonstration. But the EPA was the EPA, and they'd do things the way they wanted. "When does it start?"

"Three weeks."

"What?"

"The window starts in three weeks."

"That's way too soon."

She shrugged. "It's part of the fast-track process. We didn't realize until we'd already submitted our application."

"Evelyn, that's crazy! We don't even have the design yet."

"I'm sorry, Noah, but there is nothing I can do. The alternative would be to withdraw our application, which would mean pushing back approval."

"For how long?"

"Twelve months, maybe longer."

That was too long. We both knew it. Developing the wild dragons would take time, and the market window wouldn't be open forever. We'd make the deadline because we had no choice. That wasn't really the question. I did have one, though. I groaned and rubbed my eyes. "Why does this always happen to me?"

"This is the exciting world of dragon design," Evelyn said, as if she'd read my mind.

"Yeah, yeah. We'll get it done." I pointed at her. "But don't expect anything too pretty."

"Your code is never pretty, Noah Parker."

"Hey now, it's better than Wong's." Don't get me wrong, the guy was a genius, but following his logic was like reading Ancient Greek.

"You could learn a lot from—"

"Korrapati, I know." Her code was orderly and pristine, like the code samples from a web tutorial. "What's she working on?"

"I am not at liberty to say."

Oh, right. Security clearance. I'd almost forgotten. "How about a little hint? Mime something."

Evelyn frowned. "It's not allowed."

"I know. I was kidding."

"You should not joke about these things." Her eyes flickered to the windows behind me. "You never know who might be listening."

I followed her gaze without meaning to. My window faced out the back of the headquarters into the Sonoran Desert toward the McDowell Mountains. It was rough country out there, desert country, but anyone could be watching. Or shining a laser against the glass. When we'd first obtained security clearance to bid on the defense contracts, the whole company had gotten an overhaul to make us harder to spy on.

"I thought we secured the building," I said.

"We did, in theory."

"Then how could anyone be listening?"

"I put nothing past the U.S. government."

"That's probably wise." I recalled some of the security procedures we'd gone through during the trials for the DOD and shivered involuntarily. Whether that was discomfort or excitement, I couldn't be sure. Probably a little of both.

"So what do you think?" she asked.

"About the government?"

"No, about the timeline for the EPA."

"Oh, that." I knew she wanted me to agree, but I also felt like I should use the opportunity to get something. "Can we use the rapid gestation protocol?" We'd developed that specifically for the DOD's dragons, but it would be useful here. Otherwise waiting for the eggs to hatch would take up most of the little time we had.

She pressed her lips together but she knew the math as well as I did. "I suppose it'll be necessary."

"Even with that, it's going to be tight."

"You may have to work overtime."

I grinned. "Oh, we get paid for overtime, now?"

"It's more of an expression of how I expect you to work a lot."

"Wonderful." I suppressed a groan. I'd just promised Summer we could take up geocaching again. The weather was perfect for it, and our rankings in the local competitive boards had both fallen considerably.

"This is a design problem, so it falls with the Department of Dragon Design."

She meant me, mostly, and she was right. I had a dragon self-destruct system to build.

CHAPTER FOUR
INTERLUDE
BUILD-A-DRAGON UPDATES LIST OF BEST-SELLING[1] MODELS
By Max Rose
GenEngineering Times, Weekend Edition

PHOENIX, Ariz—The Build-A-Dragon Company released an updated list of its best-selling domestic dragon models. While the list contains the usual suspects, there are some changes. The company cited market forces for changes in demand for certain models.

1. The Rover. The iconic pet from Build-A-Dragon Company has seen a steady sales decline since the return of dogs to the world. Yet, as far as dragons go, it remains the most popular. Weighing about the same as a golden retriever, the Rover is the gentlest of Build-A-Dragon's product offerings. It brought joy to thousands of families in the dark times when no dogs could be found by anyone. In theory, the Rover model has a maximum weight of sixty pounds, though we've all seen the memes about fatter-than-usual dragons getting stuck in doors. It

---

[1] In response to some follow-up questions by our reporting team, a company spokesperson clarified that this list only includes sales numbers from its domestic retail market. Dragons produced for contracted clients, such as the Department of Defense, are not counted here. The spokesperson declined to provide what proportion of the company's output goes to such clients. A request filed under the Freedom of Information Act for details of the company's defense-contract funding was declined by the federal government, citing reasons of national security.

turns out that when Rover dragons are fed table scraps, they're subject to the same effects as their human owners. Obesity, diabetes, and heart disease remain the leading cause of death in these substitute-Labradors. Despite these quirks, they're still lovable creatures, and will remain iconic.

2. The Laptop. Moving up to number two among the pet models is one of Build-A-Dragon's smallest flying models with a tongue-in-cheek name. With a maximum weight of under twenty pounds and special modifications to its digestive system, this model is perfect for the dragon lover who's short on space. It sells best in urban areas, the target demographic being young professionals, especially women. Laptop dragons in custom-made designer handbags are a common sight on city streets. It can fly, too, as anyone who's looked up in downtown areas can testify. Although environmental activists have raised the alarm about a decline in urban pigeon populations where Laptop dragons have become popular, most citizens consider this a feature, not a bug. As one woman recently put it, "I'll take a cute dragon that doesn't poop over a nasty bird that poops constantly, any day of the week."

3. The K-10. Build-A-Dragon's answer to the German shepherd is like a souped-up version of the Rover: bigger, stronger, and with deadlier teeth. Designed specifically for security and patrol purposes, the K-10 has remained a steady seller for the "blue" market—police, border control, drug enforcement, and other agencies continue to renew their contracts. When asked why their personnel have not switched back to German shepherds and Belgian Malinois for their animal officers, most agency representatives declined comment. A police chief of a large Midwestern metropolis did not wish to be named, but offered one remark with a hint of an explanation: "In some situations, dragons are more intimidating than dogs."

4. The Harrier. Think of a Laptop model, add five pounds, bring back a normal digestive system, and you'd end up with the Harrier, a mid-level flying model most popular with Build-A-Dragon's rural customers. This highly trainable dragon has a longer flight time and a beefier build than the Laptop model, making it an excellent farm animal or hunting companion. Avid hunters, especially those who pursue ducks, geese, and small game, were quick to adapt this dragon as a retriever. It can not only fly, but swim, which makes it ideal for hunting in the swampy environments of the mid-South. But that's not the only use for this versatile dragon. A video of several Harrier dragons herding sheep on a Texas ranch made the news a few years ago, and brought attention to the fact that this dragon can be a work "horse" as well as an outdoor companion. Their scaly, intimidating appearance and ability to hover almost in place make them extremely effective herders. Various search and rescue teams have also trained Harriers to work alongside drones to locate missing hikers and fallen climbers.

5. The Guardian. Speaking of ranchers, there's another model popular in the American Southwest. It's the first synthetic dragon ever created, the brainchild of the late inventor Simon Redwood. This is not a domesticated dragon, but a wild animal designed and bred for one purpose: to hunt feral hogs in the most challenging of environments. They have been hugely effective at reducing feral-hog damage to crops and natural resources. Studies have shown that these dragons can eliminate entire colonies of feral hogs in a matter of weeks. A new innovation in this area is the use of a so-called Judas Pig—a feral hog captured as a piglet or young adult, equipped with a GPS collar, and released back into the wild. Feral hogs are highly social animals, so by tracking the collared animal's movements, land managers can zero in on the hidden refuges of these secretive animals. Then it's a matter of ordering a few Guardian dragons and setting them loose in the right location. Although a reliable seller, Guardian numbers have continued to decline, with business analysts saying that in some ways, they do their jobs a little too well.

6. Custom models (unspecified). Build-A-Dragon offers a customization service at a significant premium for the most discerning dragon owners. Virtually any feature is on the table: length, size, coloring, wingspan, diet... allowing those deep-pocketed customers to create a one-of-a kind pet. It's Build-A-Bear Workshop meets Purina Farms, or in the case of security companions, perhaps Build-A-Bear Workshop meets *Jurassic Park*. For an additional premium, Build-A-Dragon conducts supervised hatchings at their headquarters under the watchful eyes of trained herpetologists (widely referred to as "dragon wranglers"). Granted, there have been some hiccups associated with this service in the past. One family filed a lawsuit after their five-year-old daughter's custom dragon was savagely killed after hatching in the same room as an aggressive dragon. Build-A-Dragon did not admit any wrongdoing, but reached a settlement with the plaintiffs for an undisclosed amount. Custom dragon business has dwindled according to business filings and the current rank of this model in the company's bestseller list. One possible source of softening demand is the high price point. One-off custom dragon models, once a cornerstone of the company's business, remain a small but highly profitable source of annual revenue.

7. The One-way. *This message will self-destruct* is a staple of spy movies and thrillers since the early days of James Bond. Usually that involved a small incendiary and the smoking section of an airplane. In Build-A-Dragon's version, it's not the message but the courier that self-destructs. Genetic engineers at the company developed a tiny dragon that comes with a delivery tube and old-fashioned parchment paper. The idea is that you use it to send a onetime, one-way message in writing. The little dragon always makes sure it gets there, no matter the distance or the conditions in between. The only barrier the company recommends against is an actual ocean; none of the animals in their field trials could travel that far in the air without resting. Once the dragon delivers its message, an inborn biochemical reaction in its brain is triggered, resulting in a "quiet, painless expiration," according to company marketing materials. It was a clever idea made famous by the daytime talk show hosts who received missives on the air. Animal rights groups decried the model as capitalism at its cruelest. Their protests at the company's Scottsdale headquarters drew large crowds. Gradually the protests and the public appetite for temporary creatures subsided, so this model has dropped to number 7.

Other models of dragons that once made this list have fallen off in recent quarters. It remains unclear if this reflects a change in customer tastes or an overall shrinking of market share. When asked for year-on-year sales totals, the company spokesperson said that the information was not readily available, and did not respond to follow-up inquiries.

CHAPTER FIVE
Hidden Words

The breakthrough came while I was pacing in my office. A wisp of an idea, a phrase. It felt like it had legs, though, and might be the key to pushing our design into test-ready status. Naturally, I wanted to write it on my big glass wall where I wouldn't forget.

Technically we weren't supposed to write on the desks or the walls even though they were all made of tempered glass, which was pretty much indestructible. Practically speaking, sometimes you had to write down a critical piece of information before it left your brain. As I'd learned in my early days as a designer for the company, almost every surface in this glass-and-steel building responded well to a dry-erase marker. We all kept dry-erase markers on us and felt free to write or draw on any surface. I never bothered erasing anything. I figured that the janitorial staff would do that when they came along. But the janitors never erased any of my notes. Maybe they worried that hastily written phrases like *Too many bicuspids* might contain critical information. Or perhaps *wool digestive enzymes* could represent an engineering breakthrough. Regardless, they didn't do erasing.

And so the graffiti grew.

To deal with the glass-writing behavior, Build-A-Dragon's administrative staff removed all dry-erase markers from the supply closets and issued a policy that no glass in any "onstage" area should be marked in any way. They forgot to define what counted as onstage versus offstage, which didn't help their cause. At first, the new policy and lack of new markers had zero effect. We all kept our stashes and most employees, myself included, ignored memos from Admin on principle. Then, the Admin staff got clever: any time new dry-erase graffiti appeared on a surface, they blocked off the scene of the crime for seventy-two hours for cleaning.

After the infamous Black Thursday, the day of no available restrooms, everyone finally got the message. If we wanted to mark up the walls, we had to use invisible ink, the kind that was only visible under a black light. It worked beautifully. My coworkers and I kept writing on things, while the Admin team smugly enjoyed the misconception that we'd been cowed. True, I probably should have set a better example for my team, but I *loved* dry erase.

Unfortunately, I loved it a little too much and was on my last marker. I took off the cap and tested it on my glass wall. The pocket-sized black light on my keychain revealed nothing. *Damn.* I tested the tip with my finger, and it was bone dry. I'd been afraid of that. The markers we used for this looked like regular Sharpies, which is the only reason we could safely use them. They had become black-market items.

The lead supplier worked in Design behind a wall of empty beverage cans.

Neurotransmitter decline was the phrase I wanted to write on my wall, because that was the idea. I repeated it to myself as I hurried to the design lab. "Wong!"

"Yes?" He didn't take his eyes from his projection monitors.

"I find myself in need of a marker."

"For what?"

"I've got to write something down, and I'm out."

"Use paper."

I shook my head "It's more of a mind-mapping thing. You know how I am. I need wall space." I'd start with the phrase. Once it was out of my brain and onto a surface, I could write and draw and connect things with complicated lines. It was my idea process and it tended to get messy. More than one coworker had once described my office as "the lair of a serial killer."

"We are not allowed to mark on the walls here," Wong said.

I fought the instinct to roll my eyes, because I was in a hurry. "Do we have to do this dance every time?"

"We are not allowed to mark on the walls here," he repeated. "Admin policy."

Yes, I'm very aware of the policy. I cleared my throat. "I understand you're a man who knows how to get things."

"I am known to locate certain things from time to time." It was his too-formal approximation of a Morgan Freeman line from *Shawshank Redemption*, Wong's favorite movie. For some reason, a film about an innocent man who escapes a soul-crushing prison for a better life appealed enormously to him. I tried not to connect that to his former place of employment.

I lowered my voice. "I need dry-erase markers."

"Those are against the policy."

"I know."

"Are you asking me to violate this policy?" he asked.

I feigned astonishment and put my hand on my chest. "I would never do such a thing."

He pursed his lips and seemed to consider this. "I can get them, but they're expensive."

"What's it going to cost me this time?"

"I forget lunch today," he said.

"You never bring your lunch."

"Especially hungry."

"What are you in the mood for?"

"Bacon cheeseburger."

When I said that we had done this dance before, it wasn't an exaggeration. Sometimes he needed a ride somewhere. Sometimes he needed an afternoon off, no questions asked. There was always something. Because this was technically banned activity, I couldn't order him to give me black-market materials. He didn't see this as extortion; he considered himself an entrepreneur. In my case, he knew I wouldn't take the time to find another supplier, have things shipped to my condo instead of the office, and smuggle them into the building. I was hardly alone in surrendering to the will of the market, either. Despite the wall of empty energy drink cans that decorated one side of his workstation, I'd never actually seen him bring any in on his own. People tended to drop them off. He also did not own a car or have a driver's license—as far as I knew—but managed to get to and from work as much as he needed.

"Do you want fries with that?" I asked sourly.

"Yes. And chocolate milkshake."

I pressed my lips together so hard that they hurt. "A little steep, don't you think?"

He shrugged. "Supply and demand."

"Didn't you grow up in a communist country?"

"Yes." He smiled. "But now I live in America."

Half an hour later, Wong was enjoying a free lunch and I'd turned the portable black light so that it shined on my office wall glass, where I'd written the phrase *Neurotransmitter decline*. The letters glowed an iridescent blue, almost hypnotic. Most people knew about the monoamines: serotonin was the "happiness" monoamine and dopamine was the "motivation-reward" monoamine. In the brain, however, the amino aid glutamate was the most abundant by far. It powered so-called excitatory synapses—in other words, it was the spark that happened when neurons fired. Overactive synapses were generally bad news; they were associated with things like Parkinson's disease. Yet too little glutamate was just as bad, so it didn't make a very sensible drug target. Most of the big pharmaceutical companies felt glutamate pathways were too risky to modulate. I kind of agreed, but since I was in the business of finding ways to shorten a dragon's life, it seemed like fair game.

I drew lines to the other key neurotransmitters, and labeled all of the known receptors for those vital chemicals in the brain. Everything was tightly controlled and balanced in normal circumstances. But maybe there was a way to co-opt the system. The usual way in was dopamine, the so-called reward trigger in the brain. We'd exploited some of its pathways in the One-way dragons to trigger a cascade of consequences after a single reward completion. Now I wanted to do the opposite: make that reward completion a fundamental requirement for ongoing neurotransmitter balance.

It required some tweaks.

Dopamine played a central role in the so-called motivational pathways. It rewarded positive outcomes, ones that contributed toward survival and propagation. If you had a task, dopamine provided the motivation to do that task and the reward when the task was done. Since our dragons would be custom-designed to perform specific functions—historically speaking, that meant eliminating a pest such as a feral hog—they got a tiny little dopamine hit whenever they did so. We designed the goal, and the dragon's innate neurotransmitter system reinforced the motivation to achieve that goal over and over again. Ordinarily, there was no limit—if a dragon completed its task, waited two weeks, and then performed it again, the reward would be the same. All we needed was to modulate the system so that the dopamine reward system slowly decreased. The trouble was, neurotransmitter metabolism wasn't my strong suit. It was Wong's.

"Wong, I need you," I said, striding into the design lab.

"Good, good." He didn't so much as glance at me. "As it happen, I forget my dinner as well."

"No, this is for work." *You freeloader*, I didn't add.

He spun around in his chair and crab-legged himself out from the workstation. That was the great thing about Wong; he was always game for a design challenge.

"I've got an idea for the second-level fail-safe, and it involves the dopamine pathway."

"No more serotonin?"

"Nah, too risky." I explained the logic of the slow degeneration of delayed rewards with dopamine as the focal point.

"Could work," Wong said. "You want me to tinker?"

"Yes, please tinker." *Man, I'm glad I taught him the meaning of that word.* It fit Wong's trial-and-error approach to design so perfectly. Now that I'd laid out the idea, he could put it into practice, trying a series of small adjustments to the genes that regulated dopamine pathways. Each time he'd make a change, he would run the biological simulator with the behavioral modifications. Every model run generated dozens of numeric data points that Wong fed into yet another computational tool. Machine learning. He could specify a goal, a desired state for various complex behaviors, and the machines would navigate hundreds of trial data points to find the optimal path to success.

"How is the design coming?" Summer asked. We were sitting on my balcony eating a late dinner. We'd both worked later than usual and the traffic had been brutal for some reason. Sometimes when that happened, I just persuaded her to stop at my condo to eat. Hers was nicer, but farther out of town. Octavius dozed against the rails, perched on his little warming stone. He was the only dragonet we could trust not to fly off into the suburbs.

"It's in Wong's hands now," I said.

"Not yours?"

"I came up with the general scheme. He's the person to figure out how to make it happen."

"How *managerial* of you," she teased.

"Hey, come on, I've put in my time. If it was my responsibility, I'd still be at work." *Director privileges are limited, but they do exist.*

"What's the general idea?" Summer wasn't a biologist, but she was smart and had listened to me ramble on enough about work to have a pretty good grasp of genetic engineering, at least as it applied to dragons. Plus, like every American, she picked up plenty of science through pop culture.

"A gradual neurotransmitter decline as the dragons stop feeding on prey, encoded into the dopamine system."

"Oh, good, and here I was worried you'd tamper with something important."

"I'm not the one tampering, remember? Wong is, and he's our expert."

"You know what I mean," she said flatly.

"The concept is sound. Once the dragons—"

She held up her hand. "I know, I know, there's a super-complicated line of logic that explains why this is going to achieve exactly what you want it to."

"Oh." That stung a little, even if it was true.

She sighed and touched my hand. "I'm sorry, I'm tired and cranky."

"How come?"

"The dragonets. They're driving me crazy."

"You only have three!"

"I know, but they're stir-crazy. I'm working late almost every night, so they don't get to be outside very much. They need exercise, Noah. Badly."

"I can help," I said, which was a lie. I had my own share of dragonets to exercise, and with the preparation of the new dragon model I had even less free time than usual. "We can go to Tonto this weekend. Camp out overnight, and spend two days putting them through their paces."

She smiled. "Okay."

We both knew we'd probably never put such an ambitious outing together, especially if I was the one who had to plan it. But it was nice to dream.

The sun dipped below the horizon and it got chillier. The desert was strange like that, hot to the point of unbearable while the sun was shining, only to practically freeze when it set. Summer looked cold. She hated missing this part of the night, so she'd normally shiver out here for half an hour until I persuaded her to come inside. Not tonight, though.

"Well, we had a terrible fight," I said.

She snorted. Compared to one or two of our past epic blowouts, this was nothing.

"I bought you something." I reached into the little storage bin and pulled out a fluffy alpaca-wool blanket. It was hand-woven by a local tribe and thus pretty damn expensive. It had taken every bit of self control not to wrap myself in this last night. The best part, though, was that it was warm. The lid of my deck box was a sunstone like the one the dragonets used. It trapped the afternoon heat and radiated it down to the blanket.

"Ohh..." she breathed. "It's so soft, too."

I wrapped both of us in it and pulled her close. It was as soft as a well-worn T-shirt, and the warmth radiating from it felt wonderful against the cold.

"You did good." She turned her face up to me and I kissed her. She kissed me back and when we broke away, she stayed close, her eyes locked on mine with what seemed like an invitation.

Well, if you insist.

I kissed her again, gently at first. She moaned a little and pressed against me. Wrapped in the blanket and the darkness, with both of us so warm and close... it had an effect. I'd meant to wash the dishes and then work on the dragon design for a couple of hours. We should probably talk more about a long-term plan for them. Instead I slipped my arms around her waist and lifted her onto my lap. Things got really hot, really fast.

"Let's go inside," I whispered.

"Okay," she said. "Bring the blanket."

CHAPTER SIX
The Rival

None of us believed the EPA inspection team would show up right when the window opened. This was the government, after all. They liked to measure timelines in months, even when there were words like "priority" and "urgent" attached. I hadn't looked at the calendar closely, hell, I'd barely slept. We'd set an ambitious trial schedule to do two hatchings before the inspection window opened. That meant a crazy-fast design for the alpha prototype, then three days of impatient waiting, then a glimpse at the early results. Which had not exactly wowed anyone.

Wong and I dove into the code, but in the end we decided to tear down and rebuild almost from scratch. Cue more long days and near-sleepless nights. Design #2 got printed and went into the incubators less than a week before the window opened. Based on the timing, the self-destruct process would begin a couple of days into the window. Assuming the inspectors wouldn't show until the last two days, we could probably squeeze in a third design.

Out of dark instinct, I dragged myself into work early on the first day of the EPA window just in case. It was getting close to the start of the deceleration sequence—the fancy-sounding term that Wong and I had come up with for the start of the self-destruct sequence. The dragonets in batch two had spent two days doing simulated field work out in the desert. It was just catching their own food, but served the same purpose we wanted. Then they were no longer able to hunt the food and we simultaneously removed the metabolic supplements and the copper.

I'd updated the code on my biological simulator to account for these new fail-safes and project the dragon lifespan when they were activated. The modeling showed a rapid decline. It wasn't pretty, but it was quick. I told myself that it was merciful.

I planned to check on the dragonets and maybe tweak my simulator some more, but all that came to a screeching halt when I walked in the company's front door. Wong met me at the elevators in the lobby. The guy practically lived in our lab on the seventh floor, and took great pains to never exert himself more than the absolute minimum. So when I saw him, puffing and out of breath after making the trip down without even his urban scooter, I knew something was up.

"What's wrong?" I asked.

"Inspection team," he said. The guy looked like he was going to throw up.

"They gave us a date?"

He shook his head, had a minor coughing fit, then straightened. "They are here."

I found the inspection team in Build-A-Dragon's executive conference room. Naturally, Evelyn had met them there and even had a spectacular breakfast spread. She was subtle about it, but I knew the difference between starfruit that the caterer could bring and starfruit that was flown in overnight from Hawaii. The French press was new, but Evelyn held court with our guests like this was an ordinary day at the company.

The three members of the inspection team sat around her end of the conference table. On her left was an older white guy, probably midfifties, with thinning white hair and glasses. I didn't recognize him but the blue sports jacket over the Oxford shirt said East Coast academic—the look of a tenured professor. He was probably a consultant in a relevant field; the EPA used a lot of those for their inspections. The woman beside him in the purple suit was probably the agency official. They had another consultant, too, and I knew him. "Dave?"

"Hello, Noah." He smiled in a way that said this little surprise was planned.

I was proud of how quickly I recovered. "Hey, good to see you." I offered my hand.

He shook it. "Yeah, you too."

Other introductions followed. The older man was Stephen Levine, a professor of biology (like I called it) from Boston College (like I called it). His field was ecology but I recognized his name—he specialized in the impact of genetically engineered organisms on natural environments. I'd grown up reading his research papers. Now his former students were getting established in the field and his career reaped the benefits. They'd put him on grants, supporting some of his salary for his name recognition and occasional advice. As a result, the guy didn't have to chase his own funding, which freed him up to do things like inspect biotech companies applying for government approvals.

The woman from the EPA was Margaret Monroe. She went by Peggy and the name fit. She seemed competent enough, but spoke little. I got the distinct feeling that she'd lean heavily on the advice from her two consultants in making the decision. It would be her call, of course—agency officials got the final say in matters of approval like this—but we had to sell the experts first. Which would be no easy task. Levine would be tough but fair, and his editorials had a pro-genetic-engineering slant to them so I felt reasonably confident we'd get him on board eventually.

Then there was Dave McAdams, whose specialty was almost identical to mine. This was going to be tricky.

"Noah is the head of our Dragon Design department," Evelyn was saying. "He's the brains behind most of our dragon designs."

"Don't believe her. I have a really good team."

"You developed a biological simulator, too, didn't you?" Levine asked.

My face felt hot. *Stephen Levine knows about my biological simulator.* "Yes, that too. It grew out of my thesis project."

"Yes, Dave was telling us about that on the flight out here."

That took the wind out of my sails. "Is that so?"

Dave shrugged. "Just telling some stories about the good old days in the Sato lab."

I forced a smile. "Yeah, good times." I looked at Evelyn. "If it's all right, I can go make sure we're all set."

She shook her head. "Get some coffee first. We have plenty of time."

"Yeah, we're going to be here all week," Dave said. "Maybe longer."

They all laughed and I made myself chuckle with them. I turned around to set down my bag, turned back, and he was already refilling

Evelyn's coffee for her. She smiled at him. It seemed oddly strange and familiar at once. Then I realized why. That was the smile she used to give to me.

I followed Evelyn's orders to get coffee, but then excused myself to the design lab. *Fled* was a better way to describe it. Wong and Korrapati were both at his workstation but too excited to be working. Korrapati's first name was Priti, and the first time I heard it, I thought she'd said *pretty*. Which would have fit her as well. It was good to see her.

Technically she belonged in the workstation next to Wong's, but with her DOD stuff, Evelyn thought it best to sequester her on the other side of the design lab. That way passersby wouldn't catch a glimpse of things that required a security clearance. By "passersby," she meant me and Wong.

"Noah, did you see the inspection team?" Korrapati gushed. "I can't believe they came so early in the window."

"Yeah, it's almost like they wanted to surprise us," I said. Some disgruntlement must have slipped into my tone.

"Wait, do you know someone on the team?"

"Two people, actually. The senior member is Stephen Levine. Have you heard of him?"

"The name sounds familiar," she said.

"Evolutionary biology," Wong offered. "Boston."

"That's right," she said. "He's the guy who works on the impact of synthetic organisms on ecosystems."

"Yeah, perfect choice, really," I said. "He's not biased against modified organisms, or for them. It's all about the science for him. It's the other guy who might be a problem."

"Who is he?"

"Dave McAdams."

Her brow furrowed. "The name is not familiar to me."

"Never heard of him," Wong said.

That was slightly satisfying, the mean part inside of me had to admit. "We came up together in Dr. Sato's lab at Arizona State."

"Really?" Korrapati smiled, and Wong even stopped typing long enough to turn around. "Is this yet another Noah Parker rival?"

"We came up together, that's all. We're the same age, and we used to sit at the same lab bench."

"Who joined the lab first?" Korrapati asked.

A clever question. She knew how things worked in academia. Things like lab seniority. "I don't remember."

"Noah."

"All right, I did. By six months." In those six months I'd impressed a lot of people in the lab and earned some of Dr. Sato's respect. "As a matter of fact, I helped interview him."

"Did you recommend him?"

I sighed. "No." I still remembered telling Dr. Sato that we shouldn't recruit Dave. That he was a nice guy who didn't have some of the fundamentals I thought we needed. I was young and brash and felt like I should gatekeep the place where I'd landed.

"So, what happened?"

"Dr. Sato hired him anyway."

Korrapati winced. "Ooh. That's awkward."

"Yeah." I got to sit next to the guy I'd quietly lobbied against. For almost a year. We got along great, as it turned out. Dave was eager to learn, and he got along well with people. Better than me, if I'm being honest. He was a fast learner, too. I got buried in my graduate project and was dealing with life stuff, so I didn't pay attention to his career trajectory. Right up until Dr. Sato reorganized the lab. "Next thing I knew, I was reporting to him."

Korrapati gasped. Wong just smiled and shook his head. Then again, he'd come from a place where, once a month, the top ten percent of coders got promoted and the bottom ten percent got fired.

Maybe it shouldn't have bothered me as much as it did back then in the Sato lab. We all eventually reported to Dr. Sato, and he reported to the department chair, who reported to the dean... it went all the way to the top. But it rankled.

"And this is the guy who is helping decide on our EPA approval?" Korrapati asked.

"For the wild dragons, yes."

Korrapati looked at me. "What do you think he'll do?"

"He'll be fair, but tough. He has unique training."

They both shared a look but said nothing.

"Guys, you have nothing to worry about," I said. "You're going to like him."

Everybody liked Dave.

CHAPTER SEVEN
The Nickel Tour

My hopes that the EPA inspection team would keep themselves busy elsewhere were dashed before lunch. I'd gone to check the biometric readouts of the two batches of demonstration dragons that would be evaluated to make sure they were on track. The younger batch had already been hatched on-site and would serve as active prototypes. That meant they got fed the necessary metabolic supplements and were occupied with completing the environmental task for which they were designed: insect control. In an ideal test scenario, we'd have run this experiment outside to make it resemble a wild release as much as possible. However, that would mean introducing an ecological problem and taking the risk that it could bleed over into Scottsdale. Neither the city nor the EPA thought that was a good idea. Instead, we created a controlled laboratory on the sixth floor. Dragon wranglers had built out the isolation pods over the past week; one was a desert ecosystem, one was a temperate forest, and one was a swamp. Each chamber was isolated but had an array of cameras and sensors to monitor both predators and prey.

In this case, the prey meant thousands of crickets. We had considered all kinds of prey animals. Mice and rats, believe it or not, were expensive when you had to buy them in large quantities. Just like synthetic organisms, animals that were often used for laboratory research had garnered all kinds of new scrutiny after the canine pandemic. That drove up costs even when you were using them as feed for other animals. We had actually started with grasshoppers, which were a real-world pest of the kind our dragons might be asked to control. The problem was that the things could jump and fly. Someone left a container lid loose and hundreds escaped into our building. Maintenance was still trying to get them all. After that debacle, crickets seemed like a safer choice. The body composition was similar but they were inexpensive and easier to contain.

The noise was cacophonous.

There were two versions of each chamber, one with an active cricket infestation, and one without. Dragon batch A was in the active chamber, doing rounds of pest control on swarms of crickets introduced every two hours. They were the control group. Their vital signs showed it, too. Unlike most of our dragons that got shipped out as eggs, these test subjects had a number of biometric sensors. We were monitoring heart rate, metabolism, neurological activity, the works. Every metric was in optimal range, which was what we desired. Still, it put me on edge a little; after all, if our design was successful, they would not be long for this world.

Dragon batch B had been feeding for a week before moving to the inactive chambers, where there were no crickets and no metabolic supplements. Their biometric readouts offered a sharp contrast to the controls. Technically, they remained within normal range but the traces had a lot of noise to them, like the wavy lines on an old-school lie detector when the suspect told a big one. I couldn't tell if that was a good thing or not, and was pondering it when I heard voices. Noise traveled in Build-A-Dragon but my hallway was usually quiet. I followed them down to the design lab. There was Dave, leaned over Wong's workstation, chatting with him and Korrapati.

"These sliders let us adjust some of the basic dragon characteristics," Korrapati was saying. "Oh, hello, Noah. We were just giving Dave a tour of DragonDraft 3D."

"It's a nice interface," Dave said. "Was that your work?"

"No, believe it or not, that was Evelyn's contribution."

"This is Noah Parker's," Wong said. He tapped a few keystrokes and launched my simulator. The Rover dragon shimmered into existence in front of his projection monitor.

"Ah yes, the fabled biological simulator." Dave leaned close to inspect the dragon as it rotated slowly in three dimensions. "Looks like it's come a long way."

"Yeah, we find it useful sometimes." I felt a little surge of pride, but did my best not to show it. Dave had known about the simulator when it was still a janky half-assed graduate student project that hogged the Sato lab's computing allocations. He'd actually been working on a similar project of his own, a new algorithm for modeling organism-environment interactions. "Are you still doing anything with your program?"

Dave waved it off. "Nah, I've moved on to other things."

He said it so casually—letting go of a thing that he'd devoted years of his life to—that I envied him in that moment. I'd never excelled at letting go of things. "Good for you, man." I smiled. "It seems to be working out for you."

"Hey, you're the overachiever. From what I'm told, you guys only run two pieces of software in this place. You built one. The other one was built by the CEO."

Korrapati laughed. "It's true."

"She used to head this group before she got promoted upstairs," I said.

"Oh, right. She was telling me about that over breakfast." Dave grinned. "You know, after you *abandoned* us."

"I didn't abandon you, I had to check on things here."

"Sure, sure," Dave said. "You should spend some time talking to Stephen. He was asking about you."

Stephen Levine asked about me. Maybe Dave was being polite, maybe he wasn't, but it softened me a fraction. "What's he been like to work with?"

"Intimidating as hell."

"Ha! I'll bet." *But not so intimidating that you don't call him Stephen.* But I was the only one who had noticed that; from the way Wong and Korrapati were smiling I could tell his disarming manner was working. "Well, you're here. What else do you want to see?"

"Everything you can show me."

"Well, why don't we let my team get some work done, and I'll give you the tour myself?"

Wong and Korrapati seemed a little disappointed that break time was over, but I quietly told them to look at the biometrics for dragon batch B. Then I led Dave down the hall back to my office.

✢ ✢ ✢

"Whoa," Dave said. "Nice digs you have here." He'd paused on the threshold of my doorway to admire the view. "That's a million-dollar view."

"Really?" I glanced over my shoulder. "It's wasted on me." My monitors were between my chair and the doorway, so I rarely looked out the windows.

"Still. You've done well."

"Hey, I'm not the one taking calls from the EPA." I pulled my guest chair around to the backside of the desk. "Come on down."

He slid into the chair beside me and cleared his throat softly. He did that sometimes and I'd forgotten the mannerism, but hearing it brought it all crashing back. For a moment we were in the Sato lab again, working shoulder to shoulder on genetic code at two dusty workstations in a narrow aisle. Those were lean times for the lab—for the whole university, in fact—and Dr. Sato packed us in like sardines. We called them the trenches. Sometimes you had to crawl over someone to get to your spot. Dave and I spent six months together there. He was a good neighbor, and ignored my own mannerism of mumbling to myself.

Dave gave me a side-eye because he must have had the same memory. "Reminds me of the good times."

"Yeah, same." It took me a beat to work through all of those memories—good ones and bad ones both. I shook myself and refocused on what I was doing. "You saw DragonDraft3D already. You want to have a look at our new genetic safeguards?"

He waved me off. "We'll cover that later with the whole team. You should save it."

"All right, what do you have in mind?"

"Your group was telling me something about cracking domestication."

"Oh, were they?" I know it wasn't that long ago, but it felt like it anyway. Those crazy days competing with the other designers on Evelyn's team to create the most docile dragon. "Those were some wild times."

"Wong said you were the one who finally had the key breakthrough."

"He's being too modest as usual. He won that competition."

"But you helped him."

"Only a little." Wong had put in the work, systematically making tweaks and testing them on the simulator to make a better model by sheer force. "I was new around here but wanted to prove myself. You know how it is."

"Oh, yeah," he said, in a way that we both understood.

"I had this idea. Remember when they sequenced the DNA of a mummified cat from ancient Egypt?"

Dave furrowed his brow. "Vaguely."

"There was an editorial in that journal issue."

He snapped his fingers, remembering. "Written by the cat."

"Exactly." I told him how this inspired the idea of fear as a key element of domesticating an animal—not fear of humans, but fear of going back to the wild without the things we provided.

"That's genius, man. Really," Dave said.

Hearing it from him, from someone who knew, somehow meant lot more. I was aware of this even as the logical part of my brain reminded me that this was the Dave effect. This was Dave being Dave. He knew the right things to say to me just as Evelyn did. At the same time, I *wanted* it to be a sincere compliment from one of the few people in the world who could give it. The two sides warred and for a moment I couldn't decide how to respond. In the end I decided that maybe the best way to handle Dave was to be like him. "Thanks. As you know, I trained with the best."

"Yeah, you really did." Dave squinted at the monitor that showed a wall of code. "Though I think I see a typo in one of your comments there."

"Get out of my office." I grinned to let him know I was kidding.

Mostly kidding.

CHAPTER EIGHT
Flight Rules

For three days I didn't see much of the inspection team. They holed up in one of the private conference rooms, the windows tinted to opaque. They met with several groups, always bringing them to the conference room. Dragon wranglers from Herpetology. White-garbed staffers from the hatchery. Late in the afternoon, Evelyn would meet with them for a summation of the day's discussions. They seemed to be saving the design team for last, though I couldn't imagine why. We were the ones who'd ultimately try to deliver what they truly wanted: safeguards against our dragons becoming established in the wild. After the second day, my paranoia kicked in and I started to worry that they were in there talking about us. About me.

"Noah, you're imagining things," Korrapati told me.

We'd met in the break room to pretend we needed coffee and try to eavesdrop on the nearby proceedings. Which was pointless, of course. The building's tech was already pretty good, but Evelyn had gotten nervous during our tryouts for the DOD contracts and upgraded the countersurveillance measures in the conference rooms. Korrapati and I could point a laser at the opaque glass and we still wouldn't hear anything being said inside.

"But don't you think it's strange?" I watched a silhouette on the other side of the glass and tried to interpret the body language but it was unclear.

"They have a lot of people to talk to."

"We're the ones they really want, though," I said.

"Says who?"

"We're building the fail-safes."

"It's not just about the fail-safes, Noah. The government has a wide purview over anything considered a synthetic animal. That includes the marketing and the animal husbandry."

"Animal what?"

"Husbandry. The science of keeping animals healthy."

"Isn't that for cows and stuff?" I asked. "You know, meat animals?"

"They want to see the whole operation. We shouldn't fault them for being thorough." Korrapati blew on her coffee, tried a sip, and decided it was good enough.

"I'm heading back." Once she was gone, my plausible reason to be there was too, so I headed downstairs to have a quick look at our outdoor arena. Evelyn had asked Herpetology to collect physical performance metrics on our dragons. I'd missed hatching the other day but made sure I blocked out some time for today's evaluations. A small crowd of our coworkers had gathered in the outdoor arena where all of our flying dragons were being put through their paces.

The Laptop dragon had, at one time, been our best-selling model in urban areas. It had an extremely high metabolism, which made it a nimble flier with limited endurance. As I watched, a dun-colored Laptop took off from a platform and darted through three colorful aerial hoops in slalom fashion. It landed on another platform to collect its reward—three strips of raw meat—from a waiting dragon wrangler. Next up was a Harrier, a heftier dragon about twice as large. It could fly longer distances, if not with the same agility, but it was our only dragon with a very cool feature: a vertical takeoff. The hind legs were powerful, as were the shoulders, so it jumped into the air and pumped its wings to gain altitude. Today's model was bright green. It glittered in the Arizona sun like an emerald. It gained about thirty feet and then pivoted, gliding in a long arc to a distant platform where raw meat was waiting. They had equipment set up along the flight path to capture the airspeed and flight dynamics.

"How are they looking?"

I jumped, startled, but probably shouldn't have been surprised to see Evelyn. She'd probably put the board of directors on hold to come watch our dragons fly. "Pretty good, I think. I've only seen the Laptop and the Harrier."

"Then you haven't missed much. They started with the One-way."

"Are you serious?" I still felt a little stab of shame every time they came up. "That's just mean."

Evelyn looked out at the flight grounds, her face neutral. "They want metrics on all of our unclassified models."

Unclassified. That was the first time I'd heard her use that phrase. "Oh, so you *did* get exemptions for our military-grade products."

"Not me. Major Johnson made a call."

"Of course." I grinned, remembering the big friendly major and his effortless way with people. It was impossible not to like him. *Just like it's impossible not to like Dave,* I couldn't help but thinking. "How's he doing?"

She pursed her lips in a way that meant she didn't think she should answer.

So secretive. I rolled my eyes. "Fine, well, tell him I said hello, will you?"

"I can do that."

We looked back to the field to where the aerial trials continued. Next up was a Pterodactyl, a dragon that technically remained in the catalogue of production models. It was an O'Connell design and a perfect example of the flaws of the points system: so many design points had gone into the wingspan and flight capabilities that few points remained for mental acuity. Thus, though the dragon could fly well out in the open, it had a tendency to crash into stationary objects. I noticed that the handlers—no doubt aware of the flaw—tested it on the open glide course, which had no physical obstacles. Evelyn and I both watched the demonstration Pterodactyl launch, glide to the far platform, and make a decent landing. We both exhaled.

"Close one," Evelyn murmured.

"That's one model where you don't even need a fail-safe," I said.

She laughed. "You are cruel, Noah. But you are right, too."

I barely heard her, because I'd gotten a look at the next dragon getting ready to fly the biometrics gauntlet. It was as large as the Pterodactyl but somehow sleeker, with muscles that rippled in the sunlight. I almost thought it a mirage. Then it got a signal from the dragon handlers, unfurled its wings, and I *knew.* "Oh my God, that's a Condor."

The Condor was a dragon of my own design, one that had nearly gotten me fired from Build-A-Dragon in my early days as a designer. I'd gotten permission to go outside the point limits from Evelyn, but pushed well past the line to give the model strength, agility, and intelligence. Ask anyone to describe a mythical dragon from imagination alone, and the Condor usually fit.

"Don't get too excited," Evelyn said. "I only thought we should gather metrics for some of the more interesting prototypes."

Interesting is one way to put it. As much as I might hope to take credit for it, this model somehow exuded subtle confidence. Maybe it was the noble bearing, or maybe it was the eyes: look into them and you'd feel something more than reptilian intelligence. At least, I did. The Condor did have one fatal flaw, a mutation I'd placed intentionally to prove that it caused eventual muscle degeneration. But that wouldn't afflict a young dragon. I opened my mouth and then shut it again. The less I said about my Condor, the better.

I stared at it while the wranglers set up the flying course. They must have been briefed already because they were making the obstacles far more difficult—sharper turns, more pivots, smaller target hoops, that sort of thing. The dragon watched them intently. It was almost like it knew the purpose of the tests and was adjusting its flight plan to compensate. Maybe that was my imagination running wild and conferring humanlike traits to an animal without cause.

"I've never seen a dragon so calm before a trial," Evelyn said. "Usually the noise and all of the strangers make them nervous."

The wranglers finished their course setup and got clear. Without waiting for a signal, the Condor leapt from its perch and swept low to gain speed. With two flaps of its great wings, it flew up and over the starting line, plunging headfirst into the obstacle course.

"Too fast," I said to myself, and I worried that was true. The wranglers had added more target rings, decreasing the distance between them to about ten yards. Sometimes at different heights. The Condor plunged through the first and second one, then the third. But it passed by the fourth target ring, down and to the left, like it wasn't there.

"Oh, it missed one," Evelyn said.

"Did it, though?" I'd seen what the dragon had seen. The next three target hoops all slanted to the right and were spaced only a few yards apart. The Condor took them in a sharp turn, tilting its body almost ninety degrees, and continued in a sideways loop that let it dart through the target ring it had missed before continuing to the next set. The turn was so sharp and tight it didn't lose any speed. If anything, it made up time by postponing that ring. I hadn't thought to time it but now I wished I had. Then again, I had no baseline for comparison. None of the other dragons had faced the same aerial gauntlet.

The Condor landed on the finish line platform, claiming its reward of meat from a waiting dragon wrangler. Evelyn looked at me expectantly. She probably expected me to brag a little.

"Well, I should get back." I said.

Evelyn's mouth fell open. "Nothing to say, Noah?"

"Eh, got some work to do. See you." I turned and left.

I didn't have to say anything. The Condor had laid down my marker better than I ever could.

CHAPTER NINE
Inspections

I met Summer for lunch in the park outside her firm's stunning green-energy building. It was rectangular, four stories, and solar panels not only covered the roof, but extended out like overhanging eaves, lining the upper three floors. It was a kick-ass design, complete with a green walking park out front. That's where we met. I brought fried chicken, one of our new guilty pleasure foods. It was the sort of thing you shouldn't eat for lunch, which made it all the more enjoyable when you did.

"So, still no inspection, huh?" she asked.

I laughed but there was no humor in it. "What gave it away?"

"Hmm, let's see," she said. "You're picking at your chicken, you haven't said more than twenty words all day, and you still have that mopey expression."

"It's not mopey," I said. "This is just my face."

"No, you're moping. You act like this when you feel like you're not getting your way."

"Wow, you really got every cent of value from that Intro to Psychology class, didn't you?"

"I took *two* classes," she said tartly.

"Look, I'm not imagining things. Design is the heart of our company and they haven't even come to talk to us yet."

"Have you ever heard of saving the best for last?"

I shook my head. "It doesn't feel like that. It feels like we're invisible."

"Oh, how *strange*."

Uh-oh. "What are you trying to say?"

"Noah, this is the first date we've had in two weeks." She gestured at the table. "It's literally fried chicken on my company's front lawn."

"We've talked. I haven't been ignoring you."

"Once. For two hours on Sunday. When your laptop died."

It was true, I'd been a little obsessed with work. It was my coping mechanism for when I hit a wall at work. In this case, the wall was the constant boxing out from the inspection team. "It's almost like they *knew* I wanted to be in the room, so they took great pains to keep me out."

"You're being paranoid," Summer said.

"It's not paranoia if they're really out to get you."

"This inspection thing will end at some point," she said. "And then you get to move on."

"What if we don't pass?"

"Then you'll deal with it. You always do."

If we don't get this, the company will fail, I nearly said. Then I remembered that I'd said that a few times before. It was almost getting to be my most common refrain. I took a deep breath. "We'll deal with it."

"Also, you need to make time for me. You need to make time for *your dragons*, you know?"

I smiled. "Are you saying you're one of my dragons?"

"What? No. You know what I mean."

"Okay, okay." I put my hand on top of hers. It would have been romantic if we weren't both clutching half-eaten drumsticks. "I will."

She was unmoved by the drumstick-on-drumstick caress. "I'm serious, Noah."

"I am, too."

She raised her eyebrows. "I hope so."

We sat in silence for a moment.

"You know, you're my favorite dragon," I said.

She glared at me. "I'm going to call Security."

Just as Korrapati predicted, the inspection team waited until the very last minute to summon the design team to their meetings. Or rather, they asked if they could meet in the design lab. Dave had already visited a couple of times, chatting up our team and poking around in DragonDraft 3D. I kept getting messages with baseline specs from our already existing production models. He was running them through my simulator. The thing was, I couldn't exactly ask why without letting on that I was monitoring its runs. For some reason I didn't want to do that. It was also unclear to me if his poking around constituted official business or personal curiosity. The EPA enjoyed a wide scope of access to our materials for their inspection, but also Dave was a naturally curious guy.

I'd arrived early on the day of our meeting with the inspection team and found myself in the elevator with Stephen Levine. He wore the houndstooth jacket—a fixture during his time on-site—over a blue Oxford button-down shirt. When I pushed the elevator button and it opened, he was already in there, engrossed with something on his tablet. Apparently he'd never chosen a floor.

"Good morning," I told him.

"Morning." He said it automatically but remained fixated on whatever he was reading. I glanced at the screen and thought I recognized the format of a research paper, but it was digitized from print. That made it decades old. He was old school, all right.

"I was hoping to bump into you again," I said.

He glanced up, recognized me, and put his tablet down. "Well, if it isn't the head of dragon design around here."

I pressed the button for the seventh floor. "Oh, so you *do* know about our existence."

He chuckled. "Feeling a bit ignored, are we?"

"I'm just kidding." *Sort of.*

"Well, rest assured that your team gets its time with us today."

"Really? Can't wait."

"Well, we've been building up to the design team."

I smiled. "Getting warmed up for us, eh?"

"You might say that. Although Dave has been keeping us briefed."

"Ah." So that was official business. Count on Dave to make it seem like a casual pop-in motivated by sheer curiosity.

"You two worked together a few years ago, didn't you?"

"Yes. In the Sato lab at Arizona State."

He nodded, looking thoughtful. "I might have guessed that. You're alike in many ways."

"How so?"

"Smart. Ambitious. Good at finding creative solutions."

"Dr. Sato encouraged us to color outside the lines."

"Yeah?"

"Especially when we got stuck."

"He has an eye for talent," Stephen said. "He always has."

Something about his smile and the way he said it carried meaning. "Wait, do you know him?"

"For years. He didn't tell you?"

"No. I mean, we followed your work, of course, but we sort of considered your group..." I trailed off rather than finish the thought.

He did it for me. "The enemy?"

My face felt hot. I silently wished for the elevator to move faster. "I liked to think of it as more of a rivalry in the contest for scientific consensus."

"That's the beautiful thing about science. We almost never reach a consensus about anything."

It sounded like something Dr. Sato would say. In that moment I felt like they were kindred spirits, if not close friends. Making true friends in science was hard, anyway. You were naturally drawn to your peers, but routinely were asked to critique their work and their ideas. Just as they were asked to critique yours. Peer review, it was called, and it ensured the scientific rigor of published work and grant funding. Most of the time, the review was single-blind: the author of the work is identified, but the reviewers are anonymous. But science continued to grow ever more specialized, so it ended up being a relatively small group of peers who were qualified to review one another. In theory, personal feelings remained separate from the work.

But for many of us, the work was personal. For me, genetic engineering wasn't simply how I earned my living: it was something I'd worked toward for a long time and an important part of my identity. A critique of my work felt like a criticism directed at me. A lot of my scientist friends felt the same way. I knew they did. Maybe the grace of accepting peer critique was something that came with age.

The elevator dinged at last on my floor. Stephen stayed on; he must be continuing on up to Evelyn's office.

"See you soon," he said.

"I can't wait." This was going to be interesting.

✦ ✦ ✦

There was no formal invitation or notice about the inspection team's interview with the design team. Still, catching Stephen in the elevator was a stroke of luck. We had ten minutes' notice to compare notes, most of which we spent clearing the massive wall of energy drink cans from Wong's cubicle so that the space looked decent. I probably should have used it for last-minute prepping for both of them, but honestly I was still thrown by the fact that Stephen knew Dr. Sato. *For years*, he'd said.

"They're inspecting Design today," I said.

Korrapati and Wong popped out of their workstations.

"I figured," Korrapati said.

"How soon?" Wong asked.

"Any minute now. I saw Stephen in the elevator."

Korrapati smiled. "Oh, it's Stephen now, is it?"

"Not yet, but we had a nice and surprising conversation."

"What about?"

"I'll tell you later. Where are we with the inspection checklist?" We'd made it when we learned the EPA was coming—long before I knew who they'd select for consultants—as a way to make sure we had all our bases covered. It lived in our shared workspace so we could all mark things off as we reviewed them.

"Everything checked," Wong said, which of course should have been the case. I was just nervous.

We heard unusual noises from the hatchery that alerted us to something happening there. The doors were insulated but not soundproof, so I caught the unmistakable sound of Evelyn's enthusiastic voice and the muted *click-clack* of heels.

"Here they come," I breathed.

Evelyn entered first and held the heavy hatchery door open for those behind her. Dave, of course, moved up and held it so she could continue on. That was Dave. Polite to a fault. It reminded me of a time a week earlier when we'd been coming back from lunch. I'd been distracted and let the door close right in Korrapati's face. By accident, of course, and Wong shot out an arm to catch it, but I'd felt bad. As if remembering that same incident, Korrapati looked at me and pointedly raised her eyebrows. *Thanks, Dave.*

Then the team was in our space and the inspection began in earnest. The team wanted to see everything, so each of them came into a workstation and got a tour of one of our models. Wong introduced the EPA lady, Peggy Monroe, to the Rover model. Dave asked Korrapati to show him the Guardian, the original wild-hog-hunting dragon. That left me with Stephen for a tour of the newly modified fail-safe wild-release prototype.

"We meet again," I said by way of greeting. For some reason I was nervous.

"So I understand this model is substantially modified from the original dragon prototype developed by Simon Redwood."

"From the Guardian, yes."

He paused. "I was so sorry to hear of Redwood's passing."

"Oh. Yes." I kept my face somber, because I was one of the few people who knew that Redwood was still alive.

"I admired him quite a bit."

"Me too." That part wasn't a lie.

"So how has this been modified, exactly?"

"Do you know much about the original Guardian model?"

He smiled. "You can assume that I do."

"We now have developmental paths from that original model for the retail space. The first is domestication, which is aimed at producing a gentler animal for the consumer market." I proceeded to explain the so-called domestication trifecta that had finally brought dragons into an acceptable range of docility.

"That's clever, thinking back to problems that evolution has already solved for us."

"Nature knows best, right?" I regretted it the instant the words left my mouth, because I was about to make the case that nature didn't always know best.

"If you take humans out of the equation, then yes."

Touché. "Another developmental pathway is what you'll want to hear about, the biological fail-safes for wild-release dragons."

He didn't ask about the developmental pathway I hadn't mentioned, the one for the DOD's military dragons. That told me he'd already been briefed on the non-briefing agreement.

"Your domesticated models had a fail-safe mechanism, didn't they?" he asked.

"Yes, a metabolic deficiency countered by the supplements in our dragon food."

"In the food you sell."

"It wasn't my idea."

"And how did that fail-safe work, in your opinion?"

I thought about all of those dragons I'd encountered in the desert. Not to mention the herd that seemed to materialize around Redwood whenever he showed up. Plus my original Condors that had somehow survived and shown up at Connor's house. "No complaints."

"Well, of course you don't complain. Your company has an entire department for that."

"We get the summaries," I muttered.

"I think we both know what the evidence shows about your previous dragon control measures."

I held up a hand in surrender. "We're serious about ensuring our dragons can be released into the wild without major consequences, so we've redesigned the entire fail-safe system."

"All right. How?"

"The process starts at hatching when the dragonet imprints on its human handler." I went on to describe the imprinting procedure and that first critical hour, but I kept it brief. He cared less about that than the mechanisms of the fail-safe itself.

"Every dragon we release into the wild will have a specific purpose, like the eradication of pests. While the dragons are engaged in that activity, a few things keep them at peak fitness. There's the food we sell, which has two key amino acids the animals can't synthesize on their own."

"Let's have a look at that first, shall we?"

I thought the metabolic stuff would bore him honestly, so his request caught me by surprise. "Really?"

"Absolutely. I like dabbling in biochemistry."

"All right, then." I pulled up the sequence for the first of the enzymes we'd disabled to knock out a key part of the amino acid synthesis pathways. "Let's talk glutamine."

CHAPTER TEN
Bitter and Sweet

We met outside in the sweltering heat for the performance trial of the new biological fail-safes. It was 2:00 in the afternoon, and I figured the heat might help. Normally dragons enjoyed the heat—the desert in daytime made for great hatching temperatures—but it came at a metabolic cost for any animal. Heat sped up everything at the molecular level, where a lot of our fail-safes needed to start.

The on-site inspection took longer than any of us expected. Stephen wanted a walk-through of every modification we'd made in dragon survival pathways. Then he asked about genes associated with longevity, which we'd left somewhat alone. Longevity genes had, of course, been a subject of intense research for a long time. A few decades ago, scientists found a simple way to nearly double the lifespan of laboratory mice, by putting them on a reduced-calorie diet. It took a substantial calorie reduction, though, essentially cutting the normal mouse diet in half.

Some interesting things happened when you put animals on a calorie-restricted diet. Their metabolism shifted from carbon metabolism to fatty acid synthesis. Free radicals went down. Oxidative damage went down. Naturally, the mice were lean and diabetes-resistant, too. It was a perfect model for extending the lifespan of other animals. Unfortunately, the strategy didn't really translate to higher organisms like humans. It would be like living on a thousand-calorie diet for your entire life. You might see the same benefits but you'd be miserable. That was assuming you could get people to do it. Sure, everyone wanted a fountain of youth, but most weren't prepared to make a lot of sacrifices. They wanted a pill, or something easy.

The natural lifespan of our dragons derived from the source organisms, so we expected it to be in the single-digit years, maybe a bit longer if they remained healthy. We honestly hadn't had the circumstances to truly measure it because the company hadn't been around long enough. Most of our dragons were still on the early side of middle age.

We were looking at the gene called APOE—apolipoprotein E—which was famous because of its link to Alzheimer's disease in humans. One form of the gene made you susceptible to the disease, whereas another form had a slightly protective effect. The protective allele was rare in the overall population but if you tested healthy octogenarians, they often had it. APOE was one of the few genes reliably linked to longevity. It encoded a protein whose function wasn't entirely known. Something to do with lipid metabolism.

"Peculiar gene, isn't it?" Stephen had said.

"Most celebrities are."

He chuckled. "You're not wrong."

"What's your opinion of genetic longevity?" I asked.

"At best, I think it's a fool's errand. Billions of dollars have been invested in that area of research, with very little to show for it. I'd have rather seen it spent on something else. And at worst, tampering with longevity could have too many unpredictable consequences on global ecosystems. The anthropogenic effects on our environment are too large already."

"I think I agree, which is part of why we've left these genes unaltered."

"Which is wise. I'll award you a point for that."

"Thank you." I grinned. "How many points does that put me at?"

"One."

Now we approached the outdoor holding pens where the two batches of test dragons had been moved two days prior. The holding pens had running digital clocks on them that recorded how many hours had passed since the last task-associated stimulation. Dragons still under the forty-eight-hour window looked pretty healthy. They patrolled the perimeters of their holding pens for their target prey—of which there were none, of course. Holding pen number five had just hit forty-eight hours. That dragon wasn't moving as well. It stood shakily and stumbled from the pen into the shady area provided for rest. As we neared, the biometric readouts began to flash. Warning tones pealed from the monitors as the already erratic readouts all plummeted. The dragon let out a long breath and did not draw another. I felt a tightening in my stomach and looked away. Everyone else's eyes were glued to the dragon's body. Stephen pursed his lips and nodded. On Dave's face, sadness warred with admiration. *Yeah, that's about right.* I hated watching dragons die. It reminded me too much of the real deaths I'd witnessed, or the time I thought I'd lost Octavius. Even so, a small part of me felt grimly satisfied that we'd pulled off yet another scientific achievement. I checked the time clock. Forty-eight hours and twelve minutes.

"It doesn't get much closer than that," I muttered.

The team moved on to the next enclosure, where the clock read forty-nine hours. That dragon was also on the ground and clearly not moving. So were all the pens after that. At a signal from Evelyn, I drew back and let the inspection team do their thing. They were noting pen numbers, time elapsed, and the monitor readouts. A dragon handler I didn't recognize helped them run back the recordings for the dragons that had already passed on. One was forty-eight hours ten minutes, another forty-eight hours eighteen minutes. They had all crashed before the forty-nine-hour mark, except for the first one which had lasted to fifty hours. *Probably snuck a cricket after it was supposed to,* I told myself. Still, the results spoke for themselves. I felt an odd rush of gratitude for Stephen, whose questions about our designs had delayed us coming out here by a few hours. As a result, I'd only had to watch one dragon die.

Evelyn looked over at me and smiled. "Not bad, Noah Parker."

We'd all spent plenty of time sweating in the heat, so it was a relief to come back into the air-conditioned conference room. The inspection team convened for a private discussion first. For once, I didn't mind being excluded. We'd collected our own versions of the biometrics for all the test-case dragons from both batches. Plotting the deviation from normal healthy patterns over time elapsed made it clear that the lines converged on the target time of forty-eight hours post deprivation.

"I'm still amazed at how well it worked out," I said. "You two did a fantastic job. Evelyn's very impressed with your work."

"You spoke to her?" Korrapati asked.

"She was there at the end of the field trial."

"Oh." She glanced at Wong and they both avoided looking at me.

"Relax, guys. You didn't have to come to the field trials." I suppose I hadn't had to either, but I knew Evelyn wanted me there.

Korrapati offered a sympathetic smile. "Was it bad?"

"Yes, it kind of was. One of the dragons died right in front of us." I remembered how it had gone still as the biometric alarms wailed, and grimaced. "It was quick. I'll say that much."

"That's what we wanted, isn't it?"

"Yes, of course. But I still don't like it." The list of things we kept having to do to dragons simply to keep the lights on at Build-A-Dragon never seemed to end. First we turned them into pets, then we turned them into weapons, and now we turned them into mayflies.

"Me neither," Wong said.

"Really?" It surprised me to hear him say that because he'd never seemed bothered by some of our previous endeavors. Then again, Wong had always been hard to read.

"Dragon is special creature," he said. "Should be allowed to live in the wild if it can survive."

I didn't dare tell him, but I sort of agreed. The dragons we made were living, breathing organisms. If we were going to introduce them to solve ecological problems, it only seemed fair that they have a chance to compete and survive in those environments. Scientifically, it was hard to make that argument. From Asian carp to Burmese python, there were just too many examples of predators coming into new environments as invasive species. My tablet beeped with an alert, drawing my attention back from that foolish dream.

I thought I knew what the message was but checked it to be sure. "They're ready to give their decision."

We trooped down to Build-A-Dragon's largest conference room. In spite of how well the field trials had gone, and how friendly the inspection team acted, I was nervous. The EPA's initial decision was entirely their purview, and Stephen undoubtedly held a lot of influence on their discussions. Hell, so did Dave. We could always appeal their decision if it went against us, but that took months. The desert sanctuary didn't have that kind of time. Our company might not even have that kind of time, if Evelyn was to be believed about the financial situation. Granted, it seemed like every few months she told me something of that nature. I'd panic, and work my ass off to solve whatever problem she'd dropped in front of me.

The inspection team awaited us. Evelyn was already there, chatting with Stephen in a corner. Dave, ever the Boy Scout, was sitting with Peggy and reviewing something on her tablet. *Probably a detailed discussion of all the reasons they're failing us.* I shook my head, because there was no point in worrying about that now. Whatever their decision was, nothing in this room would change it.

"So, have you enjoyed your visit?" Evelyn asked Peggy as Wong, Korrapati, and I found seats along the wall and tried to look invisible. Distracted as I was, I still admired how she asked such a loaded question in such a casual way. It was almost like the next few minutes held no importance for the future of our company.

"Wonderful, thank you," Peggy said. "It's a beautiful facility you have here."

"Great lab, too," Dave said. "Clean as a whistle." Maybe it was my imagination, but he seemed to smile at Korrapati and wink at me simultaneously.

Stephen said nothing. We all knew his was the vote that mattered, so we waited with bated breath.

"After a review of your facilities and discussion with our advisory panel, your application for wild-release dragons has been approved."

Yes! I pumped a fist and shared a grin with Korrapati. Wong offered a toothy smile and clapped me on the shoulder.

"Subject to three conditions," Peggy finished.

Looks like I celebrated too soon.

"What are the conditions?" Evelyn asked.

"First, you will submit detailed design specifications for each customized dragon released into a wild environment."

When you submitted something to the EPA, it might become a matter of public record. Which meant anyone could get their hands on it. Dragon designs were my purview, so I could have asked the question, but Evelyn beat me to it.

"How much detail would you require?" she asked. "The code that goes into our dragons is—"

"Proprietary," Peggy finished for her. "Yes, we understand. I'm sure we can come up with a reasonable compromise."

"What about a detailed readout from Noah's simulator?" Dave suggested. "It would give us complete readouts of the dragon specifications and predicted behaviors. And the three-dimensional rendering is as good as a visual fingerprint, without revealing the genetic sequence behind it."

"Good enough for me," Peggy said.

We all looked at Evelyn.

"Sounds like the perfect solution," she said.

"Condition two, you agree to provide after-action reports at the conclusion of each deployment with detailed observation of the dragons' activities and any environmental impacts."

"We can do that. How soon after the end of the deployment would you want them?"

"Two weeks."

"We can do that."

So far, so good. We'd expected the EPA would want design specs on the wild-release dragons, and Evelyn had fervently hoped that wouldn't mean giving up the reptilian genome sequence. Granted, the so-called dragon genome was public already, but all of the proprietary modifications we made to make them into our products were most definitely not. As for the report, that was pretty standard stuff. Evelyn and Korrapati submitted regular reports to the DOJ—or at least, they were supposed to. Now that I was on the outside, I didn't know for sure. So both of those conditions cost us nothing we weren't prepared to give already.

"Condition three," Peggy was saying. "To facilitate communication and monitoring, we would like a neutral liaison to be on-site for the first year of the program."

Neutral liaison?

"What purpose would this person serve?" Evelyn asked.

"To monitor the initial designs of wild-release dragons and keep the review panel apprised of progress."

"With all due respect, the things we do here are fairly sophisticated. I'm not sure a government administrator would even—"

"Oh, it would be a scientist. Someone with suitable training."

Yeah, good luck, I was thinking. The expertise required to grasp genetic engineering principles didn't exactly grow on trees. I missed whatever Evelyn said next but it must have been along those lines.

"Fortunately, we've already identified someone with the correct experience who volunteered to step in."

We all looked at each other. Evelyn and Korrapati and I were puzzled. *Please be Stephen*, I thought fervently, though I knew someone at his level wouldn't take a gig like this.

"Oh, right," Dave said. "That would be me."

CHAPTER ELEVEN
INTERLUDE

Swarms of locusts have plagued farmers since the beginning of recorded history, and probably did so well before that. Many people are familiar with the plagues described in the Bible's Book of Exodus, but ancient Egyptians carved locusts on tombs 2,500 years before the time of Jesus Christ. In 322 BC, Aristotle wrote about locusts and their tendency to swarm in his book *History of Animals*. He noted that their eggs were laid in the ground and subject to destruction when autumn rains were heavy, but seasons of drought could bring locusts in massive numbers.

In China, locust plagues have been recorded for millennia. The ancient Chinese character for the locust was inscribed on an oracle bone from a 3,000-year-old Shang dynasty tomb. Chinese historians have recorded more than 800 plagues since 707 BC, especially in northern China. In 310 AD, a plague of locusts swept through the Luoyang region and caused widespread famine, contributing to the fall of the Western Jin dynasty. Ancient emperors mandated treatment programs to prevent the insect scourges; beginning in the Tang dynasty, the government began appointing "locust control officers" whose duty was to control the outbreaks. The insects even invaded Chinese literature. An ancient poem by Tang dynasty poet Bai Juyi reads:

> *Locust outbreaks distributed widely in the center,*
> *Eating like silkworms and flying like rain.*

Green crop shoots disappear,
Only black soil left for thousands of miles,
Governors worried about yield,
Demand that people catch locusts day and night.

The most impressive locust plagues in modern history are also some of the most mysterious. They happened in the Great Plains of the United States in the nineteenth century. The insect was the Rocky Mountain locust, which ranged on both sides of the mountains for which it was named. They bred in dry sandy areas of the mountains, and in times of drought descended into the prairie in search of food. These swarms became problematic in the mid-1800s as farming expanded westward into the locusts' preferred habitat. Most of the time, they were an irritation more than a devastation. Yet the locust plague of 1874 was something else. It had been a particularly hot and dry spring, followed by a hotter and drier summer.

Ideal locust breeding conditions.

The swarms glided down from the mountains in great glistening clouds that blocked out the sun for hours at a time. They cut a swath of destruction hundreds of miles wide, ravaging everything in their path: crops, tree foliage, blades of grass. Anything green was gone. The locusts also devoured wool off of sheep and food out of farmers' homesteads. The sheer number of the insects added to the devastation—their bodies poisoned water sources and fouled railroad tracks. Chickens and turkeys ate so many of them that the locust oils rendered their meat and eggs inedible. Worse, the locusts laid eggs wherever they went. The massive swarms that rose up the following year numbered in the billions to trillions—the densest concentration of animals ever recorded on the planet. Yet, like the great Roman Empire, the Rocky Mountain locust fell precipitously after this high point. Their numbers declined each year after 1875 as farmers plowed up their eggs in the spring and developed more of their preferred habitats into farmland. By the early 1900s, the Rocky Mountain locust had gone extinct. Their legacy lived on in the annals of science, and in their species name, *Melanoplus spretus*. The second word meant *despised*.

The desert locust, *Schistocerca gregaria*, remains a point of fascination for the world of science. Its historical range stretched across most of Africa and a large swath of the Middle East. Most of the time it lives as the short-horned grasshopper, a solitary green insect that generally goes unnoticed in small numbers. Every so often, usually after a period of intense rainfall following a drought, they emerge in great numbers to lay eggs in the moist earth. The presence of so many grasshoppers in close proximity triggers a morphological change from a lonely dull green hopper to a long-winged, tiger-striped migratory locust. In this form the insects are highly gregarious and mobile, forming huge bands that drift with the prevailing winds in search of food. A plague of desert locusts swept over Mount Lebanon during the First World War, causing a famine that killed hundreds of thousands of people in the Ottoman Empire. Outbreaks continued into the twenty-first century, and their range only grew.

The greatest fear for many is that the desert locust might make its way to the hot, dry areas of the American Southwest. If it did, it might very well succeed where the Rocky Mountain locust failed.

CHAPTER TWELVE
The Looming Threat

As soon as the meeting ended, I hurried back to my office to call Lisa Hashimoto. Part of it was wanting to give her the good news right away. The other part was to not think about Dave. I still hadn't processed that the idea that he was going to stay for a while. I wasn't sure how it had happened or even what was said until after they dropped that bomb.

I had Lisa's contact page up on one of my projection monitors as a reminder to myself. Even if the EPA decision had gone against us, I didn't want to keep her in the dark. Now I brought it down in front of me and requested a video call. It rang six or eight times, to the point where I was getting ready to disconnect and try later. Then she answered. In a few seconds, a new video-call window opened up. The feed was laggy, but I could see it was her. She wore a broad-brimmed hat and looked to be entirely covered with dust. She also looked tired.

"Hello, it's Noah Parker," I said.

"Oh, yes." A half smile found its way through the lines on her face. "I remember you."

I wasn't sure how to take that, so I decided on positive. *Better to be memorable than forgettable, I suppose.* "I have good news. We just won EPA approval for the wild-release dragons."

"How soon can you deploy them?"

I did some quick calculations to allow for the gestation and hatching, plus two days to review the designs we'd been working on. "Two weeks."

She frowned. "That may not be in time. We lost two more enclosures today."

My heart sank. "I thought you'd taken some precautions to buy time."

"The pesticides have had no effect on most of the swarms. I think they're resistant. And they chewed through the physical barriers like they weren't even there."

Holy crap. I'd heard about ravenous foraging insects before, but this took it to a new level. "Jeez, I didn't realize it was that bad." Forget two days to review my design, I'd do it today. And maybe get Evelyn's permission for the rapid gestation protocol given the urgency. "Five and a half days. We can deliver dragons in five and a half days if we push."

"Now you're talking," Lisa said. Her eyes shifted to the side. "Let me check where the swarms are."

"You can track them?"

"We adapted our weather radar. Turns out tracking huge clouds of bugs isn't that different from charting precipitation."

Smart. I didn't know much about radar, but I could guess it would be useful. "How predictable are their movements?"

"Not nearly as predictable as we'd like." She rubbed her eyes, looking even more tired. Almost resigned. "Sometimes it gives us a day's notice or so, and we can get in to move anything that's portable."

"You can move plants," I said, and I'm sure my disbelief came through the video.

"Some of them, if you're willing to dig."

I tried to picture getting on my hands and knees with a shovel on the burning-hot sand to pry something out of the rock-hard alkaline soil. I knew it was her life's work and chosen career, but it still amazed me how far she was willing to go. "They must be pretty special plants."

"Trust me, they are," she said. And then, more quietly, "More special than I can easily explain." She looked at me with intense focus. "Will the dragons work?"

"I think so."

"You think?"

"Lisa, trust me," I said. "Dragons are what we do."

She gave me a nod. "Keep me posted."

We disconnected, and I heard a knock on my open door. It was Evelyn.

"*Ni mang, ma?*" she asked in Mandarin. *Are you busy?*

"*Bu sheuh*," I answered, then delivered one of my favorite phrases. "*Ching tsin. Ching tsoo-ah.*" It meant *Please come in and sit.*

Evelyn did so, and smiled approvingly. "Very nice tones."

I knew she was buttering me up. My tones weren't that good, and we both knew it. Beyond that, she'd come to my office to talk. She only did that when she wanted something. "I just got off with Lisa."

"How are they holding out?"

"It's a war of attrition. I gave her the good news about our approval, but she said fourteen days might not be in time. Do you think we can use the rapid gestation protocol?"

"We didn't write that into the EPA application, but there was some language about extenuating circumstances. I'll check with the lawyers, but I think we can get away with it."

She thinks we can get away with it. Whenever lawyers were involved, there were no guarantees. Now I knew I was in trouble. "That's good. I'll have the design ready today."

"It's good we have the EPA approval, isn't it?"

"Yes..." I said slowly.

"I was talking to some of the others, after you fled the meet—"

"Okay, I did not *flee* the meeting. I wanted to let Lisa know we could help her." Why were people always accusing me of running away from meetings, anyway? When I had to go, I went. God knows Evelyn click-clacked her way in and out of meetings all the time.

"Anyway, Noah Parker, I was thinking about what to do with your friend Dave."

"What do you mean?"

"Well, he'll be with us for some time. We should make sure he's comfortable here."

"You don't need to worry about that. Dave's comfortable most places," I said.

"And I think we could benefit from his expertise."

"His expertise is basically the same as mine." Up to a point, that was. We were both in the Sato lab together for three years. ASU was the epicenter of genetic engineering and synthetic biology. Dr. Sato may not have been a scion of the field, but he ran a great lab and he knew everyone. Even Stephen, apparently. We had journal clubs and guest lectures, as well as a stable of ambitious young scientists who were all eager to master the universe. Hell, that was where I learned most of what I knew. Where I designed and built the simulator.

"Oh, you've worked for the EPA?" she asked, knowing the answer.

"No. You know what I mean. We have the same background."

"I understand. That's why I think he should sit with your team in Design."

"In *Design*?"

"Why not?"

"I thought you'd stick him in an office upstairs or something." At least, that's what I hoped. In the back of my mind, that was how I'd come to accept the fact that Dave would be joining us for a long period. Denial. If he was on another floor I could pretend that he wasn't around.

"I'm surprised, Noah. Normally you're the one convincing me that you need more people."

She wasn't wrong. I wanted another designer, and I'd probably need one if the wild-release dragon program took off. I shook my head. "This is all happening really fast."

"What was it you told me last year? Genetic engineers don't grow like trees?" she asked.

"They don't grow *on* trees." The unique mix of engineering and genetics had fallen out of fashion since the crash of most genetic engineering firms a few years back. Which had resulted in part from the canine epidemic, which was intentionally prolonged by Greaves when he ran the company. In a way, it was all kind of ironic. "It would be weird. For both of us."

"Weird to work with your friend?"

"Yes." I didn't want to tell her the whole and more complicated truth. "Can I think about it?"

"Sure, you can think as long as you like about what is going to happen." She smiled but I sensed the finality in her tone, and I knew I was beaten. She was the big boss and, as usual, she got what she wanted.

I sighed. "All right, let's go find him a workstation, I guess."

"Oh, Noah, I was actually thinking he could just share this office with you."

"*What?*"

She laughed. "I'm kidding. Oh, you should see your face. We already set him up in the workstation next to Korrapati."

Of course they did. "This just keeps getting better and better," I grumbled.

CHAPTER THIRTEEN
Chitinous

We met in the morning at Wong's workstation for a final review of the insect-eating dragons. Wong was there, of course—he'd been tinkering with the design all morning. I knew because every time he ran the simulator I still got an email with some of the basic performance stats—something we'd set up a long time ago when trying to crack domestication. Everyone else had set up filters to delete those messages, but I hadn't taken the time. That's what I told them, at least. In truth, I rather liked knowing when people were using my simulator. It reminded me of the one little thing I'd done for the company that no one had yet taken away.

"What do you think, Wong?" I asked.

"Looks good. I worked on agility this morning."

"Good. That's the one thing I was worried about." Most of nature's best insectivores had evolved special capabilities to reliably catch prey. Frogs had long, sticky tongues. Birds had specialized beaks. Even the tiny shrew, a night hunter, killed and ate its body weight in insects every day with the aid of two large front-pointing incisors.

"We still have a few feature points left," Korrapati said. "What do you think we should spend them on?"

Available feature points meant that we could boost one of the dragon's advantages. Strength was an option, though if it was too strong it might elect to choose something larger than insects for prey. If it went after birds or rodents—many of which were insectivores in their own right—that would make the locust problem worse, not better. We could add intelligence but that carried similar risks. Overall dragon size was optimal. Maybe we didn't need to use all of the feature points. Keeping some open would let us tweak things and—

"What about lengthening the claws?" Dave asked. He'd popped up from his workstation and joined the conversation of his own volition.

Yes, this was exactly what I was worried about. Someone with my experience and training jumping in to conversations that had enough people already. Korrapati and Wong both looked at me askance. Evelyn had asked me to make him comfortable, so I forced down my natural reaction. "Nice idea. How long are the claws currently?"

"Two centimeters," Korrapati said.

That might seem long enough but they were curved. That made them good for grasping prey, but ultimately reduced the reach.

"How large are the locusts?" Dave asked, beating me to it by half a second.

Wong shrugged.

"We aren't sure," Korrapati said.

"You aren't sure?" He sounded shocked.

I couldn't help but add some fuel to the fire. "To be honest, we can't be entirely certain that they *are* locusts."

"What?"

"Relax, man, I'm kidding. We're fairly confident they're locusts, but we don't know how old. Normally these swarms are mostly juveniles. But the field scientists have only caught adult insects."

"How big are those?"

"Six, seven centimeters." Those were Lisa's numbers. She'd offered to ship me some specimens in dry ice, but at the time that had seemed like an unnecessary step. Not to mention a disgusting one. Now I kind of wished I'd let her. It would be useful to get precise measurements, maybe run some tests.

"Wong, can I send you a patch?" Dave asked. "It's a module for Noah's simulator."

"It's a *what*?"

"A test module. A little something I've been cooking up, like an add-on."

I'd recently started to let Korrapati and Wong alter my simulator code, so the concept wasn't as nauseating as it could have been. In some ways, it was fitting. Dave had been there at the simulator's origins.

That's the mantra I recited to myself.

The alternative was to throw a tantrum, which didn't seem professional or collegial.

Wong's workstation beeped with an incoming message. His fingers flew across the keys, and the patch came up. Dave's code looked the same as I remembered it—efficient, lean, and completely unassuming. *Rather like the man himself*, I thought ruefully.

"What does it do?" Wong asked quietly.

I shrugged. Dave's code had always been like Greek to me. "Guess we should load it up and find out."

If Wong had an opinion about launching unknown code on his system, he didn't share it. He might have given a me a side-eye while he lined things up, but I wasn't worried. Dave didn't have a malicious bone in his body. Wong restarted the simulator and brought up the insectivore dragon design again. To me, it looked the same. Dave leaned down next to Wong and pressed the F1 key. A new but tiny three-dimensional image blinked into existence at the dragon's feet.

"What is that?" Korrapati asked.

Dave smiled and said nothing.

The image was rotating slowly—probably borrowing the movement code built in to my simulator so you could see the animal at any angle. Wong peered at it from the side. "Looks like grasshopper."

I got a better look at it and noticed the coloring, and the longer wings that only emerged in a migrating insect. There was only one species that adapted its body shape and lifestyle in response to the environment. "Desert locust."

"Noah's got it," Dave said. "Simulated dragon, meet simulated prey."

"How did you do that?" I asked.

"It's a piggyback process that will load a second genome. I used the public sequence for the desert locus."

It was brilliant. So brilliant I wished I'd thought of it myself, but even so... "Nice. Wong, see if you can move the dragon closer."

Wong tapped his keys and moved the dragon into position, then had it close its claw. Both predator and prey were illusions of projected light, but the relative dimensions were spot-on. We could see that the dragon's claws would be able to close around the locust in its middle, but not trap it entirely.

"All right, give the claws another centimeter and run it again," I told Wong.

He adjusted the slider in DragonDraft 3D and relaunched both simulated animals. Now the claws wrapped around the locust like a cage.

"Not bad, Dave," Korrapati said. The admiration was plain in her voice.

"Agreed," I said.

Dave grinned. "Glad to lend a hand. Now all we need is a name."

"Oh, I've got that picked out already."

"Really?"

"I was thinking Mantis."

"As in praying mantis?" He guffawed. "That is badass."

"I'll let Evelyn know it's ready." I put my hand on Wong's shoulder. "Start printing eggs."

"How many?"

"As many as you can."

CHAPTER FOURTEEN
Hordes

An hour in the Mojave Desert reminded me that I lived in a relatively temperate part of the Southwest. I chalked it up to the hard ground and even harder rocks that bounced the relentless sunlight up into my face. That was probably why the pop-up shelters seemed to offer little comfort out here. Well, that and the total lack of wind. There were two cliffs separated by about a half mile that formed a wide, low canyon. Probably carved out by a river millions of years ago. Now it looked dry and dusty. If Lisa's models were accurate, the nearest swarm would fly through this canyon before they threatened the next bio trove. The canyons provided a sort of natural bottleneck, so if our dragons were going to ambush them, this was the place.

Evelyn had made all kinds of preparations. She was pulling out all the stops. Our whole team plus the entire Herpetology department had come in rented dark SUVs to this area. Hatchers, too, had come in droves. Jim and Allie, the two I knew personally, now oversaw two large groups of them in their unmistakable white clothing. They had to be ready to melt, but they'd brought the dragon eggs from their transport trucks—another rental, because we'd never transported so many eggs at once—to prefabricated hatching platforms arrayed in neat rows on the canyon floor. The numbers of dragon wranglers, too, seemed to have doubled since I'd last seen them. Maybe I should have asked for twice as many designers. Well, too late for that now.

"It must be thirty-eight degrees out here," Korrapati said. She stood with me and Evelyn in the shade of a pop-up canopy tent the dragon handlers had put up early this morning. It spoke to her mood that she didn't even convert from Celsius.

Multiply by nine, divide by five, add thirty-two. Thirty-eight Celsius was about a hundred degrees Fahrenheit. I checked my tablet, which pulled real-time data from a weather station we'd set up. "Ninety-five."

"Good hatching temperature," Evelyn said.

"*Great* hatching temperature," I agreed.

Korrapati gave me a withering glare. She was not a fan of the heat. We watched Dave and Wong, who had ventured out into the sunlight to take a tour of the dragon eggs. They'd have been back by now, except Dave kept stopping to touch the various eggs. It simultaneously alarmed the hatchery staff, who never loved the notion of anyone else handling their charges, and irritated Wong, who was clearly eager to get back into the shade. I found it all rather entertaining to watch.

"How is it going with him?" Evelyn asked. She didn't have to say who she was asking about.

"Good," I said lightly, mindful that Korrapati could hear us. She was overheated and uncomfortable, but she was listening. "He had some clever suggestions for the final design."

Evelyn smiled. "I told you he would be useful."

"Well, he had the right training."

At this moment, Dave was petting another egg in its wooden enclosure. Wong looked ready to abandon him and run to the tent. Well, to speed-walk to the tent. Wong didn't run. If a bomb appeared in the middle of the canyon with a giant digital timer counting down from two minutes, he'd only walk out if he couldn't catch a ride.

He did step lively, though, when he eventually ducked under the tent to rejoin us. "Too hot."

I thought about making a comment about the weather in Chinese—something like how I personally thought it felt great outside—but I didn't think he was in the mood.

"It's amazing, isn't it?" Dave was huffing and red-faced but sounded exhilarated. "Have you ever printed so many eggs at once?"

"Not that we can tell you about," Korrapati said.

"Oh really?"

"I'm afraid you don't have the security clearance for it." She was teasing him now.

And here I thought she was in a bad mood.

"How do you know?" Dave asked.

"There's just no way you'd pass the background checks."

Dave guffawed.

Evelyn checked her watch. "They'll start hatching soon."

I knew that, though not from checking the timing. There was a rising tension in the air, an undercurrent of biological anticipation. Or maybe I was suffering from heatstroke. It was hard to be sure.

"Any sign of the locusts?" Dave asked.

"Not yet," I said.

"Are we sure they'll come this way?"

I shrugged, trying to hide my nervousness. "Lisa seemed to think so."

A cloud of dust appeared behind us over the road that led into this canyon. We heard the rumbling of a diesel engine next. Then a large, dusty brown vehicle lurched into view. It was the size of a small bus and looked like a vintage pickup truck and a beat-up mobile home had had a baby. Were it not for the modern weather station and radar antenna on the top, you'd think it belonged in a junkyard.

"I'm guessing that's her. If she's here, the plague won't be far behind." I took a breath and plunged out into the bright sunlight and the accompanying heat. The ground was hard and unforgiving but mercifully flat. Still, unlike some of the other places I'd ventured to in the desert, the ground did not seem to radiate heat. If anything, it was cooler than the air. I crouched down and put my hand on it to see if it was just my imagination, but it wasn't. Something was strange about this place.

I jogged up to meet the desert RV where it had either parked or broken down. It was angled thirty degrees off the road, facing due west. The side door opened with a cringe-inducing, metal-on-metal squeak. A man in rumpled, well-worn dungarees hopped out.

"Oh. Hey." I started to offer my hand.

"Hey." He slid past me and moved around to the back of the van. He stepped up onto the bumper and then climbed a short ladder to the roof, where he started fiddling with a piece of gray equipment. Then he leaned over the edge of the roof and said, "Try it now!"

"Still nothing," answered a woman's voice from the vehicle's interior.

The man fiddled some more, and then I heard a faint whirring noise. The apparatus was spinning. "Now?"

"That's got it." She came into view now, muttering something about "crappy government hand-me-downs."

I recognized her right away from our video calls. She was younger than I'd guessed. Maybe close to my age. Her long dusty hair was tied into a ponytail. She was the first person I'd seen all day who wasn't wearing sunglasses. "Lisa?"

She half-turned around and double-tapped the side of the vehicle. "Nice job, Kenny." Then she turned to me. "Sorry, the radar has been on the fritz."

"Everything okay?"

"Yeah, sure. The bugs are right behind us."

CHAPTER FIFTEEN
The Wave

In the semidarkness of her strange mobile science lab, Lisa showed me the radar on a jury-rigged flat-screen monitor that looked decades old. The feed was good, though, and superimposed the radar signal over a topographic map of the area we were in. The map showed a long flat area with steep increases in elevation on two sides. That would be the canyon where we'd set up. There was another symbol running through the canyon—a series of short sinuous lines, but I couldn't remember what those meant. I was distracted by the radar feed anyway—it showed a massive lime-green wall of precipitation just west of our location, moving steadily east.

Which made no sense. I'd checked the weather reports this morning and they were all clear. So were the skies. "We're not supposed to get rain today, are we? That looks like a pretty serious storm front." It was hard to say how rain would affect the dragonets' activity. We hadn't thought to test it, because this was a deployment to a desert environment.

"That's not precipitation, Noah," Lisa said. "That's the bugs."

"You're joking."

"I'm not."

I used the scale on the topographic map for a quick estimation. "That cloud is a mile wide. Maybe a mile and a quarter."

Lisa shrugged. "They must be clumping up. It was two miles wide yesterday."

Two miles wide. That was an astonishing figure. We'd never printed this many dragons before, but still, I wasn't sure we'd created enough. Well, too late for that now. "How long until they reach us?"

Lisa was already running trajectory estimates from the leading edge of the swarm. "Under ten minutes."

"I'd better go check on the eggs."

I plunged back into the heat and hurried across to the pop-up tent where Evelyn and the others waited. "Where are we with the eggs?"

Evelyn checked her watch. "Two minutes."

It still amazed me that we could predict and even control the dragonet gestation time. This was something that Nature generally set for every species and kept firm. Dragons already gestated more quickly than most higher organisms but we'd optimized it even more. It had always been an approximation, give or take half an hour, but since the DOD project, the timing had gotten far more precise. Korrapati and Evelyn hadn't said anything, but a slider for desired gestation time had magically appeared one day on DragonDraft 3D. That was a good thing, because we'd really had to make adjustments to account for printing time on so many eggs. We'd let Korrapati handle that part.

Sure enough, two minutes later there were shouts from some of the attentive hatchery staffers. Dragon wranglers ran over to confirm and gave Evelyn a thumbs-up. Then the noise of cracking eggshells seemed to fill the canyon, echoing off the walls.

"I've got to see this!" Dave pulled his hat down and ran out into the blazing sunlight. I found myself running with him to the nearest hatching station. Herpetology had custom-built them for this hatching. They were wood-framed open boxes stuffed with synthetic nesting material to protect the eggs. In the corner was another more unusual enhancement—a molded paper-board cup nestled in the corner. Biodegradable, of course. The dragon wranglers had filled each one with a handful of crickets. They were native to Arizona, wouldn't damage crops, and importantly, couldn't jump right out of the feed containers. That's what they were meant to be, feed for the new hatchlings. Dragons always hatched hungry.

Korrapati couldn't tell us officially, but she'd hinted that the military dragons that got the rapid gestation protocol came out of their eggs absolutely ravenous. Tom Johnson, our biology consultant, thought crickets were the best option for immediate sustenance before the dragonets got to work.

"Look at that," Dave said.

The egg in front of us trembled. I recognized that movement, the energetic quiver that came before every hatching. I didn't know for sure but guessed it was the dragon within testing the walls of its confinement. Looking for weaknesses. As we watched, a crack split the egg down the middle. Then a claw emerged and the crack widened.

I nudged Dave. "He's loving that extra centimeter, now."

"Yeah," he said distantly. His eyes were fixed on the egg. I watched them hatch so many times, I sort of forgot how special the experience could be.

The dragon shredded its shell and emerged into the sunlight. It was dusky brown with hints of emerald green—perfect desert camouflage. It stretched its wings out to dry. They were compact but sturdy. We didn't yet know how much the dragons would need to fly, but we knew they'd need some mobility since the swarms were always moving. There was a high metabolism cost to that, though. If the dragons ran out of food, their metabolic breakdown would happen quickly. That's what we wanted, I supposed, but I didn't like thinking about it.

One of the crickets chirped. The dragon, which had been sunning itself and stretching, cocked its head as if listening. The cricket chirped again, and the dragon moved closer. The cricket must have felt the vibration, because it went quiet. Not soon enough, though. The dragon loomed over the cup and then struck downward with its head twice in rapid succession, catching a cricket each time.

"Whoa!" I said.

"It's quick, isn't it?" Dave asked.

"They have to be."

Even as we watched, the last cricket somehow escaped its container and made a break for freedom. The dragon was still working to swallow the first two, but shot out a claw and pinned it against the wood of the hatching enclosure. In a few seconds, it scooped the wounded cricket up, swallowed it in a single bite, and looked around for more. Yeah, that's an ideal predator for a grasshopper. Similar scenes were playing out all across the hatching grounds. Some dragonets were sunning themselves, some were nosing around in their feed containers, and some were beginning to explore the area.

"Have you ever seen so many dragons at once?" Dave asked.

I started to say that I had, but paused when I realized that I really hadn't. Even the packs of wild dragons we'd encountered in the desert—feral creatures that shouldn't have been able to live on their own—were not so numerous. "Never."

"Build-A-Dragon is a pretty amazing place to work."

"You're not wrong."

Dave grinned at me. "You're lucky, you know that? I mean, you earned your place and your simulator continues to impress me. But you're lucky as hell."

I smiled. "You're not wrong about that, either." Even so, I had the distant, primal warning bells ringing inside my head. It was all too convenient and he was being too complimentary. *So what's he buttering me up for?*

"So what's the deal with Korrapati?"

His question threw me a little. "What do you mean?"

"She's really smart, huh?"

"Absolutely," I said, my nervousness decreasing a little. I'd thought he was taking that in a very different direction.

"Does she have a boyfriend?"

Okay, so I wasn't way off. I couldn't say why, but it irked me. They were both adults and could make their own choices, of course. But still. "You'd have to ask her that."

"Come on, man, if I was brave enough to ask her, I wouldn't be asking you."

Grudgingly, I acknowledged that he had a point. In his shoes, I'd have done the same thing. "To be honest, I don't know. She doesn't tell me much about her private life."

Dave sighed. "It's hard to imagine she'd be single."

"I'm going to check in with Lisa. The bugs should be here by now." I hurried off toward the beat-up trailer, as much to escape as anything else. I stalked across the hard ground but had to move slowly because there were dragons all over the place. It was like someone had flipped a switch, and they went from newly hatched to roving predator mode. As I got closer to the trailer, I began to see why. The feed crickets were long gone, but I spotted a few larger, green-and-yellow-banded insects getting chased. They looked like butterflies or maybe large moths. They flew a few feet above the ground, and the dragons were well aware. *Must be some kind of by-catch.* If it was, I should figure out what species. One fluttered near and I tried to grab it. It curved away, only to be caught in midair by one of the dragons. I spotted another one and reached out, but another dragon appeared out of nowhere and nearly took off my hand snatching it.

"Hey! Watch it!" I shouted.

The dragon spread its wings out and skittered away a few paces, then resumed its hunt. I gave up on trying to catch the insect and instead jogged to reach the trailer. Kenny was back on the roof fiddling with the radar while Lisa called out instructions.

"The dragons are about ready," I called. "They're hungry, too."

"Any sign of the insects?"

"No, just the crickets we brought. And some weird kind of flying moth."

She stopped what she was doing and turned around. "What moth?"

"I don't know. Big and brown and not very good at flying."

"Moths are nocturnal." She swung out of the van and shaded her eyes to look out across the canyon. "Shit, that's a lot of dragons."

"Well, you said you had a lot of bugs."

She tore her eyes away from the hatching grounds and looked at me. "Show me one of these moths."

Right as she said that, one flew around the front of the van, made a sharp turn, and landed in the dark shade beneath it. I pointed. "There's one right there."

She got down on her hands and knees to take a look. Without a word, she beckoned me. I moved quietly over and knelt down. The ground was hard and cracked from the dryness, but not hot against my palms. It took my eyes a minute to adjust to the shadows underneath the van, and the insect was well camouflaged. Then something moved. It wasn't a moth at all, but a grasshopper, a dusky brown color that blended in well with the desert terrain. "I didn't think grasshoppers could fly like that."

"Normally they would not. See the longer wings and the faint yellow coloring underneath?"

To me, the grasshopper mostly looked like the color of beige sand. "Uh, sure."

"That's a migratory-phase adult female."

All I heard was the word *migratory*. "That's a locust?"

"In lay terms, yes."

"What's it doing here?"

She stood up and brushed herself off. "It's a scout."

"A scout for what?" I stood up and brushed the dirt from my pants. Something was different. At first I thought my eyes hadn't adjusted from looking at the shade. Everything was dim. A massive brown cloud dominated the horizon and blocked out the sun. It looked like the cloud of dust left by a truck on a dirt road, only ten times higher. I'd never seen anything like it.

"For a plague of locusts." Lisa banged twice on the roof. "Kenny, get down from there."

Shouts came from the direction of Build-A-Dragon's staff. They were abandoning the tents and taking shelter in the SUVs. The visibility had already gone from clear to opaque as the first wave of insects swept into the canyon. As if responding to some hidden signal, the dragons all launched themselves into the air. They soared through bands of flying insects, jaws snapping left and right. Fascinating as it was, the locusts started to grow thick around us, too. One landed on my shirt, another on my pants. I flicked them off me. In theory, the locusts wouldn't harm humans but the sheer numbers of them were intimidating. They were big, too. Over two inches long. The clouds of them were getting thicker, and now I understood why everyone had fled for shelter.

"Shit!" The nearest SUV was a hundred yards away and almost completely obscured by the bugs.

"Looks like you'd better bunker down with us," Lisa said. She offered a hand and I climbed up into the semidarkness of the research trailer. Kenny hopped in after me and slammed the door shut behind us. It was a warm space but not hot, the interior cramped and lit only by the glow of the computer screens. Lisa flipped over a crate for me to sit on since she occupied the chair at the keyboard. Kenny climbed somewhere into the back in search of a flashlight. I was glad for the shelter even so. So many locusts were hitting the sides and roof of the trailer that it sounded like we were caught in a heavy rainstorm. Or a hailstorm.

My phone buzzed in my pocket, so I glanced at my watch. Evelyn was calling.

"Sorry, it's the boss." I dug the phone out of my pocket. "Hello?"

"Noah, are you all right?"

"Yes, just fine. I jumped into Lisa's trailer."

"Oh, that was smart." She sounded relieved.

"How are you guys?"

"Good. We took shelter in a couple of the SUVs. Dave, Korrapati, and Wong are in one. Tom and I are in the car behind them."

"I'm glad." Actually I was amused, too. Evelyn had once remarked about how our head herpetologist stood out in a crowd.

"These locusts are something, aren't they?"

"Something out of the Bible."

Tom must have asked Evelyn a question. She repeated it. "How long until the swarm passes us?"

Lisa's hands flew over the ancient keyboard, overlaying travel projections on the ever-shifting cloud of locusts. "Fifteen minutes, maybe less."

"I'm going to check in with Wong and Korrapati," Evelyn said. "Keep me posted."

I hung up and tried to make sense of the numbers and images on Lisa's screen. The large green blob in the middle of the screen faded a little bit, then flickered and disappeared.

"Damn, lost it again." Lisa tried some adjustments on a couple of the small black dials that were on the control board for the radar equipment. The thing looked ancient—if any of the knobs had been labeled at one time, they no longer were.

"Does that happen a lot?" I asked.

"More than we like. The swarms are always moving, so their density fluctuates."

She tried the knobs a couple more times, muttering to herself, then gave up and went with the tried-and-true technique of hitting the side of the radar screen. Which did not seem to help, probably because it was sensitive equipment rather than a cheap video-game console.

"No luck?" I asked.

She shook her head. "The antenna's probably out of alignment again. We used to be able to control it from here, but sand keeps getting in the bearings and making that difficult."

"Yeah, the sand gets everywhere, doesn't it?"

"As soon as the bugs clear off I'll have Kenny go adjust it again."

It amused me privately that Kenny spent a lot of his research internship on the roof of the beat-up trailer trying to fine-tune their janky radar antenna. Thinking of the roof made me look up, and for the first time I realized that it was now quiet. No more steady drumming of insect bodies against the metal trailer. "You know what? I don't hear them anymore."

My phone rang. Evelyn was calling again. "Hey," I answered. "We just lost the radar feed, but we're going to try to—"

"Noah, come out of the trailer," Evelyn interrupted.

She didn't sound alarmed. If anything, there was a hint of of restrained excitement in her voice.

"All right." I looked at Lisa. "How do you get this door open?"

"Kenny!" Lisa shouted. "Door."

The young fellow squeezed past us and shoved the door open. He looked around and then swung himself out to the ground. "All clear."

I couldn't believe that. Moments ago there had been a hurricane of locusts in this canyon. Now I didn't see a single one. All I saw were dragons. They were resting now, fat and contented on the sand. I knew the look of a well-fed dragon—I'd seen it with Octavius and his brothers too many times—but this was on a scale I'd never encountered. A noise from the trailer alerted me to Kenny, who had clambered back on top.

"What the hell?" Lisa produced a pair of binoculars and looked east. Whatever she saw unsettled her.

"What's wrong?" I asked.

"They don't usually move that fast." She stood up to take a look at the radar antenna on the top of the van. "What do you think?" she asked Kenny, who hadn't touched it.

"It looks fine," he said.

"So the signal is good?"

"It should be."

They turned and surveyed the rest of the valley, the dragons, and the SUVs where my coworkers were emerging with excited gestures. That reminded me I still had Evelyn on the phone. "What happened?"

"The dragons were incredible, Noah. Didn't you see?"

"Nah, we were in Lisa's . . ." I caught myself before saying what I really thought. If she hadn't offered me shelter I'd have been out in the locust hurricane. "Traveling fortress."

That won me a little smile, the first I'd seen from her.

"Don't worry, I had Darryl here to get some footage."

"Who's Darryl?"

"Our head of media relations."

"Well, I can't wait to see that."

"Why don't you bring Lisa over? I'd love to meet her."

"I'll ask."

Lisa and Kenny had made a sweep of the area around the research trailer. Now they both had pairs of high-powered binoculars and were looking east. Their expressions were a mixture of shock and disbelief.

"They're all gone," she said. "That's why we weren't getting something on the radar."

"Unreal," Kenny said.

I could hardly believe it myself. One moment there was a massive wall of locusts. Now there were hardly any. The air was clear. I spotted a small cloud of them rise up from the ground halfway across the valley. A dozen dragons leapt into the air and bore down on them. Kenny let out a whistle.

"Your dragons did this?" Lisa asked.

"My boss got some video footage," I said. "Would you like to meet her?"

"I'll do you one better. Does she like rare plants?"

"More than anyone I know."

CHAPTER SIXTEEN
The Frenzy

Evelyn hadn't been kidding about the new director of media relations. Whoever this Darryl character was, he produced results. By the time we left Lisa's incredible bio trove, it was nearly dark out. I took my phone out to check on things and had an avalanche of new messages. The first one I saw was from a friend of mine from undergrad with the subject line YOU ARE FAMOUS.

Yeah, something had happened. Most of the rest of the messages were from strangers, a lot of them requests for interviews or for comment. Once upon a time, I'd dabbled with the media about Build-A-Dragon stuff. That had been when Greaves was in charge, and a bit of a desperation move. To be honest, I thought my chances of getting the official green light to talk to the media on behalf of the company were slim at best. That was for two reasons. First, I didn't have any training on how to talk to reporters or go on camera, even though I was on camera all the time. Yet there was a big difference from being recorded for security purposes and getting filmed for public consumption. The second and probably more important reason was that I had a tendency to say what I really thought in the moment. It had caused issues for me, professionally and personally, since before grad school. Even if I managed not to say my thoughts out loud, apparently my face advertised them quite well. So I had no filter and no poker face. I knew this about myself. Most people close to me knew it, too, and that included Evelyn.

Sure, we'd come a long way since the tumultuous early days of joining Build-A-Dragon before domestication, back when it was just called Reptilian Corporation. We'd always thought alike and we usually worked well together. Even so, part of me thought that she'd always see me as that fresh-out-of-grad-school kid, not as a peer. Part of me wondered if she'd have even made me the head of Dragon Design if there had been a better alternative. It wasn't like I'd beat out a crowd of dozens of willing candidates.

These thoughts warred in my head as I made my way up to her office. It was late but I knew she'd still be working. The job of a biotech CEO doesn't stop when you want to watch a field trial. Her new-ish assistant Roger was present too, a bit to my surprise.

"Hello," I said. "Is Evelyn free?"

He glanced at me. "She is, but she's on the phone."

"I can wait." I slouched into one of the chairs, missing the days when I used to pop into her office on a whim. "Is she getting bombarded with messages, too?"

"With messages from reporters?" He shrugged. "I can't really say."

Can't say, or won't say? I wanted to ask, because it irritated me a little. Then again, I supposed that the head of our company merited a little bit of privacy. Even from me. Besides, I hadn't said anything about reporters. He did, so he'd essentially told me anyway. Which made him either careless or very clever.

"Oh, then I can't say if I'm getting lots of messages from reporters, either."

He gave a thin smile.

Clever. "Do you know this Darryl person, our new head of media relations?"

"I only met him when he interviewed."

"What's he like?" I asked.

"About what you'd expect."

"Young, old?"

He glanced at his computer. "She's ready for you now."

I sighed and got up. "Well, thanks for... whatever this was."

"Anytime."

Evelyn stood in the corner of her office, rearranging her plants on the multitiered table where the two big windows met. They were all carnivorous plants. I tried not to read too much into that. She was transferring a new plant from Lisa into a ceramic stoneware planter embossed with Chinese-style dragons. It looked a little bit wilted, but I liked its chances. The office got plenty of sunlight and besides, Evelyn had a green thumb.

"I thought you only got a new plant when you achieved something," I said.

She smiled but kept her attention on the plant. "We saved Lisa's bio trove and proved that dragons can be effective at insect pest control."

"And safer than any pesticide," I said.

"Also, you became an internet celebrity."

I laughed. "Let's not exaggerate."

"Haven't you seen the video?"

"No."

"Oh, Noah, you've got to see it."

"I will."

She moved over to her workstation and brought up a projection monitor. "It's only been up a few hours."

She pulled up the video, but it must have been the wrong one. This one had hundreds of comments and thousands of views. Before I could ask, she hit the PLAY button and the thing went to full screen. I recognized the scene right away: it was the canyon where we'd done the hatching. The camera panned the wide array of hatching boxes, then zoomed in on one as the egg began to hatch.

"These dragons were custom-built for a single purpose," a man said, in a deep voice reminiscent of a voice-over actor. "To protect a precious trove of some of the rarest plants in the world. From these." Now the view swiveled up and the massive wave of locusts seemed to block out the horizon. Even though I'd been there and seen it, even though I knew what happened, it still brought a stab of fear. Then the camera panned again and I was looking at myself. It was when Dave and I were watching the dragonet hatch from its egg. We looked good. The voice continued. "Scientists at the Build-A-Dragon Company have received EPA approval for wild-release dragons to tackle the world's toughest ecological problems." More footage of the locusts.

"Who made this?" I asked Evelyn.

"Darryl."

I didn't say anything, but I was impressed. The thing was production-grade. Daryl, or the professional narrator he'd found and hired in less than two hours, kept going. "Where pesticides and physical interventions failed, genetic engineering found a way."

In the next moment, locusts were everywhere. Whoever was filming had retreated into one of the company's SUVs. The insects threw themselves against the glass. Then a larger dark shape shot past. Another one soon followed, and this time it was clear it was a small dragon. The field of view zoomed out and now you could see dozens of them swooping back and forth through waves of locusts. The dragons were fast, and made sharp little turns with their triangular wings. They looked like stunt planes. Where they flew, no locusts remained. The video flashed ahead, probably by five minutes or so. Now the locusts flew in smaller, tightly bunched groups.

"Unlike chemical pesticides, dragons are highly selective killers," the narrator-man said. "They're intelligent, and can adapt to their environment to do their job even better."

"This is my favorite part," Evelyn said.

There was a swarm of locusts flying six feet off the ground, churning tightly together. It must have been a defense mechanism like a school of minnows. Four dragons converged on it from above. At the last moment, they reared up and backpedaled, sweeping their wings forward on top of the swarm. The downdraft forced the bugs to the ground... where four other dragons waited hungrily. It was like a game of Hungry Hungry Hippos. They didn't just eat, but killed and maimed countless bugs with their claws. When the dragons from the aerial maneuvers glided down, these fresh kills awaited them.

"Pack hunting," I said.

Evelyn smiled. "Very clever."

"But we didn't program that into them."

"Many animal group dynamics are instinctive," Evelyn said. "It makes sense for them to cooperate when it benefits a group."

"Still, I never imagined they would learn to work together so quickly. Then again, they did hatch together."

"Within seconds or minutes at most."

"I'll have to thank Korrapati for letting us borrow the gestation timing protocol."

"You should be proud, Noah. This was a big win for us," she said.

"It went better than I imagined."

"Why do you think it was so successful?"

I'd been thinking about that myself a little bit. So many things had gone right for the locust intervention. Our client had given us clear specs, and the deployment location was close to our headquarters. Besides, behavior was hardwired into dragons already. The first flying reptiles on the planet—pterosaurs—had evolved the ability to glide to catch vast hordes of flying insects in the Triassic period. "We got lucky," I said. "The right predator for the right pest, designed by the right team."

"It also helped that we knew the environment," she said.

"Like it was our own backyard."

She pointed at me. "Exactly. We know the Southwest, and we know the desert. Some of us perhaps more than we should."

I kept my face still. "What are you implying?"

"Nothing. I'm saying that we had firsthand knowledge of the deployment environment." She gestured at the projection monitor that had the video pulled up. "It's hard to argue with the results."

"Speaking of results, I've been getting some messages."

"What kind?"

"From reporters, mostly. A few of them asked about an interview."

"Let Darryl handle them. I want you to focus on our next project."

"What's that?"

"That's for us to decide," she said.

"Really? What are the options?"

"Let's see." She brought up a new projection monitor that contained a neatly sorted grid of messages, three rows of four. She pointed to the top left one. "How do you feel about a project in the Everglades?"

"What kind of project?"

"Mosquito control."

Yikes. That sounded both difficult and uncomfortable. Possibly requiring anti-malaria vaccination, too. "What else do you have?"

"Rabbits in Western Australia."

"Still? I thought they had that rabbit-proof fence?"

"That didn't work," Evelyn said.

"Didn't they have some kind of rabbit-specific virus they were using?"

"Myxoma virus and more recently a hemorrhagic virus. For obvious reasons, they're interested in alternatives."

"Alternatives to biowarfare? Yeah, one would hope so."

"There's also the Asian carp invading the Great Lakes."

"What do they want us to do?" I asked.

"Have the dragons eat them, I imagine."

"Have you seen the size of an Asian carp?" The torpedo-shaped fish reached two or three feet long when mature and averaged twenty pounds but could weigh three times that. "You'd need a dragon that's a hundred pounds, and aquatic." Even I didn't love the idea of encountering one of those while swimming at the lake.

"That's a good point." She looked back to her messages. "There's rats in Antarctica, cactus moths in Texas—"

"Wait," I broke in. "Did you say *Antarctica*?"

"Yes."

"Where in Antarctica?"

"King George Island, which is in the South Shetland Islands and home to several research bases. They have a rat problem."

I didn't think anything could live in Antarctica, but apparently I was wrong about that. "How did they get a rat problem?"

"The usual way."

"Colonialism?" I said.

Her eyes widened, as if it surprised her. "I suppose that's one way to put it."

"Whose colony is Antarctica anyway?"

"No one's, officially. About a dozen countries have research outposts there—Russia, the United Kingdom, the U.S., Argentina, China."

"Oh, sounds like a *wonderful* and harmonious place."

"They're scientists, Noah. They've figured out how to get along."

As someone who was a scientist and didn't always get along with coworkers—or people in general—I wasn't sure I agreed. Then again, I wasn't going to argue the chance to design dragons for Antarctica. How would they survive that kind of cold? It was hard not to start thinking of the challenges. "Dragons seem like overkill for a rodent problem."

"It's a pristine environment where things never thaw. They're reluctant to try anything that could persist, and any organism that might become an invasive species."

"Good thing that our dragons self-destruct." I didn't mean it to sound bitter, but it did.

"They'd never even consider dragons if we couldn't make that guarantee," Evelyn said. "Be glad."

"I know, I know. Be glad I get to design a cold-weather dragon." It did sound like a fascinating scientific challenge. Plus, a chance to see a penguin up close, which I really wanted to do.

"Be glad you get to design any dragon at all."

I rushed home to make sure that I caught the 5:00 PM news. It was earlier than I'd usually left, but the news producers couldn't tell us for sure when our segment would run. I flipped on the projection television and pointed it to my largest wall. I had a second one, picture-by-picture, that I tuned to the network's twenty-four-hour news stream.

The five o'clock show was mostly a disappointment. Even the news stream didn't run our segment. My phone buzzed occasionally with another news alert. My name and the company name kept popping up all over. But there was still something thrilling about the idea of appearing on broadcast television. Websites came and went. Social media platforms were born and then imploded. But television media carried a permanence like no other. My mom and brother were watching, too. Well, my mom was, at least. Connor had told me he'd record it and "maybe have a gander later if it's good." Brothers are like that.

Summer came a few minutes before six. She clutched her work bag, purse, and lunch box, all of which she dumped unceremoniously on the floor because the dragonets swarmed her.

"Hi there," I told her, once the dragons had had their greeting.

"Hi." She hugged me. "Did I miss it?"

"No, there was nothing at five. If it comes on at all, this will be it."

"People at work were asking about you."

Hearing this gave me a good feeling and brought a grin to my face. "Oh, yeah?"

"They saw the stories and wondered if we were still, you know, together."

So much for the good feeling. "Why would they ask that?"

She shrugged. "You haven't been around much."

"Well, I hope you told them that I'm still very much in the picture." The last thing I needed was Summer's predominantly male coworkers thinking she might be back on the market.

"I did," she said.

"Good."

"Grudgingly."

"Hey!"

She laughed, then looked at the television. "Ooh, I think this is it."

The anchor was Julie Foss, a lovely blonde woman who'd headlined the coveted evening news spot since I was in grad school. The story graphic over her shoulder gave me goose bumps. It was a photo of one of our dragons—a Laptop model—and the text read DRAGONS SAVE PRECIOUS PLANTS.

"Dragons came to the rescue in the Mojave Desert this week, when an oasis of priceless desert plants came under threat from insect pests," Julie said. "That threat? An actual plague of locusts." The graphic changed to an image of a grasshopper, zoomed in on its bright yellow head and striped body. "The desert locust, which normally lives in the Middle East, is now established in the Southwest. Their numbers, by some estimates, reach tens of millions." Now we saw an actual video of a huge cloud of the insects flying high over a desert landscape. I couldn't tell if it was Arizona or footage from elsewhere. "It's the same insect believed to be responsible for plagues of locusts in the ancient world," Julie said, with that slow news-anchor cadence that inevitably drew you in to the story. "Even the one written about . . . in the Bible."

The view zoomed out to show that the massive vertical cloud was one of a handful that billowed over the sand dunes.

"Oh my God," Summer said.

"Crazy, right?" I'd told her about the size of the swarms, and the terrifying sound of their bodies drumming against the metal roof of the trailer, but it was hard to put the experience into words. *Now you can see what we were up against.*

"Against these overwhelming odds emerged an unlikely hero," Julie said. "Dragons. With approval from the U.S. Food and Drug Administration, scientists at the Build-A-Dragon Company engineered a dragon that is a bug-eating machine."

Now came the footage from our setup in the desert valley. First there was a clip of hatchery staff in white robes lifting an egg gently into its synthetic nest. Then came a shot of Dave and Wong talking and looking at eggs up close.

"Look! There's Wong!" I said.

"Who's that with him?"

"Oh, that's Dave."

"Where are you?" she asked.

"At this moment I was under the tent with Evelyn and Korrapati." Apparently that footage hadn't merited inclusion in this little montage. Instead it showed Evelyn earlier that morning, walking among the nest enclosures with her tablet, gesturing, and looking very *executive* overall. *Like the boss that she is.*

"She's so, so smart," Summer said. "You can just tell."

Now we were looking at a sliding view of the eggs in their nests from above, which must have been taken from a drone. There were hatchery staff and dragon wranglers walking in the rows, but I didn't see anyone who looked like me.

"Jesus," Summer said. "That's a lot of eggs."

"The largest batch we've ever printed, according to Evelyn."

The report came back to Julie then, who went on to talk about the logistics of the operation, how nothing like this had been tried before, and about the remote location. This was a little annoying—I wanted to get back to the footage of the actual event.

"It's a familiar sight, though you don't hear about it as much these days," Julie said. "Dragons hatching from actual eggs. A fantastic creature brought to life by the power of science." They had a zoomed-in view of one of the eggs hatching. It was a Mantis dragon; I knew that from the shape of the head and the prominent curved teeth. Then they showed my favorite shot so far, the drone's aerial view of dozens of eggs hatching at once. The coordinated timing was incredible, and I made a mental note to compliment Korrapati on it.

"And it's not a moment too soon," Julie said ominously. "The locusts have arrived. Their numbers are too vast to count, and their appearance sends the scientists running for cover."

That, naturally, was when I made my television news debut. I was running, covering my head with my hands, and jumped into the trailer right before the door closed.

I groaned. "Oh, *come on!*"

Summer busted out laughing. "You look terrified!"

"I *was* terrified. But I'd also gone out to watch an egg hatch. I was the one who saw the swarm coming."

I stopped complaining because we finally got to the footage I wanted, the part when the dragons got to work. Everywhere little jaws snapped around locusts. Sheer carnage.

I looked at Summer expectantly. "Well?"

"Okay, that's pretty cool."

Julie returned to the screen, her big green eyes wide with wonder. "Wow, that's some incredible footage. And once the dragons eliminated the threat, it was safe for the scientists to get to work again."

Oh, no. Please tell me it's not... Yes, sure enough, the camera zoomed in on me as I climbed out of the trailer's dark interior. "Why?" I muttered. Lisa Hashimoto climbed out, too, and we chattered excitedly with one another, both of us smiling and delighted by the outcome.

"Who is that?"

"That's Dr. Hashimoto, the botanist."

"You never said she was a woman," Summer said, and I detected a slight chill in her voice.

"So what? Half the people I work with are women. More than half."

Now Lisa was being interviewed by a field reporter in a new location, which had to be her botany research field in the desert. Green plants and flowering cacti dominated the hill behind her, all of it lush and exotic-looking. "Absolutely incredible. When Noah said they'd gotten the approval to bring these dragons in the nick of time, it was like a godsend," Lisa said.

As much as I appreciated that *someone* had acknowledged me as part of this, the look on Summer's face screamed caution.

"*Noah?*"

"She knows my name."

"She didn't call you Dr. Parker, though, but you call her Dr. Hashimoto."

"Not to her face."

Summer's tone was angrier now. "It's like you hid the fact that you were holed up with this hussy in her love-trailer. She's what, twenty-seven, twenty-eight?"

"How would I know?"

"Is she married?"

"I didn't get her life story. She's just a client who needed help. Don't make a big deal out of this."

"It *is* a big deal!"

"No, it's not." I had to head this off before it devolved into a real fight. Especially because there was nothing to fight about. "I don't know anything about her personal life, and I don't want to. I'm with you and perfectly happy about that. Unlike your coworkers, mine know about us."

"Even Dave?"

"He doesn't count."

She seemed a little mollified, but still upset. "I don't want you to lie to me."

"I'm not lying. Look," I said, gesturing at the screen where Lisa was giving a tour of her bio trove, and quietly wishing that they'd run a goddamn commercial. *It's like this newscast is actively trying to ruin my life.* "Lisa Hashimoto is like the Evelyn of desert botany. You're not worried about me hooking up with Evelyn, are you?"

She broke off her glare at TV-Lisa and looked down. "I guess not."

"Honestly, if anyone's going to fall for Lisa, it would be Evelyn."

"What? Oh." She smiled a little. "Carnivorous plants. I almost forgot about her creepy hobby."

"It's not *creepy*. She's got a green thumb."

"If you ask me, it's worrisome that you *don't* find it creepy when your boss collects carnivorous plants."

"Whatever. But you get my point."

"Fine, I get your point."

"Besides, Lisa has Kenny."

"Who's Kenny?"

"Her research assistant slash trailer mechanic." I told her about how he'd banged around the trailer and the roof of the trailer while Lisa shouted orders to him. "They have a weird dynamic and I wouldn't want to get in the middle of it."

She closed her eyes, took a deep breath, and exhaled. "Fine. I forgive you."

I didn't do anything wrong, so that's only fair. It seemed advisable to keep that remark to myself. "I'm glad, because I might be going on a trip."

Her eyes flashed, and she said slowly, "If you even say with Lisa, I will hurt you."

"No, of course not. I'm not an idiot. Evelyn's been getting calls because of the press frenzy. People with other kinds of pest problems. Scientists, mostly." I wanted to add.

"From where?"

"Think *south*."

"Mexico?"

"Nope."

"South America," she said.

"Even more south."

"What the hell is south of South America?"

"One continent."

Her mouth fell open as realization came. "Oh my God. *Antarctica?*"

"That's right. The great white continent."

"Why would they need dragons?"

"They have some kind of a rat problem in the penguin nesting areas."

"Ooh, penguins. I love penguins."

"Yeah, me too," I said.

"Evelyn doesn't really expect you to go, does she?"

"I don't know."

"Because there's no way in hell." She shook her head. "It's too far and you have too many dragons to look after."

Ooh, yeah, I forgot about that. It was hard enough to share custody with our dragonets at times. "Don't worry, I think it's just the idea of doing a project for Antarctica. I seriously doubt Evelyn would need me to go."

But if she did, I sure as hell wanted to.

CHAPTER SEVENTEEN
Cold-Blooded

Like most reptiles, Build-A-Dragon's models were ectothermic. In layman's terms, cold-blooded. Their bodies adapted to whatever the ambient temperatures were rather than trying to self-regulate. In practice, it meant that they acted like lizards or snakes—they liked to bask in the sun, and they got sluggish in the cold. These instincts must have been hard-coded somewhere deep in the hodgepodge of DNA sequences that went into the dragon genome. They had physical adaptations as well—parts of their bodies that served as heat exchangers to consolidate or let off warmth as needed.

To be honest, it had never been a problem for most of our retail models. Customers had plenty of complaints, but they tended to be about dragons eating other pets or getting wedged in doggie doors. A lot of our customers lived in warmer climates anyway, or kept their reptiles indoors. Granted, we did apparently get some complaints about our dragons being lazy. Maybe we should have considered those customers who lived in cold climates.

Regardless, this new arctic dragon would have to be endothermic. Warm-blooded. Like mammals, they would have to regulate their own body temperature. In a frigid environment, that meant they had to produce heat. All that required was mitochondria.

Mitochondria were organelles that produced energy inside animal cells. In tissues that had high energy requirements—muscle and nerve cells—they were more numerous. Warm-blooded animals had, on average, many more mitochondria in every cell because they produced their own heat. They were a strange little organelle. Millions of years ago, mitochondria were their own organism. At some point they traded their independence for the safety of the cell, and in return produced the cell's energy. They still had their own tiny genome, a circular chromosome with 16,000 base pairs. That provided only enough space for a handful of genes that produced the few proteins the mitochondria needed to do their thing. Humans inherited many, many copies of the mitochondrial genome—a hundred thousand in each embryo, virtually all of them from their mother.

Because mitochondria contained DNA, they sometimes picked up damaging mutations. If enough of these defective energy-factories were passed on to a child, they could cause mitochondrial diseases. These were cruel disorders and hard to diagnose because of slow-onset, mysterious symptoms. Hearing loss. Muscle weakness. Retinal degeneration. Anemia. All this was to say that when you tampered with the mitochondria, you had to be very, very careful.

As usual, when pondering a design problem, my feet carried me over to Wong's workstation. "How can we increase the number of mitochondria in our dragons?"

Wong never took his eyes from his projection monitor. "Exercise."

"What?"

"Exercise increases mitochondrial density. Also energy capacity."

"In mammals, or reptiles?" I asked.

"Both."

Well, that was a start. However, we couldn't guarantee that the dragons would get sufficient exercise in the Antarctic. I didn't know if the humans got enough exercise there. My guess was, running as fast as possible to get back inside was the lion's share of their aerobic activity. If Wong was right, the dragons would require a serious regimen. It might not even be enough. Many reptiles got plenty of exercise but didn't suddenly become endothermic. "What if we need to add more mitochondria at gestation?"

"Into the egg?"

"Yes," I said.

"How many?"

"Five times the usual amount."

"Seems like a lot," he said.

"I was thinking the dragon needs to be endothermic."

"Which dragon?"

"The one for Antarctica."

He grunted. "Good, then, to be exothermic. One less problem."

"So, any thoughts?"

"Yes. One." He pointed past his workstation to the racks of servers and the robotic arms of the biological printer. "Start there."

When I first joined Build-A-Dragon, the company was called Reptilian and the machinery to create dragon eggs was already in place. There were three parts: the computational servers we used for the designs, the ungainly apparatus that printed the eggs, and the odd piece of technology that truly made it all possible: the Redwood Codex. This last piece was the hardest to understand. It resembled the wiring harness of a car stereo plugged into the DIY graphics chips that people hot-wired to mine cryptocurrency. Even after all this time we didn't know for certain what it did. I should have asked Simon Redwood, I suppose. It didn't seem important at the time. It instead seemed like something we'd never need to know about. Now, of course, we had to make a tweak outside the usual parameters of dragon genome modification, and I didn't even know where to start.

Redwood wasn't likely to take my calls even if I did have his number. Most of the world thought he was dead and he wanted it to stay that way. The best way I had of contacting him was to spend days wandering in the Arizona desert hoping he had some reason to want to talk to me. That didn't sound like a plan for success.

There was someone who knew the biological printer, someone who had programmed its operating code when the company first began printing dragon eggs en masse, but he didn't work here anymore. He also didn't like me very much. Still, I didn't dare go poking around in the God Machine without some guidance. If I broke it, our entire means of production would come to a screeching halt. I put it off for half the morning by trying to find any documentation for the biological printer or the Redwood Codex on the company servers. Amusingly, I found a stub of an article on our internal wiki for the Department of Dragon Design: "This page will contain information about the biological printer." That was the only content on the page, which hadn't been updated for two years. *So much for keeping up with internal documentation.*

When my designers were out eating lunch at a food truck, I'd crawled underneath the frame of the biological printer like a mechanic working on a car. The wires were easier to see from underneath. They were all slightly different colors, their groups tightly bundled and trussed to keep clear of the floor. Most ran from the master SwitchBlade server to the control unit of the printer, but five apparently random wires made a detour to the Redwood Codex before continuing on to the printer control. Five wires. That had to mean something. Maybe the fifth base, though that was mostly a guess.

DNA had four bases: adenine, cytosine, guanine, and thymine, usually represented by the letters A, C, G, and T. These paired together—adenine with thymine and cytosine with guanine—to form the "steps" of the twisted ladder shape of DNA's double helix. Naturally, most of the information in the genome was encoded in vast stretches of these four letters. When we designed a dragon in DragonDraft 3D, all of its specific characteristics were written into the dragon genome using that four-base code. Always those four bases. In higher organisms, there were also a number of chemical modifications to DNA that facilitated its packaging, turned genes on and off, and protected the genomic structure. These were called *epigenetic* marks. Sometimes geneticists referred to them as the "fifth base"—another dimension of complexity underlying an organism. For a long time, I'd wondered if the Redwood Codex produced viable dragon eggs by adding those epigenetic marks, those fifth bases. And now here, right in front of me, there were five wires running from that strange device to the biological printer.

"What are you doing, Noah Parker?" Wong asked.

"Flailing for answers," I grumbled.

"Does he do stuff like this a lot?" Dave asked Wong.

"All the time," Wong said, with mock seriousness. "He is always digging for things."

"Don't you have some work to be doing?" I asked in a good-hearted way. After twenty minutes crammed under the instrument alone I was glad for the company. I scooted out and stood up.

"I'll brush you off." Dave searched me all over, but couldn't find a speck of dust. "How are you so clean? You were on the floor!"

I felt a little surge of pride. "We keep a clean lab here." *And we have a fleet of cleaning robots.*

"Man, if you did that in the Sato lab, your shirt would look like a dust mop."

"If I did that in the Sato lab, I'd still be stuck to the floor."

We both chuckled. Dr. Sato was an excellent mentor and we'd learned so much in that time, but his lab had occupied the back corner of an ancient building on the ASU campus. With twenty grad students and postdocs, it had existed in a perpetual state of semi-chaos. Which was why most of us had worked on computational projects—they were harder to contaminate. I forced myself to pull back from the tempting nostalgia, though. The designers really did need to get back to work, and I needed to talk to Evelyn.

I took the elevator up, already dreading the inevitable confrontation with Roger. He seemed to delight in keeping me out of Evelyn's office whenever he could. When I approached her office and saw he wasn't at his desk, I figured I'd caught a break. There were voices from within, though, so I slowed my pace. Sometimes Evelyn would be on video calls or meeting with bigwigs privately, and I avoid interrupting those occasions. Like a dummy, I'd forgotten to stalk her calendar to see if her schedule was even open. That I'd spent so long chasing dead ends rather than come to her directly only added salt to the wound.

"I'm not sure we have the budget for it," Evelyn was saying.

"It's worth investigating."

I recognized the voice as Korrapati's, which was a bit surprising but meant I could probably get away with interrupting. I popped my head in and knocked on the doorframe. "Hello."

"Oh. Hello, Noah," Korrapati said. She and Evelyn sat together on the leather couch along the inside wall of the office. There were two mugs of hot tea on the glass-and-steel table in front of it.

"I'm sorry to interrupt." I managed not to add that I thought Korrapati was out to lunch, not up here talking to the big boss.

"It's no problem," Evelyn said. "What's going on?"

"Well, I came to ask an awkward question."

"I think that's my cue." Korrapati stood and straightened her dress, a lovely green floral number I knew was one of her favorites.

"Don't forget your tea," Evelyn said.

Korrapati took it and smiled at me on her way out.

I really wanted to ask what they'd been talking about, which would have been terribly impolite. Instead I looked at Evelyn and asked, "Everything all right?"

"Just fine," she said. "What is this awkward question?"

I took a deep breath and let it out. "Do you know what Brian is up to these days?"

"O'Connell?"

"Yes."

Brian O'Connell used to work for the design team. When I first joined the company, he was one of the lead designers and not my biggest fan. When Evelyn promoted me to lead the group, shortly after she became CEO, he left the company in protest. So did his longtime friend Paul Myers, a developmental biologist who'd gone by the nickname Frogman. In part, I understood that—they both had seniority over me, and I'd somewhat gone rogue to expose some of Build-A-Dragon's secrets. But Evelyn had wanted me back—needed me back—and knew that dangling the leadership position in front of me was the only way. It worked out somewhat. O'Connell and Frogman had later gone to work for Robert Greaves, who almost stole the DOD contract from us.

"I believe they're working for Suncoast Biotech down in Tempe."

"Really?"

"I made a call to make sure they got interviews."

"Wait, you helped them get new jobs?"

"Of course. They were my designers, remember?"

It surprised me that she'd not only stayed in touch but was helping those two with their careers. Especially after they'd gone against us in the DOD challenge. Even so, if she had a good relationship there, it would help. "I was wondering if you'd put me in touch."

"With O'Connell?"

"Yeah."

She smiled too much, the way she did when trying to hide that she was amused.

"I know, I know, he's not my biggest fan."

"That is certainly an optimistic way to put it."

"We need information on the God—I mean, on the biological printer."

"What sort of information do you need?" she asked.

I explained my theory about making the dragons endothermic and how it required more mitochondria.

"So, why didn't you ask me how to do it?"

"Oh." Her response had caught me off guard. "Well, I didn't think—"

"You remember who was the triple-D before you were, don't you?"

"Of cour—" I started, but she cut me off again.

"Do you think I could do that job without knowing every single aspect of the dragons we make?" She was looking at me flat-eyed, impossible to read.

I paused now to make sure she was finished. *Okay, apparently she's done.* "I apologize. Naturally I should have asked you first." I did an about-face and left her office, waited a beat, and then came back in. "So Evelyn, I was wondering if you knew how we could adjust the biological printer to give the eggs more starting mitochondria."

She wore a faint smile now. "I see."

"Do you know how we could make that happen?" I asked.

"I have no idea."

"Oh my God!" I said, while she laughed.

"You make it too easy, Noah."

I shook my head. "We need O'Connell. He's the expert, isn't he?"

"Second only to Simon Redwood, may he rest in peace."

"Ah." I put my head down, hoping to appear somber. As a matter of fact I *was* somber. O'Connell was still the only guy who could help me.

"I'll tell you what. I'll invite him to lunch, and you can crash it."

"Oh. Hooray," I said flatly. *This ought to be fun.*

CHAPTER EIGHTEEN
Lunch Crasher

"Oh, hello, Evelyn." I glanced at the man across from her and feigned surprise. "Brian! Been a while."

"Parker," he said evenly.

I smiled and kept my demeanor friendly. "It's good to see you."

"Yeah, uh, you too."

"Would you like to join us?" Evelyn gestured to the open seats. It was no accident she'd put them at a four-person table, just as it was no accident that I'd placed my order in advance.

"Oh, I don't want to impose," I said.

"Please. We insist," she said.

"Well, I can stay for a little bit, thanks." I plopped down into a chair before O'Connell could mount an organized protest.

"Brian was just telling me about his work at Suncoast Biotech."

"Oh, right, the photosynthesis improvement company," I said, brandishing my fresh knowledge. I'd spent the morning getting up to speed on Suncoast Biotech, which engineered improvements for cultivated plants. These were big business, both for agriculture and for improving cultivars. "How is that going?"

"Good. Really good, actually." He was a little shell-shocked but asking him about his work had helped. "We've been crazy-busy. Hundreds of plant genomes sequenced already, and more coming every day. Everyone wants a customization."

"With plant genomes is it much harder than animals?" Evelyn asked.

A lot of people thought the human genome was the most challenging one, but plant genomes made it look simple by comparison. They contained multiple copies of hundreds of genes, making it difficult to know where everything truly belonged. Early on in the development of my biological simulator, I'd decided not to even try adapting it for plant genomes.

"So much more complicated," O'Connell was saying. "We can't always model the effects of genetic changes, so we end up doing a lot of test germinations."

"That sounds intense," Evelyn said.

Per her instructions, I focused on eating my food when it arrived and acting like an attentive listener. She hardly touched hers—she made sure to keep him talking.

"Do you know much about the King Edward potato?" O'Connell was asking.

"No," Evelyn said.

He glanced at me and I shook my head, even though I knew it was one of their projects so I'd done some background.

"It's a major staple crop, especially in England."

"Did this King Edward make it?" Evelyn asked.

"No, but it was introduced around the time of his coronation. According to legend, the grower wrote to Buckingham Palace to ask for permission to name the cultivar after him, and it was granted."

"No way!"

"So cool," I agreed. I loved little stories that intermingled history with science. Evelyn did, too. Idly I wondered if she'd already done the background and knew all about the King Edward's potato cultivar. It wouldn't surprise me. Evelyn Chang always knew far more than she let on.

"The English growers already selectively bred the potato to be hardy," O'Connell was saying. "It resists scab, which is the main disease for tubers, and it's somewhat resistant to potato blight. But there's a nematode."

I nodded, unsurprised. Nematodes were roundworms, often less than a millimeter in size, that lived in soil almost everywhere on Earth. They could be especially devastating to certain plants, sometimes ones that were otherwise pest-resistant. The pinewood nematode was one of the most infamous. It traveled from tree to tree on bark beetles, which bored holes and introduced the nematodes into conifer circulation systems. Once the trees started dying, all you could do was cut them down, burn the wood, and replace them with deciduous trees.

"Potato root nematodes are like the super parasite. They move into the root and eat it from the inside out," O'Connell said. "We're making progress, though. We've got the crop losses down to ten percent. It's getting infections down to zero that keeps frustrating us."

"The last part is always the hardest," Evelyn said.

"We've been fighting tooth and nail to get that last ten percent." O'Connell sighed and shook his head. "I haven't banged my head that hard against a problem since..." He trailed off.

"Since domestication," Evelyn finished.

"Yeah." He gave me a rueful smile, which I took as a slight conciliation.

I smiled back. "Don't look at me, man. I don't know anything about plant genomes!"

"What about a trap crop?" Evelyn asked.

"Hmm. Interesting idea," O'Connell said.

"Sorry, a trap crop?" I asked. When I said I knew nothing about plant genetics, that wasn't an exaggeration.

"A trap crop is something you plant on the margins of agricultural fields to lure the pests away from the food crops." O'Connell looked at Evelyn. "Any suggestions?"

"I've always been partial to *Solanum sisymbriifolium*."

"Sticky nightshade?" O'Connell said. "We heard some small farms use that for hedges."

Evelyn nodded. "That's because it has thorns. The fruits are bright red and aromatic. Great for drawing out pests, including nematodes."

"Thanks, I appreciate it." O'Connell relaxed a little and leaned back, seeming to notice me again. "I'm guessing you didn't only come by to talk about plant engineering."

"Well, since you asked, I was wondering if you'd humor some questions about the God Machine," I said. "And maybe the Redwood Codex."

"The one you started with, or the one you stole?"

I wasn't prepared to hear that, and for a moment I didn't know what to say. Fortunately, O'Connell laughed.

"Relax, man, I'm just messing with you."

Thank God. "Well, we need to tweak the baseline egg component." I explained about the warm-blooded dragons and the need for more mitochondria. "I thought maybe since you did a lot of the programming for the machine, you'd have some advice."

"We never adjusted mitochondrial content."

"Oh." Then all this had been for nothing. My disappointment must have shown on my face.

"I think I know how you could, though."

"Really?"

"Yeah. The first thing you're going to need is an RC-245 cable."

I fumbled for a pen and started taking notes on a napkin. "RC-245 cable. Do they even make those anymore?"

"Any vintage computing store should have one."

"Okay." I wrote another note. *Find a vintage computing store.*

"And then you'll need the oldest workstation you can find."

CHAPTER NINETEEN
Energy Factories

"Good news," I told Wong the next morning. "I think I know how to boost the mitochondria in the dragon eggs."

He glanced at me sideways from his workstation. "What is that cord?"

"An RC-245 adapter."

"Do they still make those?"

"New? No. I had to go to the night tech market."

Wong wrinkled his forehead. "You should not be going there."

"Why?"

"Not safe."

"I can take care of myself."

Wong's expression was mildly dubious. I chose to ignore this and got on my belly to crawl under the God Machine. The air from the SwitchBlade servers enveloped me, warm and faintly metallic. It was a good thing I wasn't claustrophobic. "Hey, don't print any eggs while I'm under here, all right?"

"Relax, Noah Parker. Not printing," he said.

"Do you want to start on the dragon design for Antarctica?" Boosting the mitochondrial content was only the pregame to this dragon.

"Sure. What base model?"

I crawled close to the central hub, which naturally was the hardest-to-reach part of the biological printer's undersides. "What do we have saved under pest control?"

DragonDraft 3D saved a snapshot of every design we printed, and recently I'd tasked Wong with saving them all in a searchable catalogue. I figured why not, he'd designed more customs than anyone and he practically lived in the lab anyway.

"Junkyard dog?"

"Nah." I remembered that one well and it was designed for bigger prey.

"Gray Mouser?"

"Ha!" *Holy copyright violation.* "Anything in between?"

His fingers drummed a staccato on the desktop while I searched for the plug that O'Connell had told me about. I saw the junction box he'd described, but it was bolted shut. I didn't think to bring any tools. O'Connell hadn't mentioned the need.

"Found a terrier," Wong said.

That was good; terriers were bred to hunt rodents and other small animals. We used to get a lot of requests for dragons with their traits before the dogs came back. "What kind?"

"For rabbit and squirrel."

"Sounds promising. How big is it?"

"Thirty pounds."

"What are the feature points used on?"

More keys drummed, and I knew he was bringing the design into DragonDraft 3D. Meanwhile I'd made no progress on finding the RC-245 port beneath the God Machine, and the heat from the servers was starting to make me sweat.

"Curved teeth, added jaw strength," Wong said. "More points on sensory abilities. Night vision, sense of smell. And we have points left."

I had my own ideas, though I'd have preferred to run the model through our simulator first. But he was driving and I wanted to hear how he thought. "What do you think we should spend them on?"

"First, I change the body shape."

"Why? How does it look?"

"Like a torpedo. Needs to be thinner."

"As long as it can stay warm," I said.

"Looks like you are the one staying warm."

"Hey, man, give me a break. It's hot under here."

"What are you doing anyway?"

"I'm looking for the RC-245 port that this thing goes into."

"Why?"

"Because that's how we can make adjustments to the bio printer."

"Why don't you just use this port?"

His words took a moment to register. "What port?"

He lifted a foot toward the area just behind his workstation, which I couldn't see very well. "Right here."

"Does it look like it will fit this cable?"

"Maybe."

I sighed and crawled out from under the biological printer to come see what he was talking about. Since designer workstations were arrayed honeycomb-style around the biological printer, each one offered a slightly different view. I'd never seen much of Wong's—between the way he constantly hunched over his workstation, and the stacked wall of empty energy drink cans, it was hard to see anything. I squeezed in there anyway. He pointed and sure enough, there was a metal wall plate about the size of an old-school light switch plate, and in the middle was a port that looked like it could fit the RC-245. Even more telling was what someone had hand-written with thin black marker on the bottom half of the plate: *Access Panel*.

"Oh my God, it's right here!" I checked the plug to get the right orientation, tried it on the port, and it clicked right into place. "Bingo."

"Always wonder what that was for," Wong said.

"You didn't think to tell me that there was something here labeled Access Panel?"

"You said you need a port underneath."

"That's what O'Connell told me." Now that I said it out loud, I wondered if this was his idea of a joke. We'd been civil to each other and I shook his hand when I left, but maybe not everything was as water under the bridge as I'd thought.

"O'Connell told you this?"

"Yeah, that's how I knew about the RC-245 cable." Now that one end was plugged in, the other end constituted a standard data cable. I handed it to him. "Here, try this on your workstation."

He plugged it in.

"Anything?" I asked.

"It's connecting."

I didn't dare get my hopes up. His workstation chimed and a new projection monitor materialized. The workstation OS recognized the biological printer, read its credentials, and accepted the connection. Even better, the connection triggered a module to load automatically. A printer configuration module.

"Have you seen this before?" I asked.

"Never."

"How in the world does this still work?"

"Last year, this was O'Connell's workstation."

Damn, why didn't I remember that? "Of course. It would make sense that he set it up at his workstation." Which apparently we'd forgotten to reformat when he left the company. We'd gotten lax on security since Ben Fulton's time. He'd been the security chief of Build-A-Dragon when I first joined, an intimidating guy on the surface. Turned out, he had loved dragons as much as anyone. Man, I hadn't thought about him in a while.

"Look at this," Wong said, bringing my focus back to the new projection monitor. The control interface was nothing fancy, but it gave us control over some fundamental aspects of the dragon-egg-printing process. Baseline shell shape and thickness, for example, which we might need to think about for extreme cold environments.

"We should be careful," I said, half to Wong and half to myself. Tinkering with these elements was tempting but could break one of the few things about our company that actually worked. I forced my eyes to look only for the fields relevant for mitochondrial load and nothing else.

"There it is," Wong said, pointing.

The field said *Mitochondrial content* and it was currently set to 1.0. Which could mean any number of things, but most likely represented a proportion. Wong tapped his keys and navigated to the field. It was free-text input, and judging by the current value, allowed a decimal point.

"What do you think?" I asked.

"Must be ratio. What does research say for endotherms?"

"About five times the mitochondrial load."

He deleted the 1.0 and typed in 5.0, then looked at me. I knew what he was thinking. If this janky old-school input broke the undoubtedly fragile code that managed the biological printer interface, forget creating wild-release dragons. We'd be out of business and out of job. But I'd given so much thought to this path to making dragons produce their own body heat—so much devotion to removing one more barrier to putting a dragon on the last continent—that I refused to let fear hold me back.

"Do it," I said.

He saved the change and the biological printer control program seemed to allow it. It prompted him to ask if he was sure, and he agreed. Then the disconnection chime sounded from his workstation. Carefully, he unplugged the cable from his workstation and handed it back to me. I had to squeeze a tiny release latch on the RC-245 plug, but then it clicked free. If the God Machine noticed the difference, it gave no sign.

"Seems okay," Wong said.

"Maybe." We wouldn't know for certain until we printed an egg, though. "You know what? Let's print a Rover."

"You don't want to run through simulator first?"

I shook my head. "I never factored mitochondrial content into the model."

"Rover coming up, then." He saved the draft of the Antarctic dragon, closed it, brought up the Rover, and sent it to print. We watched the machine and both held our breaths. The arms swung into motion with their usual metallic whine. *Man, I missed that sound.* Wong was listening intently, and I imagined he felt that way, too.

Then the conveyer belt started moving. This was always the best part, the moment the newly printed egg slid out of the printer. It emerged from the darker recesses of the God Machine, a middling to large-sized egg with a near-perfect oval shape. The size was correct, and the shape looked familiar. To be honest, it had been a minute since we printed a Rover model, so I couldn't be sure.

Wong squinted at it rolled to the side, squinted again, and gave a sharp nod. "Rover egg. No doubt."

"No doubt." The egg was dusky brown with slashes of darker coloring. I took a breath, leaned close, and laid my hand on it. The dragon eggshells looked like they'd be smooth and almost slippery, but this was an illusion. To the touch, they were rough as sharkskin.

"Looks fine, but how do we know if it worked?" he asked.

"It worked." I wasn't sure how, but some primal instinct of mine *knew.* Then I realized what it was: the sensation of preternatural heat radiating from the egg to my fingertips and up my arm. The smell was different, too. Dragon eggs had a faint oily scent to them when they were printed. I'd always assumed it came from the machine. But this one had a different aroma, an animal musk. Weirdly, it made me think of woodland animals. Either way, there was no denying the warmth beneath the shell.

Wong looked dubious. "You think?"

"Go ahead, touch it."

He did, and jerked his hand back by instinct. "It's hot!"

"It's endothermic," I said.

CHAPTER TWENTY
Egghead Request

Within ten days, the first batch of dragon eggs had been printed for deployment to Antarctica. They were all warm like the first one had been, but we kept them in Build-A-Dragon's sun-powered incubators just to be sure. Evelyn had asked for an update so I ran up to her office to give her the good news.

"The eggs are all printed," I said.

She stood at the window using an eyedropper to water one of her dangerous plants. She actually counted how many drops she put on it, then squirted the rest back into her copper watering can. "Excellent. How do they look?"

"The shells are dark, almost charcoal gray with fine black spots. But they have bright skinny slashes of white as well. It's a strange pattern, but it's just uncanny how warm they are to the touch."

"Did you set the biological printer back to its default mitochondrial levels?"

"Yep, and I made sure Wong knows how to adjust it in case we need more."

"Good," she said. "Because I was wondering if you'd like to travel with the eggs to Antartica."

My heart sped up a little. *I can't tell if she's joking or not.* "Are you serious?"

"Yes, absolutely. We've never designed dragons for an environment like this. I need someone who understands the design to assess their performance."

I felt a thrill in my stomach at the thought of getting to go, but I still wasn't sure I believed her. "Antarctica is kind of a long trip. It's not cheap, either."

"The board approved the travel costs this morning," she said. "For both travelers."

Both travelers. "So you're going, too?"

"No, not me."

"Well, then who else is going?"

She smiled. "Who do you think?"

"Wong."

"No, travel outside the U.S. is risky with his visa."

"Korrapati?"

"No, the DOD just placed—" She stopped, straightened. "Well, let's just say that I need her here right now."

Ah yes, another fun moment of not having security clearance. Evelyn never knew what she could tell me and when, so she erred on the side of no information. "Fine, I give up."

"Someone you like."

I shrugged. "I like everybody."

"Really, Noah Parker?"

"As far as as you know."

"Fine, this is someone *I* like."

I laughed, because I knew who it was. "Tom Johnson?"

Her eyes sparkled. "How did you know?"

"You're not as mysterious as you pretend to be," I said. "At least in some things."

"Tom got wind of the Antarctica delivery and insisted we have some people there, including himself."

"Oh, did he ask for me?" I was kidding, for the most part, though a tiny part of me wondered. Tom Johnson was a herpetologist I'd known about since I was a kid. He counted as senior staff for Build-A-Dragon but did a lot of field work, always looking after the dragons and their welfare. Come to think of it, I wasn't surprised he'd volunteered for this assignment. Not only would it be the toughest environment our dragons had faced so far, but it was one of the last pristine places on earth.

"Yes, of course," she said.

"By name?"

"In a manner of speaking." She paused, but seemed to recognize that I was going to press and added. "He asked for 'one of the eggheads' to accompany the eggs."

That was hardly the vote of confidence I'd hoped for, but then again, I'd been called worse. "How soon do we leave?"

"On Monday, once we confirm the logistics with the Chilean authorities."

"We don't need to arrange visas or anything?" That seemed like it could take a while.

"No. I had Roger verify."

"So you're serious. You're sending me to Antartica next week," I said.

She smiled. "Yes. You want to go, don't you?"

"Do I want to travel to the last pristine continent with the world's top herpetologist? Yes, please!" *But how the hell am I going to tell Summer?*

First, I offered to take all the dragons off her hands for the weekend. I told her I'd do a couple of geocaches in Tonto and let them get lots of flying time in. She couldn't wait, because she wanted to install new curtains after Marcus Aurelius had pulled hers down to make himself a bed on top of the refrigerator. *This is why we can't have nice things.*

Then, on Saturday, I took her to a surprise dinner out at La Boheme, a French restaurant. I said it was a belated celebration of the net-plus win and the Mantis dragon deployment. We, being young professionals in our twenties, didn't do a lot of fine dining. Our idea of a nice dinner usually came wrapped in foil. La Boheme took this to a next level.

She'd called me an hour before I was set to pick her up. "Are you going to dress up?"

"I think I have to," I said. "They said something about a—" I broke off because Nero snatched one of my socks and scampered into the kitchen. "Hey, get back here!" I ran in and found him trying to build his own nest against the trash can. It already had several mismatched socks and my favorite baseball hat crammed into it. "Give me that!" I snatched my sock back from him before it became part of the fixture. I brought the phone back up. "A jacket. I have to wear one."

"Okay, then I need time. See you soon!"

I picked her up in my Tesla, which I'd washed and vacuumed. She came downstairs and I got out to open the door for her. She wore a slender black dress with tiny white polka dots and platform heel sandals that matched it. The purse, too, was the same pattern. She'd curled her hair, too. "Oh, wow. You look foxy as hell," I told her.

"Thank you." She side-eyed my khakis, button-down shirt, and dark jacket. "I didn't think you owned a jacket."

It was the jacket from my suit, but I didn't see the need to tell her that. "Sometimes I moonlight for the FBI."

She snorted but climbed in. I ran around the front of the car, feeling suddenly nervous. We hadn't gone for an overly elegant night out since... I couldn't remember when. I hoped this night would go well.

The restaurant did not help with my plans. In true French fashion, La Boheme forced its customers to sit practically elbow to elbow with total strangers. I saw the layout and panicked, but we lucked our way into a tiny respite: ours was a corner table against two walls, so it offered a tiny bit of privacy.

The menu was four courses, starting with escargot. Summer wouldn't touch them. I didn't care for the taste of the snail, but I liked the garlic-butter sauce. Even better was the fun of poking them out of the receptacles in the tight-fitting porcelain baking dish with a tiny fork. I got most of them out without incident, but one of them flew over Summer's shoulder and onto the table behind us. Which, mercifully, another couple had just left. Summer and I suppressed our laughter behind our hands, trying to keep our decorum.

The main course, a large fancy steak called Chateaubriand, was one of the most delicious things I've ever eaten. Summer ordered it, too, medium, and said the same thing. Dessert was a fancy and warm chocolate cake drizzled with both chocolate frosting and some kind of liqueur. It had a subtle alcohol flavor but the cake seemed to melt in my mouth.

"God, that's good," I said.

"You can have the rest of mine." She pushed her cake across to me; only a tiny bite was missing.

"You don't like it?"

She smiled. "Not as much as you will."

"You're the best, you know that?"

"This is fun." She shifted and started running the toe of her shoe up the inside of my leg. "We should do this more often."

I'd go broke if we did this more often, but didn't have the heart to tell her that. "Sounds good to me."

She picked up her wineglass. "To our successes." I found mine and we touched glasses. It was a very French thing to do, and we both enjoyed it.

"Speaking of successes, I was wondering if you might do me a favor."

She moved her foot again, now caressing my *other* leg in the tiny booth. It was very distracting. "I might. What kind of favor?"

"Look after the dragons for two weeks."

"What?" Her foot moved away from me. "Why?"

"We finished printing the eggs for the Antarctica deployment, and Evelyn asked—"

"Well, tell her no. She can't make you go."

"No, but..." I took a breath, summoning my courage. "She wants a designer on-site. I'm really the only one who can go."

"I *knew* this would happen." She kicked my leg, which hurt like hell.

"Ow!" I said it louder than intended, and I could feel people looking at us. I lowered my voice. "Listen—"

"No, *you* listen," she hissed. "I am not going to babysit a pack of unruly dragons! Not while you go off adventuring."

"Two weeks. That's all I'm asking. You won't even notice I'm gone."

"That's a long time, Noah. Work is crazy right now, too. It's like *the worst* possible timing."

"I know, and I'm sorry. But I just... really want to go."

She scoffed. "Yeah, you want to go. Of course you want to go. You probably planned this whole thing."

"I didn't plan it, I—"

"Forget it." She held up her hand. "Just stop." She got her purse, tore the napkin off her lap, and stood. "I'll be at the car." She stormed out. Several of the other couples nearby watched her go, glanced at me, and then pointedly looked away.

This was a new level of humiliation. The waiter brought me the check. I paid the exorbitant amount and left a good tip because it wasn't their fault the meal was ruined.

Summer was waiting at the car with her arms crossed, still fuming.

I unlocked it and would have opened her door, but she pushed me away and got in on her own. "Take me home, please."

The drive to her house was long, quiet, and extremely uncomfortable. She gathered her purse and took out her keys as we neared her building. It was a clear signal that I wasn't coming up. I pulled up in the circular drive and stopped. Four hours ago we'd been so happy here, and now it was the complete opposite. She opened her door and started to get out.

"Summer—"

She stopped and looked over, but not at me. At the dashboard halfway between us. "You can bring the dragons over Sunday afternoon."

"I was thinking we might—" I started, but she'd already gotten out of the car and slammed the door.

CHAPTER TWENTY-ONE
The Long Way

Monday morning. I met Tom Johnson at Build-A-Dragon's headquarters at the ungodly hour of four AM. Mind you, our flight was not until seven AM but he insisted on riding together to the airport. And driving, of course. Which was probably for the best. I knew the head of the Herpetology department well enough to guess what he'd think of my modern electric car.

The thing about me is that I'm not a morning person. After I'd dragged myself out of bed and driven to work in complete darkness, I found myself regretting most of my life choices. Dropping off the dragonets at Summer's place had been a pretty miserable experience. She greeted the dragons with kindness but hardly said a word to me. At last, she gave me a cool, half-hearted hug and said, "Be safe."

The coldness of that departure robbed my travel day of most of its excitement. The sun showed no promise of rising and my coffee hadn't done the trick, either. I parked in the cold, empty parking garage beneath our building, which yawned dark and silent against the starlight. It was cool as always this early in the morning. Or this late at night, whatever you wanted to call it. Eerie to come here at this time. Unnatural. I hauled my travel bag out of the trunk and shouldered my backpack. They were both a drab olive green synthetic canvas, sturdy, but heavily loaded with all my gear. Never in my life had I spent so much on what was essentially luggage. From the outside they looked nondescript. I'd left them out in the sun and sand for hours to get rid of the new fabric smell. The straps felt good, though. Solid. I shouldered them and checked my watch. I'd be on time but I had to hustle.

A large, battered pickup truck waited in the visitor lot outside Build-A-Dragon. Its engine was running. The sight of the tall, bearded man leaning against it made me quicken my step. Yeah, it was early and I felt crabby, but only part of me believed I'd get to spend the next few days with Tom Johnson.

"Morning, Parker," he said affably. "Glad you're on time."

"Early is on time," I said. It was more of a statement of how he felt, not how I did. In my world, two minutes late was on time.

"Good man." He offered to take my duffel so I handed it to him, and he slung it into the truck's bed below. His own bag was there, a travel-worn but expensive duffel. It was even the same brand as mine, but obviously had seen more mileage. That perked me up a little.

I slung my backpack in beside it, trusting the impact foam sleeves to protect my precious tablet. *God, if that breaks I'll have no purpose down there.* It wasn't like you could just order a new piece of tech and have it overnighted. Commercial flights rarely went anywhere near Antarctica. There was no point. Never was it convenient or economical to route a flight over the most out-of-the-way continent on the planet.

The passenger side door squealed in protest when I opened it. I climbed into the seat and pulled it hard so that it closed with a loud *thunk*.

"Good, you remembered," Tom said.

"You ever think about getting a new truck?"

"Why would I do that? This one's fine."

No electric locks or windows, no GPS, and two doors that barely close. He had a strange definition for the word *fine*. I shook my head. "If you say so."

"Besides, too many memories." He patted the dashboard fondly. "You ready?"

"Where are the eggs?"

"Already being loaded onto the plane. The handlers wanted to see to it themselves." He put the truck into gear manually, seemingly oblivious to the metallic grinding noises that followed. "You know how they are."

"I certainly do." Even though it was God-awful early, I started to feel better. Remembering that you worked at the same place as a childhood idol tended to do that.

"You ever been to South America?"

"No. I'm excited to see a little bit of it." *And you've been all over.* "What's your favorite part?"

"For work, it's a tie between Patagonia and the upper Amazon."

"Some of the animals for the Dragon Genome Project came from the Amazon, didn't they?"

"More than half. The biodiversity down there is incredible."

"Incredible and dangerous," I said.

"Yeah, a couple of snakes got me down there."

"*Venomous* snakes?"

"That's pretty much all they have down here."

I chuckled. "I'm surprised you didn't ... lose a leg or something."

"Well, you don't even get off the plane without two snakebite kits."

"How long since you've been down there?" I asked.

"Couple of years." His brow furrowed as he stared at the road. "Come to think of it, might be closer to three."

"Time flies, doesn't it?"

"It's this job, man." He shook his head and gave the road a thousand-yard stare. "It's got me putting down roots."

"You say that like it's a bad thing."

"It's not all bad. Regular pay is good. Benefits are good. I've just never lived this long in one place."

I understood what he was saying, though I couldn't help but feel insignificant. After all, I'd spent most of my life in Arizona. "Well, we like having you around."

"Thanks, Parker. Right back at you."

Hearing that brought a flush of warmth to my core. I looked away out the window because I knew it would show on my face.

"I don't think this is a good idea, though," he said.

The warm fuzzy feeling disappeared, washed away by a wave of cold uncertainty. "Wait, what? Why not?"

"Antarctica is the last pristine continent, and we're about to introduce a new predator."

"To control their rat problem and protect the native species."

"Yeah, I know the sales pitch." His tone said what he thought of it.

"But you don't buy it."

"You know how many times we've introduced a predator species to a new environment and had it blow up in our faces?"

"Um—"

"Let's talk cane toads, for example. Do you know those?"

The name sounded vaguely familiar, though I couldn't place it. "I don't think so."

"It's a large toad native to the Americas, mostly South and Central America. Voracious insect predator. In the early 1900s, sugarcane farmers in tropical climates started releasing them into the wild to help control insect pests that destroyed sugarcane crops. The toads got established and their populations grew exponentially."

"Did they at least control the insect pests?" I asked.

"It seemed to help in Puerto Rico where they had a major beetle infestation. That was around 1930. Even the scientists were on board. Cuba and many Caribbean islands were gung-ho to import them. Then Hawaii, then the Philippines and other places in the Pacific. The results for insect control were mixed. The truth is, cane toads eat just about anything they can swallow. They don't just prey on the pest insects, if you know what I mean. In most places, they go after easier food than cane beetles, so they end up a net neutral. Worse than that, they're poisonous."

"They bite people?" I asked.

"Animals that bite or sting are technically called *venomous*. Did I say venomous?"

"No, Professor Johnson, you said poisonous."

He chuckled at that little jab. "Good, you were listening. *Poisonous* animals make toxic chemicals for defense only, and they only get you if you go out and touch one. Or eat it, which is the mistake a lot of the Australian species make." I wondered if this was going to turn out like the fable of the woman who swallowed the fly. "Let me guess, they introduced a snake or something to control the toads."

"No, there was no point in that. Snakes that eat them usually die. And the toads breed like crazy. Now almost all of those countries that imported them for sugarcane control consider cane toads to be their biggest pest."

"Now this is starting to sound familiar."

"It took decades to figure out the scale of the effects on other species, the ones that tried to eat the toads." He sighed. "Australia got hit the hardest. Yellow-spotted monitors, which are really important for ecological maintenance down there, died off in many areas with cane-toad infestations. The northern quolls were wiped out in the top half of Australia."

"Is that a bird?"

"No, a furry little marsupial. Bigger than a rat, smaller than a possum. They're shy and mostly nocturnal, but cute little things if you get the chance to see one."

"Have you seen one?"

"Once when I was down in Kakadu National Park, in the Northern Territory. We were hiking in to catalogue nests of pig-nosed turtles, which are endangered there. Made camp at the base of a rocky hill. I was the first up an hour before sunrise, and saw one foraging among the rocks."

We rode in silence for a moment. Then I asked, "Is there really a pig-nosed turtle?"

"*Carettochelys insculpta*. The only living member of its genus."

"Does it really have a pig nose?"

"Oh, yeah. A round snout with two nostrils at the end. They have flippers, too."

I laughed. "Come on. Only sea turtles have flippers."

"All sea turtles, and one freshwater turtle. It's part of why they're endangered. Reptile smugglers are always after them, for the exotic pet market and sometimes for their meat."

"People are the worst."

"You don't have to tell me."

He exited the freeway then, which didn't make sense, if we were headed to the Phoenix airport at least. "Hey, we're not going to Sky Harbor?"

"No, Scottsdale Airport. Less air traffic."

He pulled right up to an unmarked gate where we showed our IDs to a guard in a beige uniform. Then he parked outside the private hangar.

"Want to know something about the northern quoll?" he asked as we climbed out of the truck.

"Sure."

"Every year after the males breed, they die off."

"Why?" I shouldered my backpack.

"Nobody knows." He swung my duffel out of the truck, handed it to me, and gave an enigmatic smile. "Something to think about."

It was my first time riding on a private jet and it ruined me for air travel. Tom carried his luggage right up the motored staircase into the passenger cabin, so I followed suit. The plane was bigger than a standard private plane, at least by my guess. There were twenty-four passenger seats. Six rows of two on each side of a central aisle. The cargo hold was pressurized and climate-controlled. We had a pilot and copilot already locked in the cockpit together. The flight attendant, a crisp matronly woman in a navy blue uniform, informed us that they were already starting their startup checklist.

A man and woman occupied two seats in the last starboard row of the plane. They were both huddled over a tablet.

"Recognize those two?" Tom asked.

I stared at them for a moment, then realization dawned. "Oh, that's Jim and Allie. Two of our hatchers."

"Takes a minute to recognize them when they're not in all white, huh?" He walked up to say hello and I followed him.

"How's it going?" Tom asked.

They glanced up at the sound of our approach. These two were a study in opposites, which had always helped me recognize them at work. Jim was probably in his midthirties, a stout fellow with dark hair and eyes, who always had a slight frown on his jowly face. Allie was five or six years younger, also brunette, and very pretty. Her eyes were sky blue but they spared us only the fleetest of glances. She offered a smile but glanced around nervously. Everything she did was nervous, like a rabbit crossing an open field.

Tom seemed a bit flabbergasted at the nonresponse. I guess he was accustomed to bigger reactions.

"How are the eggs?" I asked.

"Holding steady at ninety-five degrees," Allie said.

"We had a slight dip in their temperatures during the loading operation, but they stayed within acceptable parameters," Jim said.

"Were they heavy?"

"Somewhere between a Rover and..." He trailed off and looked at Allie.

"The smallest of the ones we can't talk about," she said.

"Anything unusual about them?"

"Hell, yeah. They were warm," Jim said.

Allie smiled at him. "Like little hot pockets."

I told them about the endothermic design, though I left out the part about tampering with the God Machine. Something told me they might not appreciate it.

"We wondered if that's what it was," Allie said.

"You didn't think to ask?"

Jim shrugged. "Not our department."

Yeah, they work at Build-A-Dragon, all right. "Have a good flight."

I moved up and picked a seat in the front row, figuring that if I was going to fly first class I should go for the whole experience. The flight attendant had already buckled herself in and gave us a pointed look like we should do the same. I dropped into the starboard seat by the window, leaving the aisle for Tom if he wanted it. He slouched into the window seat opposite on the far side of the aisle. I felt a twinge of disappointment but tried not to take it personally.

In minutes, the engines were powering up. The jet accelerated quickly and practically leapt into the sky. I took out my tablet and started to do some work. The first time I looked up, Tom was reclined in his seat, his hat over his face, sleeping soundly. *Lucky bastard.* I could never sleep on planes, nor did I dare admit to him that I'd rarely flown anywhere. Eleven hours is a long flight time but I hardly noticed. I spent most of it working, my tablet hot-linked to Build-A-Dragon's servers and using both the projection monitor and the keyboard. I'd been working on some modifications to the simulator that would let us stress-test the dragon designs in extreme environments. The extreme cold was already working well, even if it kept predicting my dragons would go to sleep and freeze to death.

The next thing I knew we were descending into Buenos Aires. The flight attendant shook Tom awake and made him put his seat up. The guy had taken the flight like a man on a leisurely vacation. He slept, ate dinner, thumbed through a dog-eared field guide to Antarctic wildlife, and then slept again. Then again, he provided more entertainment than Jim and Allie, who hadn't so much as ventured up to the front of the plane.

We dropped through the cloud deck into an emerald green landscape. A strong crosswind buffeted the plane as we made our final approach. My stomach rose into my throat. I panicked and gripped both armrests. I glanced around wildly. The flight attendant was strapped in, not looking at me. Jim and Allie had shrunk against their seats, white-eyed and trembling. They were whispering fiercely to one another. The only word I could make out was *eggs*. Last I glanced at Tom, who was reading his goddamn book again. Cool as a cucumber.

"There's always a little chop when you land in Buenos Aires," he said to no one in particular. "Nothing to worry about."

I felt a little silly but his casual reassurance helped. I forced myself to take a few deep breaths and loosen my grip on the armrests. Then the plane touched down, the wheels holding solid on the pavement. I lurched against the restraints as the pilot braked.

"We're not getting off here, are we?" I asked Tom.

"Nope. Just a pit stop."

"Do we need to... check the eggs or anything?"

He laughed. "If there were a problem, don't you think they'd have told us?" He hitched his thumb toward the back of the plane.

"Good point."

They turned us around in less than an hour, and we took off from a different runway, now flying south-southwest. Tom settled in with his book again. I should have worked but got distracted by the view out the window. *South America*. I'd always wanted to visit this place. To say it was verdant green didn't do it justice. Glittering, deep blue rivers snaked through an emerald landscape, interrupted only by checkered squares of farmland. Everything was in full bloom, too. I had to remind myself that the seasons were flipped in the southern hemisphere. Our winter was their summer. Granted, it never felt truly cold in Phoenix but we didn't have greenery like this. At some point I must have finally dozed off. I woke up when we started descending. Bright azure waters glittered outside the oval window. Ocean.

The landing was much smoother this time, though for most of the descent it looked like we were heading straight into the water. The plane couldn't have been more than thirty feet off the ground before white sand, a green strip, a fence, some vehicles. Then dark asphalt ran beneath us just as the wheels touched down. So, smoother but still nerve-racking. I closed my eyes and exhaled. *We're here.*

The plane taxied off the runway and stopped, then the engines powered down. I stood and stretched. Every part of me felt stiff, and dozing had somehow made me more tired. Tom was already on his feet, claiming our duffel bags from the overhead compartment.

"This was a long way," I said.

He set my bag on the empty seat in front of me and shouldered his own. "That's why they call it *Fin del Mundo*."

"End of the world?" I guessed.

"Right."

"That's a fitting name."

"How's your Spanish?"

I winced. "Ooh, not my strong suit." I'd picked some up here and there—in the Southwest it was impossible not to—but Summer spoke it well. She did everything well. "I'm more into Mandarin."

"That might prove useful on the island, but won't help you much here."

The flight attendant, acting on some signal we couldn't hear, moved to the plane's door and put her palm on the biometric lock. It chimed in affirmative. The locks cycled open, and she pushed the door outward. We were not at a gate, but still on the tarmac, with the rail of a portable staircase waiting outside. A warm breeze sighed into the cabin, carrying the faint smell of ocean salt and the cries of distant birds. It was somehow familiar and foreign at the same time.

Tom breathed in audibly. "Sea breeze."

The flight attendant gestured out the door. "Welcome to Ushuaia, everyone. Please have your passports ready."

I followed Tom out the door. The warm, moist air wrapped around me like a blanket. It was early evening, and the sun was setting in a light blue sky behind mountains that rose up to the west of us. Big mountains, too, some with the bright white of snow near the peaks. The airport was rather small, with only a few runways and a single central terminal. Ours was the only plane on the central tarmac at present, though others were parked neatly along a chain-link fence that ran around the perimeter. A huge canvas-wrapped cargo truck was parked right beside the plane near the cargo area, its diesel engine rumbling. Four dark-haired, mustachioed workers in drab olive uniforms were latching a large metal ramp to the back of the truck, chattering back and forth in Spanish.

I poked my head back in to where Jim and Allie were slowly

collecting their luggage, looking as stiff as I felt. "There's a truck here that I assume is for the eggs. They're—"

A blur of motion was my only warning before the both of them shouldered me aside against the metal rail of the staircase, limbs flying, baggage akimbo. They passed Tom on the stairs and thus were the first to reach the ground, where a man and a woman waited with digital tablets to officially record our arrival. Moments later they were through, and quickly took charge of the egg-unloading operations. Whether there were any language barriers or not, I couldn't tell.

Meanwhile, Tom greeted the customs agents with a flurry of Spanish. They responded in kind, which suggested in that brief moment he'd demonstrated enough fluency to be trusted with official questions. My measure of him went up a notch, if that was even possible.

The man and woman took me in with a glance and greeted me in English.

"Good evening, sir. May I see your passport, please?" the man asked.

"Of course." I handed it to him and tried to hide my relief that I wouldn't have to muddle through the conversation with my forty-word Spanish vocabulary.

The man scanned my passport while the woman pulled up something else—possibly the flight manifest—on her own tablet. They glanced at each other and both nodded.

"Welcome to Ushuaia," the woman said.

Welcome to the end of the world.

CHAPTER TWENTY-TWO
The Pole

The race to the South Pole was arguably the greatest extreme contest of the early 1900s. In the so-called Heroic Age of Antarctic Exploration, reaching the geographic pole first was, for many, the ultimate prize. The first serious effort was in 1897, a Belgian-led expedition that was the first to spend the winter in Antarctica. They sailed from Antwerp in August and their ship, the RV *Belgica*, became stuck in ice at the end of February. Over the next months, the men endured harrowing conditions of extreme cold, perpetual darkness, and the growing toll of scurvy. When the captain and commander became too ill to perform their duties, the twenty-four-year-old first mate—a Norwegian named Roald Amundsen—stepped up to lend a hand. They returned to Belgium to receive a hero's welcome, two years and two months after departing.

Germany, Sweden, France, and the United Kingdom sent their own expeditions to Antarctica over the next decade, each country hoping to claim the prize. In 1907, famed explorer Ernest Shackleton led the *Nimrod* Expedition. Their ship was an old seal-hunting vessel bought on the cheap when Shackleton's sponsor pulled most of his funding. They had no government sponsors. Their crew was half the size of preceding expeditions and had far less experience. Yet, somehow, Shackleton's team achieved the farthest southern journey recorded to date by a significant margin, reaching the magnetic South Pole at 88° 23' S. They not only set the record for the southernmost reach, but also calculated the location of the true South Pole for future expeditions. When they returned to England and the full scope of the achievement was recognized, Ernest Shackleton was knighted by King Edward VII.

Yet the famous contest for the South Pole, the story most often told, involved two expeditions that began in 1910. One British, one Norwegian. The British *Terra Nova* expedition was led by Robert Falcon Scott, a Navy officer who had been part of the first British Antarctic venture in 1901. He not only wanted to be the first to reach the South Pole, but hoped to continue the scientific studies he'd begun on the previous voyage. To haul their gear, Scott brought thirty-four dogs, nineteen Siberian ponies, and three prototypes of a new invention, the motorized sledge. One of the sledges immediately broke through the ice and was lost upon arrival, heralding a series of mishaps that would plague the expedition.

Scott attempted to establish at least three supply depots ahead of their pole push. It was a chaotic effort that took two months, killed several ponies, and led to the most important supply depot being set thirty miles short of its planned location. The motor sledges that didn't fall through the ice only managed to travel around fifty miles. The ponies died and became food. As a result, most of the expedition members had to haul the gear and supply sledges by hand. It was exhausting work in a frigid environment. In spite of all the setbacks and warning signs, Scott and a party of four hand-picked men made their push. They reached the South Pole on January 17, 1912. When they arrived, they found the black flag of the Norwegian expedition already planted. They had reached the South Pole almost a month earlier.

The Norwegian team was led by Roald Amundsen, who had survived the arduous Belgian expedition years earlier and knew the dangers of the Antarctic. His careful preparation for the journey began in Europe, when he purchased a specially built ship with a round hull to resist the pack ice. He packed 3,000 books to stave off boredom. He ordered a special kind of pemmican that included vegetables and oatmeal. He also stocked considerable amounts of wine and alcohol to keep the men in good spirits. And he brought 220 pounds of chocolate.

Amundsen's plans were meticulous, and he established three depots—containing 7,500 pounds of food and fuel—at regular intervals. Over the winter, he kept his men fit, worked to improve their sledge equipment, and gathered even more supplies. Their push to the South Pole used mainly lightweight sledges pulled by large teams of dogs. They focused on speed rather than research or sample collection, covering fifteen nautical miles a day even on the glacier. On December 14, 1911, Amundsen and his team planted the Norwegian flag at the South Pole. They spent the next three days taking sextant readings to fix the exact position of the pole. They also pitched a tent at their best estimated position, and left equipment and letters for Scott's party. Amundsen and his own party had nearly returned to their ship by the time Scott's team reached their tent at the South Pole.

The British party planted their flag and began their return journey. In spite of the disappointment of coming in second, they made good progress at first. But the weather turned poor, and the exhausting labor of hauling their sledges by hand began to take its toll. Edward Evans, second-in-command, died when they reached the glacier. That was mid-January. A month later, Lawrence Oates—who could barely use his hands and feet due to frostbite—said, "I am just going outside and may be some time," and left the tent. He was never seen again.

Scott and his two remaining companions reached a point eleven miles short of their closest supply depot, but could not go any farther. In his final entry on March 29, 1912, Robert Falcon Scott wrote, *We shall stick it out to the end, but we are getting weaker, of course, and the end cannot be far. It seems a pity but I do not think I can write more. R. Scott. Last entry. For God's sake look after our people.*

Amundsen returned a national hero to Norway, a country that had only recently won its independence. He then turned his attention to the Arctic, and led several efforts to reach the North Pole by land. In 1926, Amundsen and fifteen other men flew a semirigid Italian airship named *Norge* over the North Pole, making him the first explorer to reach both poles. He disappeared two years later while flying on a rescue mission for survivors of a second airship that had crashed on return from the North Pole.

CHAPTER TWENTY-THREE
Sea Unworthy

I clung to the rail of the ship's stern deck and hoped I wouldn't get sick again. The ocean rolled with four-foot swells and the occasional whitecap. The wind whipped at my jacket. Everything was gray. The ship, the sky, the water... probably my face as well. I hadn't spent a lot of time on boats. Apparently I was one of those people who did not take it well. A pair of terns glided gracefully behind us, diving occasionally to capture something churned to the surface by the ship's propeller. I didn't have the energy to try to identify them. In theory, terns were one of the bird species that were at risk from the infestation here. The dragons should help them. I wasn't sure I'd survive long enough to see if that was true.

"How are you feeling?" Tom appeared beside me at the rail.

"I've been better."

He looked at my face and did not seem reassured by what he saw. "Still no sea legs, huh?"

"Not yet." In my defense, when I'd seen ship travel on our itinerary, I assumed it would be on something larger, like a cruise ship. Two of those had been docked at Ushuaia, massive thousand-foot vessels with white hulls and brightly painted decks. Instead we'd boarded the ugly gray cargo ship that was moored in their shadows. *Part transportation vessel, part torture device.*

"We're lucky to have such mild conditions."

"This is *mild*?"

"Drake's Passage is one of the most volatile and unpredictable sea routes in the world." He shaded his eyes and scanned the horizon. "Imagine doing this on a wooden sailing ship."

I could have, but I didn't want to. I was trying to keep my eyes on the horizon, which they said was one of the ways to reduce seasickness. It didn't seem to help any more than the wrist pressure bands or the horrific ginger gum. The only good news was that I wasn't cold. The air sure was—it had to be near freezing, or below that with the wind in your face—but I'd zipped myself into a down-lined synthetic all-weather suit with a built-in heater. My arms, core, and legs were plenty warm, and I didn't even have the temperature set to high. Of course, the air was frigid where it blew against my face, and no amount of warmth helped with the wrenching pain in my stomach.

"You're still looking a little green, kid," Tom said.

Go to Antarctica, they said. *It's a once-in-a-lifetime trip*, they said. That last part was right, for sure. "I just want to get there."

Tom shaded his eyes and looked ahead. "I think you're in luck."

Forward on deck, someone shouted, "Land ho!"

Finally. I prayed that stepping onto solid ground might bring an end to the endless gastrointestinal torment. I covered my eyes and looked ahead to where several unmoving white peaks rose from the churning waves. At first, I thought they were icebergs, but they gradually revealed themselves as the snow-capped peaks of carbon-gray rock formations. To my surprise, there was more gray than white. "What am I looking at?"

"Fildes Peninsula, King George Island."

"It looks..." I searched for the right word. Barren, inhospitable, and foreboding all would have fit. "Um, cold."

"Don't worry, this is the peak of summer." He clapped me on the shoulder. "Might even get above freezing a couple of times, you'll see."

The land seemed to bounce up and down as the boat pitched, which only made the rocks and crags more threatening. *A perfect location for a shipwreck.* "How close can we get?"

"Not much closer. They'll use Zodiacs to ferry us ashore."

"What the hell is a Zodiac?" I was hoping it was some kind of extremely safe helicopter.

"It's a semirigid boat with a big outboard motor. They're good for landing on beaches."

Even as he spoke, the deep rumble of the ship's engines lessened, then faded away. I hurried back into the cabin to retrieve my duffel bag and satchel. My dreams of reading or getting work done had been dashed the moment we pulled out of Ushuaia harbor. I thought maybe now that we'd stopped, the motion of the boat wouldn't bother me as much. Instead, the ship rocked sideways with the waves, which was far worse. *I need to get off this damn thing and onto solid ground.*

By the time I'd returned to deck, a motorboat had appeared between us and the peninsula, its low hull punching through waves. There were two crew aboard, both wearing royal blue life jackets over bright orange all-weather suits.

"There you are." Tom strode toward me. He wore a life jacket himself and threw me a spare. "Put this on. We're going first."

"First?"

"Captain's orders. The hatchers are going to supervise off-loading of our cargo here. You and I get to make sure they're ready to receive them on land."

Which is how I found myself jammed in the corner of an inflatable boat as it roared across the waves. Tom had produced large orange waterproof bags for our gear. Now I understood why. Every bounce of the craft brought a wave of ocean spray across the rigid hull. Not full-on waves, but enough to keep everything in the little craft good and wet. I had to face forward so I couldn't really gauge our distance from the ship. The jagged white piece of land loomed ever larger in front of us.

King George Island was part of the South Shetland Islands, an archipelago north of the main white continent. Instead of researching the most common modes of transportation when going to Antarctica, I'd foolishly looked into the history and politics of the place we were headed. Ushuaia belonged to Argentina, and our destination on King George Island belonged to Chile, so I'd figured the island must belong to one of them. Or maybe both in some special arrangement.

Turns out, it belonged to no one, officially speaking. The 1959 Antarctic Treaty was one of the most significant international accords that was signed during the Cold War. Seven of the twelve initial signing parties made territorial claims on Antarctica, all of which were ignored by all other parties. Now more than fifty states had joined the treaty, which prohibited military operations, territorial claims, economic exploitation, and nuclear testing in Antarctica. Everyone agreed that the main purpose was research. Nowhere else in the world would you find outposts from dozens of countries all within driving distance of one another.

Of course, I'd have settled for any country's base right now. The ocean grew more turbulent as we neared the island but the pilot of our tiny boat never slowed. The Zodiac shot up a wave and went airborne. My stomach dropped.

"Whoa!" I shouted.

The boat hit the water, which sent a huge wave of salty spray over the bow. Because my mouth was open, it choked me. I spluttered and coughed, trying not to gag. I looked up and Tom had a huge stupid grin on his soaking wet stupid face.

"Isn't this great?" he shouted.

I shook my head. "You're crazy, man."

The boat caught one last wave and nosed onto the beach, if you could call it that. It had dark gray pebbles rather than sand. The two crew members jumped over the side and hauled the boat up onto shore. I might have felt sick most of the way, and crouched in salt-soaked misery for the final approach, but I'd been waiting for this moment. *Solid ground at last.* I vaulted the side and onto the pebble surface. It was a little jarring—the pebbles didn't have as much give as sand—but I held my footing.

"First!" I called to Tom, who was still gathering his bags.

He looked up from where he was gathering his bags. "Oh, so you can move fast when you want to."

"Hey man, I'm just glad to be off a boat for once." It was snowing steadily now, the thick flakes more visible against the dark slate of the terrain. I retrieved my gear, glad that it was ensconced in waterproof plastic. Otherwise, everything would have been soaked. As soon as our bags were out, the crewmen began pushing the boat back into the water. Tom tossed down his bags to lend a hand, so I did the same. We pushed the boat back enough and then, at the rapid instructions of a crew member, spun it around and gave it one last shove out into the waves. The pilot pulled the cord to start the outboard. Nothing. I readied myself in case the thing wouldn't start and the waves pushed it back on us. On the second pull, though, the engine roared to life. The pilot and crewman waved their thanks.

Tom and I returned their wave. Then we turned around to get our gear and saw a penguin. A *wild* penguin. It stood there looking at us from about thirty yards away like a maître d' in a tuxedo. I grabbed Tom's shoulder and pointed.

"Oh yeah, it's your first time," Tom said.

"There's a penguin over there," I said helpfully. *Brilliant observation.*

"That's a gentoo. See the triangular white patches at the eyes?"

"It's... bigger than I thought they'd be." Probably three feet tall if I had to guess. The only penguins I'd ever seen in person were at a zoo, and those couldn't have been over a foot.

"That's a mature male." He squinted against the snow, which was falling more heavily now. "Probably seven or eight kilos. They don't get much bigger."

The penguin apparently didn't care to be the subject of further examination. It waddled to the water and swam away. I felt sad seeing it go, but I was glad for the glimpse of what we came for. I shouldered my duffel and satchel. "Guess we should get a move on."

We hiked away from the water. The rocks of the moraine were fist-sized and occasionally unstable. I stumbled a couple of times until I got the hang of it. You put your boot down and gave it a side-to-side wiggle to make sure the rocks wouldn't slide out from under it. It made for slow going, but with the wind-blown snow pelting me in the face I couldn't move much faster anyway. Tom either knew where to go or was one of those people with an innate sense of direction, because in a couple minutes we spotted several bright red buildings nestled in a flat area surrounded by taller rock cliffs. Off the beach, the ground was hard rock and more stable. More of the settlement came into view as we approached. There had to be thirty or forty buildings, most of them about the size of a trailer and also painted bright red.

"Here we are," Tom said, as we neared the main door of the largest central complex. Impressively, we had not walked on any snow so our boots were clean and I didn't feel bad about going in. The outer door opened into a small anteroom with another door to the interior of the building. Tom tried it as I was stepping in, but a buzzer sounded and it wasn't open.

"Is it locked?" I asked.

"Sealed." He gestured without looking. "Pull that door tight."

I crammed myself into the enclosure space—moving around in the heavy parka and weather suit made me feel like an overstuffed penguin myself—and pulled the exterior door shut. Then the interior door made a loud *ka-chunk* as it unlocked.

"They don't like to waste energy here," Tom said, and pulled it open.

Compared to the desolate exterior, the inside of the base buzzed with activity. It was large but highly organized into different sections. The module on the left drew my eye right away because it was a glass-walled laboratory. A long steel table ran along the front of it, stacked with plastic intake bins for materials from the outside. These could be deposited through airtight doors in the glass wall reachable from the foyer. On the other side of the table was an array of equipment for processing whatever came in. There were sifters, some kind of fancy imaging machine, and even a glass holding tank filled with cloudy salt water. They had a 3D printer that reminded me, oddly enough, of the God Machine.

To the right of the doorway was a compact laundry facility, its machines churning, the already-laundered parkas and jumpsuits hanging in neat bundles. Beyond that was a modern kitchen and small dining area with three tables. A man in a white apron worked the stove currently, and whatever he was making smelled peppery and delicious. My stomach grumbled as Tom and I approached the steel reception desk opposite the door. A young dark-haired man, presumably Chilean, looked up at us and smiled. "*Bienvenido!*"

"Hello," Tom said heartily. "Tom Johnson and Noah Parker."

"It's good to see you, *señores*. Welcome to Montalva Base. How was your journey?"

"*Bien,*" Tom said, and then rattled off something more in Spanish, gesturing at me. Then both of them had a good laugh.

"Yeah, yeah, no sea legs." I was too tired to put up a good fight, and the smell of fresh cooked food from the kitchen was disrupting my brainpower.

"In seriousness, *señores*, we are very glad to see you. I am Manuel Soto Flores."

"Pleased to meet you," I said.

"Yeah, glad to be here," Tom said.

"Are the dragons with you?"

"On the ship," I said. "We're here to make sure the hatching facility is ready."

"Yes, of course. It's two buildings over. I can take you right away."

"Great," Tom said.

"Or, we could eat something first, and then I can take you over."

Tom started to answer, but I put my hand on his shoulder. "I've got this." I turned to Manuel and said, "*Bien.*"

CHAPTER TWENTY-FOUR
Montalva Base

The food was good. Amazing, really. Some kind of tiny, delicate pink shrimp fried in butter with several unidentifiable spices and peppers. The cook's name was Julio and he always made enough for everyone. Cooking was not his job; it was his passion. His official business purpose here was an astronomy fellowship. By night he manned a telescope at one of the outer bases. All that was good. Eating hot freshly made food reinvigorated me. Then we got to the hatching facility and the good feeling went away. Everything was all wrong.

The interior of the building was a single room. Inside were about a dozen steel tables pushed together toward the middle, and... nothing else. No nests, no individual enclosures, no nesting material. Beyond that, it didn't feel warm enough to meet the specs of hatching, which required ninety degrees Fahrenheit minimum. Optimal hatching temperature was even higher. *Maybe we came to the wrong building.*

"Where is everything?" Tom asked.

"Pardon?"

"The materials for hatching. We sent wood and fibers and feeding bowls," he said. "Did the cargo container not arrive?"

The materials had been flown here directly from Ushuaia and literally dropped from the cargo hold of an aircraft. We didn't risk that with the eggs, but for sturdy materials the base managers preferred an air drop. Now that I'd experienced the harrowing journey from ship to shore in an inflatable boat, I understood. That didn't explain where all those materials had gone, however. They were supposed to be here.

"We received the cargo container, *señor*," Manuel said. "Everyone was very confused with what was inside."

"How was it confusing?"

"Insulation and bundles of wood did not seem to make sense."

"Those are frames and synthetic nesting material," Tom said.

"Ah, I see." Manuel nodded agreeably, but did not exactly go running off to find the materials.

Tom looked at me in exasperation.

"So," I said. "Where are the materials, exactly?"

Manuel shrugged. "Gone."

"How are they gone? It was two days ago."

"We had a swap meet."

"You had a what?"

Tom jumped back in. "What the hell is a swap meet?"

Manuel adopted the tone of a parent explaining something to a young child. "Every few weeks the personnel of the bases on King Edward Island meet to trade materials and equipment."

"Really?" I asked. I couldn't decide if it was cute or sad or somehow both.

"Supplies are hard to come by here. We support each other."

"I know, but still," I said. "Why did you trade our stuff?"

"We didn't understand what it was for. Nothing grows here, so wood is in short supply. And we can always use insulation."

"It wasn't insulation. It was..." I couldn't bring myself to finish because it didn't matter. The eggs were probably on their way. "Never mind. What can we get quickly?"

"What do you need?" Manuel asked.

We need what we sent you, I didn't say.

Tom took over because this was his area. "Sturdy materials to make a two-foot-by-two-foot box."

"There may be some storage crates about that size in the warehouse."

Tom nodded. "That'll have to do. Next, it needs to be a lot warmer in here."

"Are you not comfortable?"

"It's not me, it's the dragon eggs. We need at least ninety Fahrenheit in here. Didn't you receive our specs?"

"We thought that was a mistake," Manuel said. "Most buildings keep it at sixty-five. Even our warm buildings are below seventy."

"Where's the thermostat?"

Manuel gestured to a discreet metal panel on the wall. "Right there. Digital. But I will need approval from the base commander to set it so high."

"We can worry about that later," Tom said.

I imagined I knew what he was thinking: we had to get the eggs here safely, and then it was up to them whether they wanted their rat problem solved or not.

"Anything else?" Manuel asked.

"We need some soft materials to cushion the eggs in their enclosures," Tom said. "Cloth, leather, neoprene, or something like that."

"We can ask around."

That's how I found myself walking door-to-door in the freezing cold to beg and borrow materials for dragon nests. Manuel led us back to the main building where we'd first met. Julio the cook had a crate that would do in his glass-door refrigerator. He had to unload it first. Ironically, it held cardboard boxes of eggs. While he unloaded it, Tom and I sidled over to the laundry station.

"Let's ask if we can borrow clothes," he said.

"Maybe don't tell them the exact purpose," I said. Dragon hatchings were messy affairs.

Two young women looked up from their sorting table as we approached.

"*Buenas dias*," Tom said. "My name is Tom and this is Noah. We're from the Build-A-Dragon Company." He smiled at them. I did, too, though neither of them could tear their eyes away from Tom.

"You're a long way from home." The older of the two women, maybe twenty-six, was taller than me and kept her hair in a long, dark braid over one shoulder. "Please, call me Antonella."

"I'm Isidora," said her companion, another Chilean by my guess. Shorter height, shorter hair, and more of a shy smile for the handsome dragon wrangler.

"You look very familiar," Antonella said.

"Ever watch Animal Planet?"

"Of course. We're zoologists."

Then Tom did something I'd never seen before. He grabbed a rolled-up blanket from the top of a stack of laundry and slammed it down on the steel table. Then he grabbed a rag, twisted it into a rope, and wrapped it around the end of the towel. "Stay down, fella!" It was a perfect reenactment of probably his best-known video segment, the time he'd subdued a full-grown caiman. The clip still played in the opening of *Tom's Wild World*.

"*Dios mio*," Isidora breathed. Then she whispered something to Antonella in rapid Spanish.

"You—you're Tom Johnson." Antonella's voice had a touch of wonder to it.

I felt a little star-struck myself. I'd spent so much time with Tom that I sort of forgot he was a celebrity. Before I knew him professionally, I'd only known him from his wildlife shows. Hell, that caiman was one of the animals whose DNA contributed to the Dragon Genome Project. Now both women smiled at him, and I could not have been more invisible.

"We were wondering if we could borrow some soft materials," Tom said.

"Yes, whatever you need ... Tom Johnson," Antonella said.

They loaded us down with as many linens as we could carry: towels, rags, bedsheets, and curtains. They told us we could come back for more, whatever we needed.

In the meantime, Manuel had obtained some leads on where we might find more holding boxes. We suited up again, and Tom offered to carry the borrowed linens back to the hatching building. I piled my load on top of his, and he told me in low tones he was going to "goose the thing" while he was there. It was just a vague enough reference that I understood, and Manuel did not, that he'd be pushing the temperature up to ninety and worry about the repercussions later.

Manuel and I put our backs to the wind-blown snow and trekked to an unusual bowl-shaped building. We met two Chilean astronomers who let us borrow some boxes that were used to store telescope lenses or something—honestly, I missed some of the discussion while measuring their dimensions, which were just large enough. Next door was a storage facility for "ice tools" according to Manuel, which included hand tools like ice axes as well as a larger pneumatic drill for taking core samples from the glaciers.

The woman in charge of this was the first person I'd met who was not openly friendly at introduction. She was also French and went by the name Rousseau. Manuel told me that she was an "alpinist," a fancy word for a mountain climber. She'd come to Antarctica to scale the Vinson Massif, the highest mountain peak on the continent. She was blond and undoubtedly European, with a Gallic face and stunning ice-blue eyes. Possibly a bit older than everyone else or maybe that was just the weathering.

"Hello, I'm Noah Parker."

"Rousseau," she said.

"There was a bit of a misunderstanding, and we've misplaced some of the materials we need to hatch our dragon eggs."

"What materials?" she asked, in a clipped voice. She had a hint of a French accent and a healthy dose of French arrogance.

"Well, synthetic padding, which we've managed to replace with..." I stopped myself, because for all I knew, she was the one waiting on sheets to come back from the laundry. Something told me this lady wouldn't like it much. "Something else. But we still need boxes or some kind of sturdy container." I showed the approximate dimensions with my hands. "Two feet by two feet."

"I know how big two feet is. I also know its proper representation in meters. Do you?"

Her quick riposte took me aback, but I'd been making English-to-metric conversions since I was a kid. "Zero point six."

She'd already started to turn away from me, but turned back and stared a moment. "Lucky guess."

While I was being nonverbally dismissed from existence, I'd scanned the room and already spotted several crates in the area behind her that looked about the right size. They were filled with tools and equipment, but not to the brim. Some looked nearly empty. If we combined their contents, we could free up five or six crates. Maybe enough to finish the job, which was good because the Zodiac had to be inbound by now.

"Rousseau." I put on my best imitation of Tom's charming smile. "That's a beautiful name. It means 'redhead' doesn't it?"

"And?"

"Well, I can't help but notice that your hair, though lovely and golden, is not red."

Again she gave me a stare, though it felt a bit less icy this time. "It is a common name where I come from."

"Ah, I see." I was doing my best to maintain the smile but my facial muscles were starting to ache. "I suppose that would be somewhere around Chamonix?" It was a guess, a Hail Mary, but I took a shot. Chamonix was an area in the French Alps and home to many of the country's elite mountain climbers. The village called Chamonix was located at the base of Mont Blanc, the highest peak in Western Europe and a rite of passage for many mountaineers.

"How did you know that?" she asked.

Bull's-eye. "Well, Manuel told me that you're an alpinist, and that's where most French alpinists are from."

"We are from Argentière, which is in the Chamonix commune. Do you climb?"

"Only some rock climbing. I'm not a mountaineer, but I read a lot about them." I didn't add that most of what I knew came from an old-fashioned blog, written by a veteran climber who chronicled the spring climbing season in the Himalayas. "You came here for Mount Vinson?"

"I summited almost two years ago."

"Wow. Are you going for the Seven Summits?" This was a popular challenge among climbers and adventurers, to scale the highest mountain on each of the seven continents. At 4,892 meters, Mount Vinson was one of the lowest peaks... but obviously, one of the hardest to get to.

"That's what I was doing."

"How many have you climbed?"

"All of them. Vinson was my seventh."

That *was* a surprise. "That's incredible!" I didn't have to feign my astonishment. It meant she had risked the conflict-ridden New Guinea to reach the Carstensz Pyramid, scaled the "Mountain of Death" Aconcagua in the Andes, and of course, climbed Mount Everest. I offered my hand. "I've never met anyone who has done that."

She shook my hand and offered the first hint of a smile. "Now you have. Your name was... Mark?"

"Noah. Noah Parker."

"And you are looking for boxes."

"Just to borrow," I said quickly. "We'll bring them back, good as new."

She looked at me in silence, and I felt all but sure she was going to refuse.

"You may have six."

Manuel and I managed to stack and carry the crates, which were bulky but not heavy once emptied of the ice tools. We started the trek back to the hatching facility.

"That is a major... *hazaña*," Manuel said.

"*Hazaña*?" I didn't know the word but loved the sound of it.

"Word for... accomplishment," he said. "That was a major accomplishment."

"I know, right? Seven summits, one on each continent."

He laughed. "I meant getting Rousseau to lend you anything. That is the real *hazaña*."

"Really?"

"She is not known for lending out equipment. We call her the Ice Queen."

"I can see that."

"To even get twenty words out of the Ice Queen is a great thing. Not to mention six crates!" He whistled. "You and the famous Tom Johnson are making many friends here."

Even with the crates, I felt like I was walking on air the rest of the way. We clomped into the hatchery building, where Tom and the two zoologists—who'd taken it upon themselves to bring over more linens—were pushing steel tables into a widely spaced grid.

Tom saw us carrying in the crates and grinned. "Nice work!"

"Yeah, you too."

"Is it warm in here?" Manuel asked.

"Feels fine to me," Tom said. "Hey, would you grab the other end of this table?"

Manuel set down his crates and ran over to help. Tom made eye contact with me and I took his meaning. *Let's keep him away from the thermostat.* He was right, though; it *did* feel noticeably warmer in this building than it had in any of the others we'd visited so far. Hell, it might be close to ninety, which is what we needed. Once the tables were in place, we spread out the crates and boxes so that they weren't too close together. Our written specs recommended six feet of open space between dragon eggs. Here, because the room was smaller and we were going to hatch a dozen, we could only manage about five feet of spacing. Manuel and I laid out the crates. Antonella and Isidora doled out the padding material—sheets, pillowcases, work shirts, and a few towels—and then Tom shaped the nests to have the right-size indentation in each. It might seem like overkill, but after bringing the eggs this far we didn't want to lose any to a silly mistake.

The radio at Manuel's belt crackled, and he answered. There was a quick back-and-forth, which everyone in the room but me understood. Manuel signed off, then looked at me. "The eggs are here."

The thing that happened next truly surprised me. I figured that we would have to make several trips to carry the eggs up to this makeshift hatchery. They traveled in specially made shipping crates: flat-sided, armored cubes with reinforced corners, about sixteen inches in diameter. Each one had a control panel with a combination lock—Jim and Allie had the combination but thus far had been unwilling to share it—and a constant readout of the environment within. A tiny rechargeable heat pump kept them right at the optimal incubation temperature, no matter the ambient conditions.

These containers, as we learned, had audible alarms for temperature deviations or low batteries. The latter was especially irritating. It started out as a short beep, increasing in volume and frequency every few minutes. The trouble was, with so many cubes jammed into the hold of our cargo ship, figuring out which one was alarming was a constant chore. Then you had to run a long power cable from the cargo hold's generator/inverter appliance to the crate responsible and give it a charge. Jim and Allie handled this boring task most of the time—their ability to know which egg needed attention bordered on supernatural—but Tom and I split the shifts when they were sleeping. It gave me a new respect for the patience of our hatchery staff.

All this was to say that when the eggs came ashore at King Edward Island, they were still in their transport cubes. These were not fragile. Tom had promised me I could throw one on the rocks without damaging the container or the egg inside. I didn't try it myself, but I believed him. The material was some kind of advanced polymer, softer than metal but harder than rubber. It was surprisingly resilient. I hadn't exactly been gentle when searching for alarming cubes in the middle of the night sometimes, and God knows the airport baggage handlers had shown even less care. In spite of all that, no cube had a mark. The only downsides were that they weren't large enough to facilitate hatching, and they all had to be returned to the ship immediately. Evelyn didn't say why. She also didn't say where we'd gotten these cubes, though I had an educated guess.

Because of the strength and heater, the egg cubes were heavy—maybe twenty-five pounds each. Tom and I suited up as quickly as we could and headed out the door to the hatchery to start carrying the eggs up. Ten yards from the door, we saw that wouldn't be necessary. Jim and Allie swung into view, each of them holding an egg cube like it was a newborn baby. One of the Chilean women, probably Isidora, was directing them to the hatchery building. Behind the two of them walked a long line of base researchers and staffers, all bundled up against the weather, all carrying one egg cube. They looked like a winding line of leaf-cutter ants moving between nests.

"Well, that saves us a trip." Tom turned and strode back to the hatchery's outer door.

I followed him and took up the opposite position. We knew better than to try to take the eggs from the hatchers. Instead, Tom pulled open the outer door, and I snuck in to pull open the inner one. The hatchers came in, and if they were surprised by the haphazard, borrowed-material nests they didn't say anything. Jim set down his cube against the far wall. Allie handed hers to him and hurried back to take the one that was coming in the door. They hit a rhythm and had all the eggs inside in less than two minutes.

"We've got it from here," Jim told me.

"Are you sure?"

"Yeah, it's going to be tight. If you guys want to stand outside, we'll bring out the cubes as we unload."

You just don't want me to know the secret code, I nearly said. But he was right, there was hardly any room to maneuver between the crates and the makeshift nests.

I stepped out and took Tom with me. A minute later, Allie started handing empty cubes out the doors to us. We took the first two and joined the line of volunteer movers for a hike down to the beach. Two

Zodiacs waited on the moraine, and we tucked our crates into these. By the time we got back to the hatching facility, all the crates had been carried down. We called our thanks to the now-empty-handed people in bright yellow or orange suits, and they waved. Then everyone filed back to the main building or other ones elsewhere on the base.

Manuel found us. "That's all of them."

"That was so nice of everyone," I said. "You saved us about a million trips to the beach."

"How do we thank them all?" Tom asked.

He waved this off. "No need. Everyone helps around here. Now, may I show you to your bunks?"

"Yes, please." I stopped myself. "Oh, but I have to send a message first. What's the network password?"

"Password?" he repeated.

"Yes, if you don't mind. I should let people know we got here safely."

He laughed. "The network is called Glacier. You don't need a password."

"Seriously?"

"We don't have hackers here, *señor*. Only friends."

He showed us to a small building that was about the size of a construction trailer. "Welcome to your home."

The inside was sparse: metal shelves on the walls, two bunks opposite each other, and a little table. Soft motion-activated lights had come on when we entered. Someone had even brought our bags here, and I was especially proud to see that my duffel had taken on *some* of the weather-worn character of Tom's. I tugged off my outer gear so that I could use my fingers properly, and dug my tablet out of my knapsack. *Yes, I still have battery power.* I connected to the Glacier network and saw he was right, no password required. "This place is wild," I said.

"Make yourselves comfortable, my friends." Manuel pointed to a little panel on the wall. "This is the light switch." He pointed across to a larger display. "That one is the thermostat. I should tell you that, unlike in some other buildings, it will not go higher than sixty-five Fahrenheit."

"I don't know why you're telling us that, but thank you for the information," Tom said casually.

"Sure. I'll be in the main building if you need me."

"Thanks, Manuel," Tom said.

I waved at him and went back to typing my message to Summer, letting her know that we'd gotten here finally. I didn't know how long it had been or even what time it was back in Phoenix, but I sent it anyway. The speed was terrible, laughable even, but it went through. A minute or two later, I got a delivery confirmation. I waited a couple of minutes, my eyes dragging downward, my head starting to ache.

But no reply came.

CHAPTER TWENTY-FIVE
Moraines

I'd been awake twenty-seven hours at that point and I was flat-out exhausted. I crashed hard and only woke when Tom shook me.

"What?" I asked, both irritated and confused.

"It's go time."

"For what?"

"For the dragons to get to work. They all hatched, can you believe that?"

"Wait, they *hatched*? Why didn't you wake me?"

"I tried, but you were dead to the world," he said.

"How long was I asleep?"

"Eleven hours."

"Damn it. I can't believe I missed it."

He put his hand on my shoulder. "You've seen dragons hatch before, right?"

"Yeah..."

"They pretty much all look the same hatching, don't they?"

"I suppose."

"Then what are you worried about?"

"All right." I rolled off the sleeping pallet and started suiting up for the extreme cold. Tom helped me find my boots, which I'd kicked off on two different sides of the room.

"How much time do we have?" My stomach was empty and I still had fond memories of the spicy shrimp dish from when we'd arrived.

"Enough for this." He handed me an unbranded bar in a white wrapper with the label PROTEIN BAR and no other details—no ingredients, no nutritional advice, nothing. It had the consistency of cold molasses and was an unnatural tan color when unwrapped. I figured beggars couldn't be choosers, so I took a bite. It had a faint honey taste, but no overt flavor otherwise. Or maybe my recent exposures to South American cuisine had dulled my sense of taste. Either way, I forced it down in four bites while lacing my boots, chewing all the while.

I followed Tom out into the too-bright sunlight. It reflected off the bright glaciers around us. I dropped my polarized sunglasses into place, grateful again that I'd remembered to bring them. We hurried to the hatchery building and I poked my head in to get a glimpse of the dragons. They were dozing still, some in their makeshift enclosures, others on the floor. Their seemingly casual repose may have been a ruse, though. The one nearest the door was watching us with catlike eyes. Another had its back to us but stirred, its head cocked as if listening. They were three feet long snout to tail, slender, with narrow heads and strong jaws. The room felt much warmer than ninety degrees, and I imagined I could see the heat radiating from their bodies. I backed out to find Tom talking to Manuel, who had brought two steel buckets filled with something that, even in the frigid air through layers of clothing, absolutely reeked.

"*Buenas dias*, Manuel."

"*Buenas dias*. Did you sleep well?"

"Like the dead."

He smiled. "You know, someone came looking for you last night."

"What? Who?"

"A certain alpinist." He then nudged Tom with his elbow and said something in Spanish, just to be that way.

Tom chuckled and asked something about the *verdad*. Which it probably was not, but Manuel assured him it was.

"What's in the bucket, Manuel?"

"Ah, a special request from *Señor* Johnson. My team worked through the night."

"Our destination is three hundred yards that way." Tom pointed at the ridge to the southwest. "Major nesting site and fresh signs of an active infestation. I already scouted it."

"Of couse you did." I took one of the buckets, glanced inside, and regretted it immediately. The thing was filled to the brim with ragged strips of a grayish meat. Some of it still had hair. Not cute fluffy fur, but the wiry, disheveled hair of a wild beast. "What the hell is this?"

"You should know," Tom said.

"What?"

"What are these dragons specifically bred to hunt?"

Oh no. "Rats."

Tom pointed at me. "Bingo. Manuel and his capable team caught several rats and were good enough to cut them into strips for us."

"It's no trouble, we do it all the time," Manuel said.

"You said the dragons already ate," I told Tom.

"They ate some. Enough to sate them initially, but they'll be hungry again soon." Tom hoisted his bucket. "These are the breadcrumbs we'll use to lead them to the nesting site."

The work that followed was, in a word, rather disgusting. We started leaving a trail of rat-meat right at the door to the hatchery, then down the main path toward the beach. When we had covered some ground, maybe halfway to the cliffs that protected the base from the shore winds, Tom gave Manuel the signal. He first took out his radio. Then an overhead alarm klaxon rang, three short blasts accompanied by red flashing lights. That was the shelter-in-place signal; everyone knew to stay inside. The dragons shouldn't be a threat to them, but they were wild animals and we wanted to minimize distractions. Then Manuel opened the hatchery door and retreated to the shelter of a nearby building.

Tom and I watched eagerly, but nothing happened.

"Maybe you fed them a little too well," I said.

"Be patient," he said.

Sure, be patient. It's ten degrees below freezing and all I can smell is dead rat meat.

Motion blurred in the doorway, and then a dragon approached the first pile of meat, its tongue flicking in and out. It put its snout to the ground, crept close, and then snapped up a piece. Another dragon appeared and took the next piece in nearly identical fashion.

"They seem to like the meat," I said.

Tom nodded. "And they don't mind the cold."

The two dragons ate a few more "breadcrumbs" before turning

back toward the hatchery door. If they made a sound, we couldn't hear it over the wind. The rest of the dragons poured out of the doorway, jostling one another to get at the meat. In seconds, they were halfway to our position.

"Move!" Tom said.

I didn't need to be told twice. We ran for the beach, flinging handfuls of meat behind us. I told myself that it was to prevent these dragons from associating humans with food. Preserving the wild nature of these dragons was critical for them to perform their intended function. They were custom-built to kill and eat rodents alone. In theory, there was no physical threat to me. That being said, I had no intention of getting pinned against the cliffs holding a bucket of chum.

Plus, Tom dealt with dangerous animals all the time and he was running full-tilt.

When we rounded the cliffs, the freezing wind hit my exposed face like a physical slap. The surf churned, whitecaps cresting the swells, the noise of the waves thunderous.

"This way!" Tom took off to the right, cutting a diagonal between the cliffs and the beach. We left the solid rock and stumbled onto the moraine, the pebbles large and slippery. I dropped another fistful of meat and noticed a round indentation lined with a border of larger stones. *An empty penguin nest.* Soon there were others, left and right. Tom slowed and held up a hand to warn me. The footing was more treacherous. I had to watch where I stepped, so I didn't see the penguins until we were almost on them, when the birds began honking in alarm. We skidded to a halt. The oblong black shapes that I'd mistaken for large stones began to move. They were penguins. Hundreds of them. Most sat atop stone-encircled nests like the ones I'd just seen. They apparently were accustomed to humans, as they didn't flee outright, but a tremor of anxious watchfulness swept over them like a wave.

"We need a path through this," Tom said. "It's best not to scare the penguins off their eggs."

Now that I knew what to look for, I saw the penguins on nests were packed in tightly, with no more than a few feet between them in most places. The only break was a long rock formation that ran up the middle of the beach like a high-tide mark. The penguins seemed to build their nests away from this, on the flat ground. The head of the rock line was to our left. I pointed. "How about along those rocks?"

Tom looked back and I followed his gaze. The dragons were entering the beach now, still leap-frogging one another to get at the piles of dropped meat. Their appetite seemed to know no limits.

"It'll have to do." He stalked to the start of the ridge and climbed it.

I followed, scattering meat behind me in a line so the dragons wouldn't miss it. My bucket was running low. *Never in my life have I wished to have more rat meat.* We made it about fifty yards along the rock ridge before we ran out. We shook our buckets out to make one final pile of bait, more or less in the middle of the nesting grounds. By this time, the dragons were almost at the start of the ridge.

"Where do we go?" I asked.

Tom made a quick survey of the grounds around us. "Let's work our way to the shoreline. Move slowly and keep your eyes on the water." He scrambled down the edge of the ridge and I followed, dislodging a small avalanche of dark pebbles. The two penguins guarding nests at the base of the ridge looked at me harshly.

"Easy, easy," Tom said softly. "Let's just keep up a nice soothing conversation."

I did my best to mimic his calm, reassuring tone. "Lead the way."

"Here we go. Nice and easy now." He moved in a cautious but deliberate pace, keeping as much distance from the penguins as he could.

"This is crazy. Really crazy." I focused on putting one foot ahead of the other.

"You should have seen the adder colony on the banks of the Nile, just outside Cairo. Hundred and ten degrees on the sand on one side, rushing current on the other, and every inch of ground pocked with snake holes."

"I'm glad I didn't see that, actually."

"You said you loved reptiles," Tom said.

"I like the ones with legs. Or flippers. Snakes, not so much."

The penguins watched us the whole way, their heads turning to follow our progress. Some honked and shifted on their nests, but they stayed. I kept my hands to my sides and my bucket in front of me, trying to look as non-threatening as possible. At last, we reached the high-water line, which was wet and cold but free of judgey penguins. Back on the rock ridge, the dragons had reached the end of the meat trail. They milled around, nudging gravel with their snouts, tongues constantly working, searching for more. As we watched, one lunged into a rocky alcove and reared back with a dark, wriggling furry shape.

"It's got a rat," Tom said.

"A fresh one," I said.

Another dragon cocked its head and then darted forward into the rocks. It came out with two rats by their tails, both screeching. The dragon tossed one to its neighbor and swallowed the other. The other dragons had watched these proceedings. Now they spread out along the rocks, hunting for more of the rodents.

"You know what, Parker?" Tom asked. "This just might work."

CHAPTER TWENTY-SIX
Never Rest

I'd love to say that the next day we kicked back and celebrated the hatching, shared some kind of feast, and maybe took booked a whale watching cruise or something. Instead, Tom decided to build an observation blind on the beach from which to survey the nesting areas. Personally, I'd seen enough. As long as the dragons did their jobs, why did we need to observe them? Maybe it was the wildlife guru in him. Or maybe he just missed being in the field. I didn't share that sentiment. My hands and arms smelled like rat meat and it was starting to nauseate me. I asked around and learned there was a shower facility. It was, naturally, in the main building where almost everyone I'd met would see me walking through in a bathrobe and flip-flops. Okay, maybe that was an exaggeration. *Showers are normal here. This is normal.*

I stopped by our quarters for a change of clothes and my towel, which I had *accidentally* forgotten to volunteer for the hatching materials. Now I had a clean towel and a date with a hot shower. At least, I hoped it was hot. I had to suit up, of course, for the brief walk to the main building. It was twilight—as dark as it got in Antarctica in the summer season—and the temperature had dropped considerably. The moderately temperature-controlled main building was a welcome respite from the cold.

Manuel looked up from the desk. "The dragons were most impressive, *señor*."

I saw the genuine pleasure on his face and felt a surge of pride. "They did well, didn't they? I would go so far as to call it a . . . *hazaña*."

He laughed. "Yes, great *hazaña*. Everyone is talking about it."

"Really? Didn't seem like anyone even saw."

"We sounded the alarms, remember?"

"Oh." I grinned. "Right."

"In fact, technically you broke the law by remaining outside when the sirens sounded," he said.

"This is Antarctica. I thought there were no laws."

"You're under Chilean law while you're at our base."

"I'm good with that. Chileans are cool as hell." I gave him a fist bump.

He noticed my towel. "Oh, you're here for a shower?"

"God yes, I just flung out a bucket of rat meat. They're in this building, aren't they?" I'd read that in my Antarctic Station Catalogue, which was published by the Council of Managers of National Antarctic Programs. That group comprised representatives of all the countries with bases here, and it had a stellar short name: COMNAP. It sounded like the codename for a U.S. military force or something.

"You want to shower now?" Manuel asked. "Right now?"

He was being weird and I didn't understand why. Maybe there was a shower rotation, or it was frowned upon to shower this time of day. Honestly, I didn't care. "Is that a problem?"

"No. The showers are in the back, behind the blue door."

I spotted it on the far side of the weather station. "Thanks." I walked quickly and tried not to make eye contact with anyone. People were super friendly here and I didn't want any more introductions while I smelled like this. I pushed the door to the shower room, which opened with a metallic groan. Inside was a narrow central aisle and four shower stalls, two on either side. One shower was running already, so I ducked into the stall opposite. There were no doors to the stalls, only an opaque polyester curtain that was neck-high and only reached down to my knees. So, not a lot of privacy. I'd be able to see the head of the guy in the other shower, and vice versa.

I resolved right away to avoid that at any cost.

I hung my towel and clothes on the hooks provided, stripped, and examined the shower control screen. It had a single option: ON. When I pressed it, a countdown timer appeared on the screen.

4:59

Then three things happened in quick succession. First, I realized that the metal protuberance I was facing was a light fixture, right as a jet of extremely cold water hit in me in the back. Second, I yelped and spun out of the way by instinct. Third, I locked eyes with the person opposite me and it was the French woman, Rousseau. Right there in the other shower, four feet away. She was washing her hair and visibly amused at my reaction. *Good God, why!?* It hadn't occurred to me that there were no gender markings on the shower door, so of course this was a coed facility. My face burned. I'm sure it was bright red. I took a breath and forced myself back into the water. I couldn't help gasping, but at least kept it quieter this time.

4:30

There was an unmarked dispenser high on the wall to my left. I tried to use it, but the arm was already all the way down and wouldn't move. Nothing came out. I tried lifting it, but no joy. It must be broken or empty.

"You have to twist it," Rousseau said.

I couldn't look at her or speak. I twisted the spout to the right, then to the left, and it remained stubbornly in the down position.

"Like this," she said.

I couldn't not look. She spun her soap dispenser counterclockwise in a full 360.

I'm an idiot. "Thank you," I managed to say. I twisted the dispenser all the way around and it popped up, ready for action.

4:00

"Or you can use mine," she said.

I pumped the dispenser twice. Nothing came out. I said a prayer and pumped it again. At last, it spouted white foam into my hand. "You know, I'm good. Thanks, though."

"Aw, too bad." Her eyes sparkled.

At that point, I knew she was messing with me. I had half a mind to go over and take some of her soap just to up the ante. But with my luck, the Chilean women would choose that moment to come in. I wasn't brave enough. I think she knew it, too.

3:30.

Her shower beeped and the water shut off. You'd think that would be the end of my humiliation, but you'd be wrong. She took her sweet-ass time toweling off, too. I'd swear she drew the process out on purpose.

1:00

The water never really warmed up. I wouldn't call it pleasant. The only good part of it was getting clean. The soap, embarrassing as it was to obtain, lathered up nicely.

0:30

"See you later," Rousseau called on her way out.

I had no witty response because I was doing my best to finish rinsing before the timer went out. Five minutes went by quickly, especially when you were being hazed by a female French alpinist. I dried myself off, got dressed, and went out to read the riot act to Manuel.

He sat at his desk and grinned when he saw me. "How was your shower, *señor*? Refreshing?"

I'd planned to give him the what-for about sending me in there without any warnings about strange controls, frigid water, or stray French women, but there were people around within earshot and something about his grin told me he'd withheld that information on purpose. "Yes, it was a real adventure, thank you."

He adopted a fairly unconvincing look of concern. "I forgot to tell you, the showers are shared by the entire base, so it's possible someone was in there."

Now that I was sure, I absolutely refused to give him the satisfaction of admitting the full extent of my recent trauma. "You know, Manuel, that *would* have been a useful heads-up, but I learned to roll with the punches."

"There were punches?"

"Not at all." I added with a touch of bravado I didn't feel. "As a matter of fact, it was nice to have some help getting the soap."

A rapid procession of puzzlement, surprise, and uncertainty flashed across his face, which I enjoyed thoroughly. *Now you're really wondering what happened, and I'm the only one who can tell you.* God knows, Manuel wasn't brave enough to ask the woman he called the Ice Queen.

"Well, ah, that is... good. Yes, good to have help," he said uncertainly. "Oh, and *Señor* Johnson asked me to give you a message."

"Where is he?"

"Setting up cameras to monitor the dragons in the nesting colony. He said they are resting now on the rocks, but he wants to record their first hunt tonight."

That was smart. Honestly, I should have thought of it myself. I knew I should go help him, but now that I was clean and warm all I could think about was bed. "Did he ask me to assist?"

"No, he probably does not need help. When he came to pick up the camera equipment several of my Chilean colleagues volunteered."

Well, more points for the Chilean researchers here. They were friendly as hell. Or maybe they were like me, and simply wanted to spend a little time with a visiting celebrity. "Good for them."

He sighed. "I would have gone myself but I'm on shift here."

"What message did he leave?"

"He asked if you would arrange a call tomorrow with someone named Evelyn."

Crap, of course. Evelyn would definitely want to know how the hatching went. God bless Tom; he'd remembered. "Can we do that?"

"Yes, of course. Our conference room is in the northwest corner of this building."

"Which corner is that?"

"In the back, on the other side from where you had your adventurous shower."

I saw it past the weather station, a small glass-walled room with a large monitor. "Can it do video?"

"It may be choppy, but yes."

It occurred to me that the conference room was another common resource here in this place where everyone shared everything, even the showers. "Is there any time free tomorrow?"

He nodded approvingly, and pulled up the schedule on his own tablet. "I can get you an hour at eight in the morning, but you will miss breakfast."

I didn't want to miss breakfast, but we were nineteen hours ahead so that didn't leave much of a window. "Is there anything a little later?"

"Ten AM?"

"Perfect."

He tapped the schedule and typed something rapidly in Spanish into the calendar. Probably *Gringos want the conference room.* "It's all yours."

I looked at him pointedly. "No surprises this time, all right?"

He put his hand over his heart. "I promise."

"Thanks." I suited up against the cold—Manuel had arranged for a loaner cold suit while mine went through the laundry—and went out. The base was quieter than usual. More than likely, every able-bodied person was down on the beach with Tom. Which was fine with me; I'd catch the video tomorrow. I hurried to our bunk, found my tablet, and shot Evelyn a quick message. It was early for her, but she'd still appreciate an update.

HATCHING SUCCESSFUL! CAN WE DO A CALL AT 4 PM?

It took a minute to send on the base network, which was appropriately named Glacier. No sooner than it had gone through that her reply came back.

YES! SEE YOU THEN.

"Yes, you will." I set an alarm on my tablet, hit my bunk, and was out.

I don't know what time Tom got in, but it was late. We both smelled like the white foamy soap from the communal showers, so when I woke up I wondered idly if he'd had as many adventures as I did. I suited up quietly and let him sleep while I set up the conference call in the main building. True to Manuel's promise, the conference room was unoccupied. Evelyn, bless her, asked her DOD contacts to talk to their Chilean counterparts since this was technically a military-built installation. Long story short, we had a secure video uplink via satellite with the best encryption available. The only downside was that the Antarctica connection quality left much to be desired. It was still connecting when Tom strolled in.

"Morning, Romeo." He'd brought me a little expresso from the coffee station on the other side of the building.

"*Gracias*," I said fervently. Despite only being here a few days, we were both hooked on the midafternoon expresso. The Chileans knew their way around a coffee bean, that was for damn sure. "Wait, did you call me Romeo?"

"Yeah, that's your nickname around here."

"Why is it my nickname? You're the one with hordes of adoring fans hauling cameras out to the beach in a snowstorm."

"Yeah, but I wasn't the one showering with the Ice Queen."

"What is this about showering?" Evelyn asked.

I froze, because her face had appeared on the digital screen and *apparently* the audio was already working.

"Evelyn!" I coughed nervously. "Nothing. Hey, it's good to see you." Maybe it was weird, but I'd been away from the company long enough that I rather enjoyed hearing her voice and seeing her smile again.

"How are my great Antarctic explorers faring?"

"It's gorgeous down here. You should come," Tom said.

I wasn't sure I agreed with either statement, but I didn't feel the need to say so. "A bit of a rough journey in my opinion."

"Romeo's still trying to get his sea legs," Tom said.

"Romeo?"

"See, there's this French woman—"

"It's a long story." I interjected. I could tell Tom was gearing up to tell her all about Rousseau. Not only was none of it true, but this satellite call probably cost a fortune.

"So, tell me about the hatching," she said.

I let Tom handle this, because technically I slept through the hatching.

"All twelve eggs hatched. The gestational timing was spot-on."

I liked hearing that, though part of me wanted to point out that the design team handled the gestational timing so maybe Tom could have told *me* that. Then again, it was good to have his attention on Evelyn, not me.

"The hatchlings were fed a small amount of target animal source material to reinforce their selective predatory behavior."

Target animal source material was a hell of a way to say strips of nasty rat meat.

"How did they do in the cold? That's what we're all wondering here," Evelyn said.

"Surprisingly well. A moment of hesitation when we opened the door, which is natural."

"After that?"

"They were agile and quick. Not lethargic at all. We lured them to the nesting site and they immediately caught some rats. But the real action happened at night." He queued up a video on his tablet. "This is about two hours after sunset."

The feed was from three stationary cameras. I recognized their shared focal point, the rock formation in the middle of the nesting colony. The sky was darker, but the snow still bright in the half twilight that this godless continent took for night time. You could still easily see the black-and-white penguins milling around against the snow. The dragons were nowhere to be seen.

"Penguins, like us, are diurnal. Their adversaries, the Antarctic rats, are primarily nocturnal," Tom said. "They wait until the penguins are drowsy and least alert."

I was lulled by the tone of Tom's voice, the same one he used when narrating videos about cheetahs hunting gazelle on the African savannah.

"You can see the first few rats venture out near the top of the rock formation," Tom said.

I looked where he said but couldn't see anything. "Where?"

"I don't see them," Evelyn said.

"Let me try something," Tom said. "The biologists here let me borrow a pretty sweet animal recognition algorithm." He was tapping on his tablet and then made a swiping gesture I recognized because it was how we loaded additional modules in our development programs. The video feed blinked out for a moment. When it came on, white polygonal outlines were superimposed on the feed. Inside them I caught a glimpse of movement: a little oval shape with a long tail.

"It's hard to appreciate on the video, but the rats we can see now are juveniles," Tom said. "They're always sent out first to learn if it's safe. It's a survival instinct for social animals, everything from ants to white-tailed deer."

"Where are the dragons?" Evelyn asked, which was my question as well.

Tom smiled. "Wait and see."

More polygons appeared on the video, tagging other rats as they emerged from their hiding places among the rocks. They moved chaotically along the rocks, but as a group were descending toward the penguin nesting areas. A penguin honked but it was quiet, a sharp contrast from the loud calls we heard when we approached the nests during the day. Based on the dozens of rat-tracking polygons, they were swarming out of the rocks and into the nesting areas now.

"Why aren't they raising the alarm?" I asked.

"It's complicated," Tom said.

"How so?"

"First, this is the most inactive time of day for penguins. Most of them are trying to sleep and conserve energy. Second, because these two species normally don't have much contact, so the penguins don't have an innate fear of rats honed from thousands of years of evolution."

"Don't they remember what happened last night?"

"Some might, but most of the penguins that lost their eggs are gone."

"Eaten?" Evelyn asked.

"No, they leave to hunt for food. When they lose their eggs, they have no reason to stay."

That was a morose thought, but we didn't dwell on it. Something was happening on the video feed. Rats were among the nests now, away from the safety of their rocks. Suddenly, a new set of polygons, larger ones in green, bloomed into existence all over the rock formation. In some of them I couldn't see anything, but others had the telltale sinuous movement of dragons.

"Oh my God," I said.

Evelyn gasped. "They were there the whole time!"

"I don't know how I missed them," I said.

"They concealed themselves among the rocks and kept perfectly still," Tom said. "I was watching through infrared binoculars. Otherwise I wouldn't have seen them either."

"Incredible," I said. "Hiding is hard enough, but then waiting when the first few rats appear..."

"Predator instincts counter prey instincts," Evelyn said.

Tom nodded. "Watch this."

Now the dragons flowed down the rocks, their snouts low to the ground, tails twitching with anticipation. Caught in the open with the route to their holes blocked, the rats had nowhere to go. The dragons moved systematically through the open spaces, killing rats with frightening speed. They didn't even stop to eat. They kept pace with the rats, deftly avoiding the penguins on their nests. The penguins, either hopeful or terrified, remained where they were. In under a minute, all of the polygons that had tracked the rats were gone. Only the dragons remained. They started their cleanup operation, eating rats as they went. That part was a little gross. Mercifully, the video ended.

"Are all the rats gone?"

"It's hard to say, but the dragons certainly devastated the population at this nesting site. I'll monitor their activity for the next few days."

"What do your hosts think about all this?" she asked.

"They were glad to see us," I said. "The rats have been a known issue for years, but their numbers were growing. Manuel said some of the funding agencies were on the verge of pulling grants."

"We put everyone else on lockdown for the hatching. The dragons had a long way to go and I didn't want any unintended distractions," Tom said.

"How did you get them to the beach?"

"In the most disgusting way possible," I said.

"We created a direct line of organic material enticements," Tom said.

Oh my God, talk normally. It was a hell of a fancy description for the running, scrambling, and rat-meat tossing we'd endured. "I just hope no one caught it on video."

"I can't say, but I do know that the Chilean research agencies are very pleased."

"Already? How do you know?" Tom asked.

"My contacts already reached out to ask if dragons can be deployed at a second location. An island called Deception."

"Oh yeah, I know that one," I said. Deception Island not only had a cool name but sat atop an active volcano. "Somewhere southwest of us, on the far end of the South Shetland Islands archipelago."

She smiled. "Someone has been reading his COMNAP station listings."

"I had a lot of downtime on the ship ride out here."

"He spent most of it in the head," Tom added.

I'm not sure that detail was necessary. Even if it was technically correct.

"Deception Island is only seventy-five miles away, but you have to go there by boat," Evelyn said.

"More boat rides. I can't wait," I said.

"I'm told it's a seasonal station. They're open now, but there are not many facilities."

"Sounds lovely," I said.

Evelyn ignored my sarcasm. "How soon can you get there?"

"Half an hour out to the ship, three hours sailing, another half hour to make landfall," Tom said.

I was doing the math in my head and came up with the same answer. Only I was slower due to a wave of anticipatory nausea, so all I did was nod. "The only thing is, we're going to need nest-building materials."

Her brow furrowed. "Can't you reclaim what you already have?"

"Yeah, no. That stuff sort of didn't make it."

"The shipping container never arrived?" Already her fingers flew across the keyboard, no doubt pulling up a shipping manifest.

"No, no, it made it. There was a miscommunication." I paused, because I could feel Tom looking at me. He didn't say anything, or give a signal. But he was really *looking* at me. It occurred to me that there was no real need to blame the researchers at this base for what had happened. They didn't understand what the wood and synthetic nesting materials were for, but they could think of ways to use them. So they used them. And when it turned out that we needed some materials for hatching, they came up with some. I sighed. "It's my fault. I told them we didn't need to keep any of the materials after the hatching. My, uh, Spanish needs a lot of work." *Both of those are true.* "Sorry."

Tom gave me a wink and a tiny nod.

"It's all right, Noah." Evelyn's focus had already shifted to another screen to her right, her fingers typing rapidly. "We can source more materials from Buenos Aires and get them air-dropped directly on Deception Island."

"Thanks." It sounded like this was happening whether I liked it or not.

Tom clapped me on the shoulder and grinned at the screen. "We'll start packing our bags."

"Don't forget your life jacket," Evelyn said.

CHAPTER TWENTY-SEVEN
The Glacier

There's some saying about the best-laid plans and how they go to crap in a hurry. I couldn't remember the saying, but I knew it applied. The day had started off so promising. We woke up balls-early with a plan to depart at 0800. I didn't understand why Tom woke me up two hours before that until we suited up and tromped into the main building. The delicious aroma of grilled Chilean sausage touched my nose before I'd even gotten unzipped. It drew us into the building, which buzzed with activity. Turns out, a lot of our friends had come to see us off over breakfast.

Manuel greeted us with a grin. "Right this way, *señores*. You are the guests of honor today."

"Really?" I felt a little groggy still but this was starting to perk me up. Especially when I saw there were espressos waiting for us at the table beside the kitchen. "You didn't have to do this."

"*Che*, we always celebrate when someone leaves the base. You never know when you gonna come back."

"Decepción isn't that far, is it?" I asked, trying my hand at the Spanish pronunciation for the island.

"Every island is far."

I felt a little surge of affection for him. We hadn't been here that long, but Manuel was a constant fixture and he'd solved a lot of our problems. "I'm going to miss you, *amigo*."

"No, you won't."

"I will!" I insisted.

He laughed and shook his head. "I'm coming with you."

"*Che*, are you serious?" I'd been dying to start working that word into a conversation. The Chileans here used it all the time, and it could mean "hey" or "dude" or simply an exclamation of surprise. Plus, it sounded cool.

"I worked there last summer, so I know the place."

I put my hand on his shoulder. "With you along, everything is going to go just fine."

A few hours later, I gripped the handle of the Zodiac as it bounced across the waves and felt none of that bravado. Manuel was piloting at the back. He shouted something I couldn't make out over the roar of the engine.

"What?" I yelled.

He pointed over my head in the direction we were headed. Deception Island rose from the rolling surf like a molar tooth, low and wide. The tawny brown cliffs made a sharp contrast to the gray water all around us. Higher peaks rose beyond them, their glacier-capped peaks swathed in mist. This was a volcanic island, a former whaling base that was once inhabited year-round. Manuel turned east as we approached. The cliffs were lighter in color than any of the terrain we'd seen so far, but they loomed over us like the walls of a fortress. The black sand beaches at their feet were tiny, with nowhere obvious to access the shore. *Where the hell are we going to land*? Then a gap appeared in the impenetrable wall. Manuel veered us toward it. We were in the shadow of the imposing cliffs now; they had to be hundreds of feet high. We zoomed past into the open area beyond. The wind died to nothing. The water was completely calm. Manuel cycled down the motor to a soft hum. The sound of waves crashing against the cliff faded until it was almost quiet.

"Welcome to Port Foster," Manuel said.

I pulled back my hood. "It's so calm in here."

"This is the caldera. You will find no better port in Antarctica."

The water looked like it should be warm. I pulled off my glove and dipped my fingers in. No, still frigid. I shook my hand dry and tugged the glove back on. *Well, it's still Antarctica.*

A distant rumble sounded. I thought maybe it was thunder. It grew louder and resolved into the hum of an aircraft. Distantly across the water came the wail of the air-drop sirens. A bulky olive green plane soared into view over the cliffs behind us. It passed overhead and banked left. The rear cargo gate was open, and as we watched, a bright orange crate tumbled out. It had a rope with a tiny mushroom-shaped parachute trailing behind. It was in free-fall for a couple of seconds before a large white parachute popped open. It swung wildly then slowed, drifting toward the shore ahead of us.

"Wow!" I said. "That was awesome."

Then something less awesome happened. The crate still drifted well above the tops of the cliffs. Winds buffeted it, pulling the chute and its cargo eastward. It overshot the low plateau where we could see the tops of buildings and continued drifting, still high up.

"Uh-oh," Tom said.

Manuel tugged his radio free of his belt, hailing the base. "*Buenas dias,* Decepción. This is Manuel from Montalva Base."

"*¡Hola, Manuel!*" was the enthusiastic reply. Then a bunch of things I didn't understand.

Manuel responded quickly, in urgent tones, and the only part I caught was *el avión*. There was further conversation in Spanish while Tom and I watched the crate descending. It landed perhaps a third of a mile east of the settlement but high above it on some cliffs. The chute drifted down around it. I guess it could have been worse, if the crate had ended up in the ocean or something. But that was hard to imagine.

It diminished what would otherwise have been a thrill: pulling up to a relatively smooth beach of black volcanic sand beside an actual jetty. Unloading and loading might not be so hard here. We dragged the boat up onto the beach, and followed Manuel up the gentle slope to a long, low building painted olive green with a bright maroon-and-yellow striped roof. Two men in red-and-yellow snowsuits came out and embraced Manuel, clearly glad to see him. He brought us over for introductions. They were brothers, as it turned out, named Juan and Mateo. Good-looking young guys with easy smiles and outstanding handlebar mustaches. When Manuel made introductions, both of them wrapped me in bear hugs. It was a bit of a shock, so much so that I laughed.

"Argentinians are very friendly as you can see," Manuel said.

"We are the most friendly people in South America," Juan said.

"Much more friendly than Chileans," Mateo added.

"Yes, yes, it is only a shame that Chileans are better looking," Manuel said.

"*Che*, are you kidding me?" Juan asked.

Manuel raised a finger. "Oh, and we are more athletic, too."

Both brothers roared with laughter.

"Remind me, Juan, how many times has Chile won the World Cup?" Mateo asked.

"That is easy to remember. No times."

"No times? How can they be so bad at *football* if they are so athletic?"

This went on for a couple of minutes; it was easy and casual the way conversations go between old friends. I enjoyed listening in—they were courteous enough to stay mostly in English—and it distracted me from the situation. Then Juan finally got down to business and gave us the bad news.

"I am very sorry, but your crate of supplies landed off target."

"Yes, we saw that," I said. "How long will it take to retrieve them?"

"It may not be possible, *amigo*," Mateo said. "It landed up on the glacier."

"Very dangerous, especially in summer," Juan said. "More rock is exposed, and there can be crevasses in the glacier."

"Well, how are we going to get our supplies?" I asked.

"Sorry, but we're not," Mateo said.

"Unless you are an experienced high-altitude ice climber."

Tom looked at me and raised his eyebrows. "Well?"

My stomach dropped. "No."

"We need the crate, don't we?"

I sighed. "Juan, can I make a call?"

Rousseau's Zodiac zoomed through the gap in the island cliffs—which was officially named Neptune's Bellows—and didn't slow. The boat was piled with equipment and rode low in the water. A wide V-shaped wake spread out behind the boat, disrupting the otherwise calm waters.

Tom checked his watch and whistled. "She made excellent time."

We walked down to the black-sand beach to meet her. The sand was surprisingly fine-grained. Manuel told me was not true sand, but volcanic ash. We greeted Rousseau and hauled the Zodiac up the beach. It was astonishingly heavy, not because of Rousseau, who had the rangy athletic build of a climber, but because of the equipment. I'd love to say that I knew what it all was, but I did not.

"Thank you for coming," I told her.

"It's no problem," she said.

"I mean, it's a long way, but we were desperate. You're the only ice climber I know."

"Relax, Noah." She offered a hint of a smile. "You had me at 'climb up the glacier.'"

We helped unload the equipment from the boat and carry it up to the single main research building. Manuel had been right, this was a lightweight base compared to some of the others. Its command center, housed beneath the two-tone roof, was an actual constructed building. The other "buildings" outside it were converted steel shipping containers. Almost like oversized shoeboxes. There was a medical shoebox, and a geology shoebox, even a bio-lab shoebox. I walked inside one, saw how cramped and cold it was, and decided I didn't need to see any others.

Besides, the expedition to retrieve the box was about to begin. Juan had sent up a camera drone to tag the crate's position. It was not a great distance away, but about twelve hundred feet above sea level. Rousseau had brought enough gear for three climbers, which I assumed would be me, Tom, and her.

"Oh, sorry, I'm not going," Tom said.

"Wait, what?"

"Extreme climbing is a young man's game. Someone has to oversee our ground preparations anyway."

"If we don't retrieve that crate, I'm not sure how many ground preparations are necessary."

Tom lowered his voice. "Look, kid, I'm not great with heights."

"Seriously?"

"Haven't you ever noticed all of my expeditions are at low elevations?"

"Honestly, no," I said.

"Well, they are. So you'll need someone else for this ridiculous adventure."

I looked at the others. The Argentinian brothers made a conscious effort not to make eye contact with me. Manuel glanced around, and then raised his hand.

"Count me in."

Thank goodness for Manuel.

Rousseau supervised our gearing up. We all had insulated clothing, of course, but she insisted we bring extra gloves. We each carried a pack with rope, pitons, hammers, and a pair of crampons, which were strap-on metal spikes for our boots we'd put on once we reached the glacier. Then we moved over to the base of the cliffs. Rousseau had watched the drone video but wanted to look at the slope with her own eyes. She looked at it a long time, her ice-blue eyes almost unblinking. She could have been a statue in those moments, her face chiseled out of marble. For my part, I tried not to look too much at the wall we had to climb. I was a decent rock climber, but had never tried anything this ambitious.

"You said you've climbed?" Rousseau asked me.

"Rock climbing, yes. Mostly on belay."

"Any free climbing?"

I remembered the time Summer and I had free-climbed boulders to reach Build-A-Dragon's deep desert facility. We'd had no support then, no equipment, nothing. "Some."

She grunted, clearly unimpressed by either what I said or how I said it. "Right, here is how this will work. I climb lead and I set the route. You follow one at a time, five meters between us. You use the same holds and the same steps. Got it?"

"Got it," we answered.

She nodded, and it was like we no longer existed. She faced the slope, checking her harness and straps by touch. The slope in front of us was steep and rocky, but not vertical. Most of this would be scrambling as opposed to outright climbing. Still, I took her point and was glad she wanted the lead position. She was a professional compared to me, and her route choices would determine our safety. Then she walked forward and got to work. In just a few seconds she was five yards up—which seemed close enough to meters to me—and moving at a good clip.

Manuel was watching her with too-wide eyes, the uncertainty clear on his face. I put my hand on his shoulder. "I'll go second, all right?"

He nodded. "*Gracias.*"

I set myself to work, copying Rousseau's route exactly. She took a winding path up the slope, choosing firm holds, avoiding the loose parts of rubble. It's hard to describe how much a competent climbing leader takes the pressure off. I still had to be cautious and pay attention to what I was doing, but the hard decisions were all hers. When we'd gone up may be fifty yards, she paused.

"Hold here a minute." She took out a bright orange metal spike with a loop at the end and hammered it into a crevice. Then she pulled a rope through and tossed it back to us. "Safety line." I clipped in, and passed the end of the line to Manuel. He put it through his harness and tied the correct knot.

"You've done some climbing," I said.

He looked up and gave me a shaky grin. "A little. But I don't like heights."

Sure, a little. Just like he spoke a little English and knew a little about Antarctica. God bless the Chileans. They were all so humble, at least when there were no Argentinians around. We made solid progress in the beginning when it was solid rock. As we ascended there was more ice and snow to contend with. Rousseau moved with preternatural grace up the jagged terrain, always confident and comfortable. This was her element, and it was hard not to admire. She avoided the ice when she could, and tested every bit of snow carefully. I knew the reasoning. You couldn't trust the snow when mountain climbing, especially in summertime. It drifted and froze to form bridges across gaps, or cornices on the edge of a steep precipice. This was hard to see while you were crossing it, because winds swept the surface of the snow flat.

I was breathing hard. Part of that was the sheer exertion of hauling up the slope. The other part was a rising sensation that I was increasingly behind on my breath. *It's the thinning air,* I tried to tell myself. That didn't help with the sensation, though. I forced myself to take good deep breaths rather than light panting. I focused on taking each step as Rousseau did while keeping my weight centered.

At last, we cleared the rocks and reached a wide, climbing expanse that was almost entirely snow and ice. That was the bad news. The good news was that we could see the crate, maybe three hundred yards up the glacier. We stood on a shelf of rock that was almost flat. Rousseau took off her pack and sat down, gesturing for us to do the same.

"Crampons," she said.

I sat down and fished mine out of my pack. Crampons were

essentially metal plates with about a dozen serrated, slightly curved steel spikes. You strapped them to the bottom of your boots and they bit into the snow whenever you took a step. I was more than a little excited to try these, as I'd never had the opportunity, though part of me wished it were under less dire circumstances. It took me a minute to figure out how the bindings worked, but once I aligned them with the toe and heel of my boot, it was easy to figure out. Three spikes protruded forward under my toes like buck teeth. I touched them and could feel the sharpness even through my gloves.

"For vertical climbing," Rousseau said. She already had her crampons on, and came over to inspect mine. "These need to be tighter." She tugged the straps on both of my boots until she was satisfied with the snugness of the fit before calling it good. She moved to do the same for Manuel, so I stood up and tried out a few steps. It was a strange sensation, both because the spikes required that I lift my foot higher while walking, and the way they bit into the snow to hold my foot in place.

"We'll rope up before we go." Rousseau tied herself to a rope, measured out a few arm lengths, and handed me the rest. I quickly tied a figure-eight knot, pulled it tight, and slid it into the right part of my harness clip. This won me a nod from Rousseau. Manuel got himself on, and then we set out across the glacier.

"Ice axes," Rousseau ordered.

I unclipped mine from my belt and tested the heft. It was about two and a half feet long, the shaft aluminum, the spiked head forged in dark carbon steel. I tried it a couple of times on the snow. The way the head plunged into the hardened snow crust was immensely satisfying.

"Ready?" Rousseau asked.

"Ready," Manuel said.

I grinned. "Let's do this."

She set off at a brisk pace that we, being roped to her, had to match exactly or risk falling. This was a little complicated because the crampons forced me to walk differently, lifting my knees. A couple times I had to ask her to slow, but once I got the hang of it, we made steady progress. The crate was closer now. I couldn't see any damage. The ground had leveled off some and the crampons worked beautifully. Even better, the out-of-breath sensation had waned after our break to put on the crampons. I hardly noticed it now. *I'm climbing a glacier in Antarctica.* To do so in the company of a real-world mountaineer made it an even greater thrill somehow.

Rousseau halted suddenly and held up her arm. We stopped.

"What's wrong?" I asked.

She stared to turn, and then the glacier collapsed underneath her with a loud whoosh.

"Crevasse!" she shouted.

We were tied together so the rope yanked me forward as she fell. I hit the ground hard and started sliding forward to the edge of the narrow crack in the snow. I heaved myself over and swung the ice axe with both hands. It bit deep into the snow. I clung to it as hard as I could. The weight of the rope was enormous. It felt like I'd be pulled in half but I refused to let go. Doing so would send me into the abyss. But the burden was too much. I felt my grip starting to slip. Then I remembered my crampons. I kicked my left leg down hard and felt the toe spikes catch. It helped me hold on long enough to kick my other leg in. I forced my legs to take some of the weight. I was splayed out face down on the snow, the harness crushing me. It hurt like hell, but I stopped sliding. I felt the rope swing and then some of the weight subsided. For a frightening moment, I thought the rope had snapped. There was still tension in it, though. She must have kicked into the snow like I had. Even so, I was too terrified to move. If it had just been the two of us, I don't know what we would have done. But we weren't alone. Snow crunched as Manuel ran fearlessly past me.

"Hold on!" he shouted.

I tried to answer but my mouth was full of snow. I braced myself in case Rousseau lost her hold and rolled my head back to watch. Manuel reached the edge. I wanted to scream at him to be careful. What if the edge collapsed? I knew I couldn't hold both of them. He crouched at the edge of the precipice and grabbed the rope. Rousseau said something to him, her voice remarkably calm. He leaned back and heaved. *God, he's strong.* He gained a foot of rope, then two. The pressure came off my harness. I forced myself up to my knees, tugged my ice axe free, and crawled until the rope grew taut. My shoulders were on fire. I reached as far as I could and swung the axe into the ice for grip, pulling with Manuel. We gained three more feet. We did it again. Then there was enough room for me to stand and take the rope in my other hand. I didn't want to let go of my ice axe.

"Ready?" he asked.

"Yeah."

We dug in our crampons and heaved together, gaining rope. We moved back one pace, then two.

"Slowly!" Rousseau shouted. The rope shuddered and went slack. She was climbing. We backed up, keeping the rope nearly taut. Then her ice axe swung over the edge and bit deep. Her head appeared. Her face betrayed no fear, only determination. She kicked in another crampon. We all moved together and then her upper body was out and over. One more kick, one more pull, and she was out. She scrambled clear and we all collapsed, panting.

"*Merci*," she said, her voice as steady as if we were having tea and I'd passed her the sugar.

"You"—I gasped, still gulping air—"are a badass."

She laughed. Manuel did, too, and I joined them. We took a minute to catch our breath. Then Rousseau stood, brushed the snow off her suit, and said, "Well, let's get moving."

We gave the crevasse a wide berth. I wanted to ask her how deep it was, but was too afraid of the answer. The rest of the climb was without incident, and we reached the drop crate. It was a hard material, either plastic or fiberglass, a perfect cube four feet to a side. It had made a dent in the snow where it landed. Manuel and I gathered the parachute, which was surprisingly lightweight material. I managed to cram it all into my backpack. Rousseau had unlocked the carry handles. We could lift the crate easily with each of us on a different side.

"Slow and steady," Rousseau said. "Keep your legs under you."

It seemed like a nonsensical piece of advice, but I understood the meaning the first time I got off balance and slipped. "Ah!"

Luckily, both of them had good stances and held the crate fast. I used it to regain my footing. "Thanks."

After that we hit a rhythm, moving back the way we'd come. Descending was a little easier because gravity helped. We reached the rocky shelf and set it down to take a break.

"Can we keep our crampons the rest of the way?" I asked.

"I would recommend it." She took a small hand tool out of her pack. "Here, bring them to me." I lifted my feet over and she adjusted a screw on the bottom. The toe-spikes pivoted inward and the others spread out to make room. "Rock mode," she called it.

She adjusted her own crampons and then Manuel's. Then we got underway again. The bulky crate only got awkward when we had to navigate around boulders and across the rocky ridges. We stopped frequently to remove the safety anchors Rousseau had installed on the way up, so there were frequent breaks. Still, my arms and legs ached from the exertion. It was late afternoon by the time we reached the final safety anchor. We heard shouting from below. Juan and Mateo were waiting. It was good to see them and not feel quite so alone. Now we had backup.

"Can you two hold it a minute?" Rousseau asked.

We changed stances and took the weight. She unshouldered her pack and took out another long rope. She fed it through the hammered-in anchor and then tied it to the crate handle that faced uphill. At her signal, we set the crate down. She took the coil of the rest of the rope and offered it to me. "Are you up for it?"

Now I understood. *A pulley system*. Someone had to carry the rope down. To let me do it was a nod of respect.

I smiled. "Absolutely."

She took over at my handle; she and Manuel would hold it steady to belay me. I fed the rope through my belay harness and then leaned back to test it. The tension was good. I backed down, feeding line, and when I reached a steep part, rappelled out and over. I landed clean and steady—this was something I'd done at the climbing wall back home. Juan and Mateo whooped their approval from below. That gave me the confidence to go again. Two more jumps, and then I landed at the base of the cliffs. *Back on flat ground at last.*

Juan and Mateo applauded, then ran up to wrap me in a bear hug.

"Great job, guy!" Juan said.

Mateo squeezed my shoulder. "Very nice rappelling!"

"Thanks." I about sagged with relief, but remembered I had a job to do. I freed the rope from my harness and would have taken the belay position.

Juan waved me off. "We got this. You rest."

They took up the rope and assumed belay stances, with Juan in the primary and Mateo backing him. Mateo put his hand on Juan's shoulder, Juan signaled to Rousseau. They pushed the crate. The brothers took the weight and fed line steadily. It got down even faster than I did. They belayed Manuel down. He was more timid about it than I was, but looked equally relieved. They would have belayed Rousseau, but she insisted on pulling the rope back up, removing the anchor, and free-climbing to the bottom. I stumbled up and gave her a hug, which caught her by surprise. Manuel appeared and wrapped both of us in a bear hug. Then the brothers joined in, wrapping around us, squashing us all together.

"Rousseau!" I shouted, and they took up the chant, jumping around us in a circle. "Rousseau! Rousseau!"

The expression on her face cycled from alarm to acceptance to joy. She actually *smiled*. A full-on, toothy grin of happiness. And that, truly, was how we thawed the Ice Queen.

The rest of our time on Deception Island passed too quickly. I got to see the dragons hatch and witnessed their first night hunt in the penguin nesting grounds. Later, Manuel took Tom and me out in a Zodiac to see Baily Head, which was on the southeast corner of Deception and held one of the largest penguin breeding colonies in the world. Fifty thousand pairs of chinstrap penguins milled in a massive semicircular area shaped like an amphitheater. I'd never seen so many birds in one place, let alone penguins. I took a million photos and promised to send some to Summer the next time I had a decent network connection. There were fur seals, too, forming a nearly impenetrable wall along the black-sand beaches.

That's when Tom broke the news to me that we were leaving Antarctica but not heading home.

"What do you mean?" I asked. *I have to get home. I promised.*

"Evelyn sent a message. The press got a hold of our success here and we've gotten a lot of media attention."

Uh-oh. "Good or bad?"

"Good, for the most part. Most serious outlets see it as a coup to remove invasive species since we were the ones who introduced them."

"Hey, good press for once. I suppose there's a first time for everything."

He laughed. "Yeah, surprising."

"We picked up decent coverage after the swarm of locusts," I said.

"True, but that was local news. Evidently the media interest dissipated rather quickly."

"How?" I'd been there and seen the footage. Our locust-eating dragons had been next-level. Even the embarrassing footage of me diving into the trailer for cover should have had staying power.

Tom shrugged. "The thing is, that intervention ultimately served to protect a bunch of plants. People can only get so excited about green things that grow in the ground."

My fifteen seconds of fame were not only humiliating, but short-lived. "Well, that sucks."

"This win will gain a different kind of media attention, trust me, because we have a far more sympathetic victim."

"Penguins."

"Bingo. Everybody loves 'em."

Looking out at the massive colony spread before me, I didn't need convincing on that point. "It's hard not to."

"Word's already spreading about what the dragons did on King George Island. Evelyn already landed another contract for cane toads from the Australian government."

"Oh, right, your favorite poisonous amphibian."

"After we talked about them, I floated the idea of using dragons on the toads to our boss."

"Oh, nice." Apparently I wasn't the only one who pitched ideas to Evelyn.

"I put her in touch with some friends at Parks Australia. They're ready to try anything."

"Like a dragon that will kill the toads but not eat them," I said.

He nodded. "That could work, but a dragon that eats them without dying would be even better."

"All right, tell me about the poison."

"The Chinese call it *chan su,* but the technical name is bufotoxin. It's produced by the parotoid glands." He touched the upper part of his jaw. "Right by the ear."

"All right, so we teach dragons to cut off the head first."

"Won't work. It builds up in the skin as part of the toad defense." He grimaced and shook his head. "Nasty stuff. It blocks ion channels in the heart muscles and causes arrhythmia."

"Are there any animals that survive it?"

"Some of the lizards that co-evolved with cane toads in Asia."

Beautiful. I was already planning out the design process. "So we figure out which ones those are, compare their genomes to susceptible lizards—"

He held up his hand. "There's already a dragon designed. Dave's team cooked it up last week."

I heard the first part and was still dealing with the emotional slap of missing out on a cool design. Then I processed the rest. "Did you say 'Dave's team'?"

"Yeah, I think that's his name. The new guy."

Jeez, I'm gone a couple of weeks and he's already running my team. "It's *not* his team. It's mine."

"Well, I guess someone had to play assistant egghead while the main one was, you know, out climbing glaciers."

It was a little appealing for Tom to acknowledge me as such, though it surprised me that Dave was now stepping in to handle things in my absence. Or maybe it didn't. Everyone got along with him, and even I had to admit he had the right background to do this sort of work. Still, it nagged at me a little. "I guess that's true." I just didn't know why it had to be Dave. I shook my head. "Ugh."

He frowned. "Are you unhappy you came?"

"No, it's not that. This has been incredible."

"You have good people back there, don't you?"

"Yes. The best," I said, and I meant it.

"So do I. You've gotta trust 'em to do the right thing in your absence. That's what being a leader means."

"What about a paranoid leader?"

He barked a laugh. "Especially a paranoid leader. Besides, Dave covering for you means that you get to take a trip down under."

Down under. "Shut up. We're going to Australia?"

"Not only that, but we're going on the dime of the government of Queensland."

"And we already have a prototype."

"That's what Evelyn said. The eggs are being printed as we speak."

If that was right, we were already on the clock. Eggs would get printed and shipped, and we'd meet them in Australia. It gave me a pang of sadness to think about leaving. It felt too soon. We had another batch of eggs en route already, and several more locations with nesting seabirds where Antarctic researchers were clamoring for us to intervene. Word about the success on King George Island had apparently spread even on the Glacier network. "What about the other deployment locations here?" I asked.

"The base teams can handle that. Jim and Allie will stay to oversee the delivery."

"Who's going to oversee the hatchings?"

"What I hear is that a local researcher has already stepped up." He looked meaningfully over his shoulder at Manuel, who sheepishly raised his hand.

I grinned. "You volunteer for everything, don't you?"

He winced. "The Argentinians nominated me. I just hope I do a good job."

"You'll be great," I told him. "I couldn't think of a better guy."

"*Gracias, amigo.*"

Australia. I had to go. I couldn't not go—we were already more than halfway. But it was going to add time to our trip, probably another week. More time for Dave to supplant my place and for Summer to get even more pissed. But this was down under. "Manuel, we'd better head in. Tom and I have to pack."

CHAPTER TWENTY-EIGHT
INTERLUDE
BUILD-A-DRAGON
PIVOTS BACK TO ANIMAL CONTROL

PHOENIX, Ariz—The Build-A-Dragon Company has a new type of government gig, and no, it's not another defense contract. The company formerly known as Reptilian Corporation has been in business for only a few years but has frequently adapted to changing conditions. The company's founder, Simon Redwood, initially developed the synthetic organism colloquially called a dragon to address a significant agricultural threat: feral hogs, which had plagued farmers and ranchers for decades. These animals trace their origins to domestic pigs, but adapted quickly to wild environments where they have few to no natural predators. A group of adult feral hogs could devour two acres of farm crops overnight. Efforts to control them with hunting or containment efforts failed, which gave Redwood an in. Of course, those hog-hunting dragons were so effective that they killed a major source of company revenue as hog populations plummeted.

Next the company pivoted to the exotic pet market, developing and selling several domesticated dragons to serve as family pets. This was the company's biggest growth phase, when revenues more than quadrupled. Families out walking their "Rover" dragons instead of a canine companion was such a commonplace occurrence, it even ceased to be a meme. Other smaller breeds of dragon followed, and the company offered a lucrative custom-design program for the discerning customers with deep pockets. Yet, as usual, the company quickly undercut its own most promising business models. Former CEO Robert Greaves, who helmed the company after Redwood's departure, allegedly concealed crucial information about an effective treatment for the canine epidemic. The criminal and civil trials have been delayed twice as both sets of attorneys cast blame elsewhere, yet the release of crucial trial data led to fast-track approval of the drug. We all know how that part of the story ends: dogs are back.

While that was good news for the world, it had a catastrophic effect on Build-A-Dragon's revenues. Shareholders quickly saw the writing on the wall: once dogs were back, the appetite for scaly replacements diminished considerably. This brought about another pivot for the company, one that has seen far less press. Possibly because the company and its well-financed clients prefer it that way. Freedom of Information Act filings yielded some tantalizing details of the contracts between Build-A-Dragon and the U.S. Department of Defense. Those contracts gave the company a lifeline as it searched for its next act.

Turns out, that next act might involve a return to the company's roots: pest control. First it was an outbreak of invasive desert locusts that threatened the precious oasis flora in the desert. A small army of custom-made dragons made the difference, and word about their potential for pest control began to spread in the scientific community. The true proof of principle for this new dragon application has just arrived from the most unlikely of places: the frigid depths of Antarctica.

Cold. Lifeless. Inhospitable. It's the last place you'd expect to see a reptile first developed in the sunny desert climate of the American Southwest. Yet it's here that dragons scored an important ecological victory. What's more, they righted a previous wrong introduced by early generations of Antarctic explorers.

That wrong? An infestation of rats.

The first man-made ships visited Antarctica in the nineteenth century. Like most ships, they carried intrepid explorers and more than a few stowaways. Rats soon made their way to the moraines on the shorelines where dark stones trapped the sun's heat each day, making life hospitable for animals that could find food. Trouble was, those moraines happened to be where many of the world's penguins meet up to breed every year. Chinstrap, gentoo, and other penguins have come to these frigid islands since time immemorial for their couplings that serve to propagate the species. Like the feral hogs, it was a problem of devastating impact for which no viable solution had presented itself. Antarctica represents the last pristine environment on the planet, a place where all of the world powers have agreed that research should come first. The various treaties that keep the peace on the frozen continent forbid colonization, exploitation, and military activities. Yet this decades-old treaty did not foresee the problem the rats would become, nor the need to introduce a predator to control their populations.

In some ways, cats would be the perfect solution to the rat problem. They seem to like humans well enough, and their rodent-hunting abilities are without equal. Yet the same treaty system that keeps the peace prevents the introduction of any new, potentially invasive species. Are the dragons a new species? That remains a matter of some debate. No matter how it ends up, the research teams and their nation-sponsors decided that the temporary introduction of short-lived dragons did not constitute a violation of the treaty. The challenge was designing a dragon that would survive the harsh environment, where temperatures rarely get above freezing even in the summer season.

"This was one of our most challenging designs," said Evelyn Chang, Build-A-Dragon's CEO. "We had to make some fundamental changes to how our dragon eggs are printed simply to pull it off." She should know. Before stepping into this leadership role, Chang headed the team of genetic engineers who customized dragons for their niche roles. It may have been a difficult design, but it was a successful one. Videos of the dragons ambushing the invasive rats—while penguins watch from their nests mere feet away—have gone viral. Even the animal rights groups that normally might vociferously protest these activities were largely silent on the matter. PETA and the World Wildlife Foundation declined to comment. Perhaps because, when it comes to animal protections, people will always choose penguins over rodents.

Now the designers at Build-A-Dragon have another tall order: developing dragons that can prey on the infamous cane-toad population of northern Australia.

The cane toad (*Rhinella marina*) has a humble appearance. These squat amphibians are native to South and Central America, where their appetite for insect pests is legendary. In the early twentieth century, cane toads were imported to islands in the Caribbean as a means of controlling the cane beetles, whose larvae are devastating to sugarcane crops. The adult beetles have a hard exoskeleton and lay their eggs deep underground, making them difficult to exterminate. A study in 1932 reported good results in Puerto Rico, where the toads had been imported for several years. Soon after, they were tried in Hawaii, whose sugarcane crops faced similar infestations. Then, in 1935, the first cane toads were brought to Queensland, Australia. Their spread was slow at first. By 1959, they had colonized most of Queensland's northeast coasts. Soon after, they began to push westward.

Australian native species had never seen a cane toad until humans introduced them. Cane toads, in contrast, had been honing their toxic defenses for thousands of years. In their native environments in South and Central America, most predators know to avoid the cane toad. As a result, it rarely has to hide. Australian predators saw this as an easy meal. The secondary effects of toxic toads on biodiversity were not appreciated for many years, until scientists noted that the invasion of cane toads coincided with precipitous declines of birds, such as the northern quoll, and numerous types of large lizards (often called *monitors*). The yellow-spotted monitor, once a stable of Queeensland's wild areas, declined by ninety percent.

In retrospect, it's not hard to understand what happened. Cane toads seemed to solve the insect problem of a major export crop. All they were doing was eating bugs that otherwise ate plants the Australians needed. Yes, the occasional human was poisoned accidentally after touching a cane toad, but those issues could be addressed through education. But how do you teach a bird or lizard to pass up what looks like an easy meal? One by one, Australia's frog-eating predator species fell to the toxins secreted behind cane-toad ears. A few native animals proved resilient to the toxin. Others, like the Torresian crow, adapted a technique to safely eat the toads by flipping them onto their backs and eating only the safe undersides. Yet the toxin produced by toads, named bufotoxin, is simple but effective. Again, thousands of years of evolution. Scientists pondered ways to counter the invasive threat while the toad population in Australia swelled to an estimated two hundred million. They need a predator that will selectively target the toads and eat them before something else does. They need a resilient animal that can somehow negate a highly effective toxin. They need, it seems, to Build A Dragon.

CHAPTER TWENTY-NINE
Insomnia

I gripped the safety handle as the small single-prop plane shuddered and jerked, buffeted by the hot winds of Queensland's northern coast. Tom had conveniently forgotten to tell me about the final phase of our journey, which involved flying deep into the outback's rugged terrain in this pack of gum. He'd also helped himself to the copilot seat and headset, citing his private pilot's license. That left me crammed in the rear of the tiny plane with our luggage. The window was tiny and I'd long since given up trying to see anything meaningful through it. Instead, I spent my time plotting ways to get even with Tom and listening to the sound of the engine. It had the sputtering uneven tone of a car on its last legs. Basically, I was listening for it to die so I'd at least know my own fate was sealed.

Tom and the bush pilot knew each other. Of course they did. As a herpetologist, Tom had lived in Australia for nearly as long as he'd lived in the U.S. His story about the fin-swimming turtle whose name I'd already forgotten was one of hundreds. He was telling one now, but I couldn't hear most of it. He and the pilot had the only two headsets. Something about a snake and a bottle of whisky.

We were flying into a place called Cooinda, a settlement located on the Yellow Water billabong in Kakadu National Park. This was the epicenter of the cane toad invasion, at least in central Queensland. Kakadu was Australia's version of Yellowstone—people here went nuts for it, and the impact of the cane toads was widely feared. When the government had called Evelyn to ask for her assistance, they'd specifically requested that this be the first area of deployment. The impact on predator reptiles especially had been devastating, to the point where people were worried about the crocodiles. Getting out of Antartica had proven more difficult than we realized, so the eggs had beat us here by nearly a week. The replacement hatchery staff, whoever they were, had had to handle the initial hatching. Tom walked them through it from the pitiful cabin on our ship as we chugged against the waves. I was probably throwing up at the time. My seasickness had improved, but only a little.

Of note, we'd flown into Darwin International Airport and were supposed to rent an SUV to drive here. For my part, I couldn't wait to see some of Australia's wild country. However, we never even made it out of the airport. We got our bags—which had been held by security. The problem was Tom's bag, which was half-filled with knives of various kinds. I hadn't known or had occasion to ask, but it turned out his well-used duffel was essentially a portable arsenal. Since we didn't so much as use a single knife in Antarctica, part of me wondered if he intended to get to Australia the whole time. They didn't bat an eye at my bag, but I'd been invited to speak with security first since I was Tom's traveling companion.

"How well do you know Mr. Johnson?" the man had asked.

"Pretty well. We work together at the Build-A-Dragon Company."

"Is he... well?"

"What do you mean?"

"Is he mentally stable?"

I nearly laughed, but managed to keep a straight face. "Absolutely. He's an outdoorsman. Do you really not recognize him?"

"No."

I'd apologized and made further reassurances to the security personnel, because I sort of had a weapon of my own that I hadn't declared. Rousseau had given me the ice axe as a parting gift, in memory of our "adventures" together, and I sure as hell wasn't going to lose it to some rent-a-cops at airport security.

Evidently my assurances concerning Tom's need for bladed weapons were not sufficient, so we were ushered in to see a supervisor. She was a husky, no-nonsense woman with gray hair tied back in a severe bun and a grim face that brooked no back talk whatsoever. She was also an avid nature lover who recognized Tom from his shows, fawned over him like a teenager, and ensured our rapid release from their custody with all of our luggage relatively unmolested. I opened my bag and put a hand on my ice axe just to be sure.

We were nearly to the rental car section when a man called out to Tom. The next thing I knew they were shaking hands and clapping one another on the back. His name was Andrew and he'd been the bush pilot for some of Tom's conservation work down here. Yes, he knew all about the cane-toad problem and had heard about the efforts to bring in dragons to control them. Yes, he was still flying, and as a matter of fact was on his way to Kakadu and could drop us there. It took me a minute to realize that this offer meant flying in yet another plane, this one tiny, as opposed to renting a large, comfortable SUV.

"What do you say, mates?" Andrew had asked genially.

I pictured myself refusing, forcing the long awkward walk to the rental car counter with Tom frowning at me the whole time, and then an even more awkward three-hour drive out to the park. "Sounds great," I said.

We took a tram over to the noncommercial section of the airport. Andrew had called ahead so his plane, a Cessna, was already out on the taxiway, its engine warming. It was bright blue and cute and everything, but it didn't sound good to my ears. I didn't know anything about airplanes, but I also valued my life.

"Does the engine sound okay to you?" I whispered to Tom as we walked nearby, hauling our luggage.

"Eh, I've flown in worse, that's for sure. Don't worry about it. Andrew's a top-notch pilot."

I wanted to point out that the quality of the pilot might not matter if the plane crapped out at five thousand feet, but I'd committed to this route and already canceled our rental car.

Tom knocked on the ceiling of the plane to get my attention. "We're going to do a flyover!"

"Of what?"

"Kakadu!"

I crammed myself against the side of the backseat to get a better look out the window. The landscape was stunning and vibrant green. We'd spent so long in Antarctica that my eyes didn't want to believe so many colors existed. A wide, glittering azure river meandered through the landscape, separated occasionally by long skinny islands and shallow rapids. To the north of that rose stunning cliffs and rock formations, all of them covered with trees. It honestly reminded me a little bit of Arizona, but where our rocks were clay-colored, these were the yellows and tans of sandstone. The sun had bleached the cliff faces to nearly white. Across the river to the south was mostly dense woodland savanna in gently rolling hills. Here and there a cliff broke free of the canopy, but it was much flatter and lush with vegetation. Andrew circled and then told us we were landing. I couldn't see the airstrip until we had touched down. That's how small it was.

Andrew taxied off the narrow landing strip and guided the plane to a large, open hangar where three other planes were parked, all small aircraft about the same size as ours. He and Tom both hopped out of the plane, and then I shoved their baggage out to them like a bag boy.

"My Jeep's over here," Andrew said, beckoning us toward a chain-link fence. There was no customs, no security. No one around at all. It was a strange experience coming from American airports and having spent time flitting between so many continents where I'd been carded, interrogated, frisked, and borderline violated by too many security personnel to count.

"It's over there?" I asked. "Is it the red one?"

"Yep, that's it."

"Shotgun!" I grinned at Tom.

He muttered a curse. *Yeah, I spent the last half hour planning that move.*

We piled into the Jeep, which had seriously rugged tires that belonged on a monster truck. They were splattered with mud, as were the sides of the vehicle and part of the windshield. I found this highly alarming but Tom didn't seem to notice. To his credit, he did climb into the backseat. Which naturally was easy for him because he's super tall and the Jeep had no roof on it. He swung in comfortably like it was no big thing, which partly ruined the effect for me. I made a mental note to call shotgun on the plane when it was time to fly back.

"Buckle in, mates, it's a bit of a drive," Andrew said, and fired up the Jeep. The characteristic rumble of the engine, and the sensation of riding in the open air, reminded me too strongly of Summer's Jeep. It twisted my stomach in an uncomfortable way, a rising feeling of unease that I couldn't shake. Maybe I was homesick. But there was a job to do, and the sooner we tackled that the sooner I could head home to Arizona. Now that the first hatching had taken place, our job was to determine if the dragons were having an effective impact on the environment. That was the fancy way Evelyn had put it.

Tom had put it more simply: *They need to know if the dragons are truly resistant to bufotoxin.* There were examples in nature, though they came few and far between. Australian meat ants were resistant to the poison. Their genomes had not been officially assembled yet, but the raw data had been generated by a government-funded project. Dave had pulled some strings to gain early access to it, and with help from Wong had tracked down the gene they felt was required for the toxin resistance.

"Are you sure you found it?" I'd asked on our video call. This was shortly after we'd boarded our Antarctic transfer ship, before it had even gotten underway. Thus I wasn't yet starting to hurl on a regular basis.

"As sure as we can be," Dave had said. He'd come in early so that we could connect in real time. "It was the only commonality with the other known resistant species with genomes sequenced already."

"What does it encode?"

"A cytochrome enzyme."

That was a good sign, as whatever protected ants from the toxin likely produced some kind of enzyme that broke it up before it caused organ damage. True experimental testing would require months of experiments with appropriate controls, isolated systems, and other things we didn't currently have the luxury for. They'd dug up the best answer they could find and integrated it into a wild prototype that was specially designed for frog hunting.

"I'll let you know what we find," I said. "It's good to see you, man."

"Thanks. Everyone says hi, by the way."

It warmed me a little to hear that. "That's nice. Tell them I'm still alive, but barely."

He laughed. "We can talk soon. Let us know when you arrive."

"Will do."

I replayed the conversation as we drove away from the airstrip. The Jeep bounced along the road, which couldn't seem to make up its mind on whether it wanted to be dirt or gravel.

"Are all the roads this bad?" I asked.

"This here's a good 'un," Andrew said. Now that we were away from the busy airport and outside the grumbling airplane, I figured I'd be able to understand him better. But I'd grown so accustomed to South American accents that it was practically a foreign language. He reached behind his seat and came up with a broad-brimmed hat that he placed on his head. Between the accent and the hat, the resemblance to Crocodile Dundee was uncanny. Part of me wondered if he knew it and was leaning into the resemblance.

"Have you seen cane toads in the wild here?"

"Everyone's seen cane toads in the wild here. They're all over."

"Ever lick one?"

He laughed. "Not in this lifetime. You don't go about licking things in Queensland if you value your life."

The canopy closed behind us. The air was warm and smelled strongly of eucalyptus with an undercurrent of something sweeter—hints of honey and flowers. Bottlebrush, maybe. It made a nice contrast to the eucalyptus, which was the aerosol equivalent of a cough drop.

"How bad is the problem?"

"Bad enough that the citizens are starting to notice the disappearance of predator populations."

"Really? Got a lot of reptile enthusiasts down here, do you?"

"More than you think, but I'm mainly talking about the budding community."

"What the hell is the budding community?"

Tom tapped my shoulder from the backseat. "He's saying *birding* community, as in birdwatchers."

"Ohh," I said. "That makes a lot more sense than budding." The accent shock still hadn't worn off.

"Sorry, mate," Andrew said. "Didn't know you were hard of hearing."

I decided to let it pass, just as I decided to ignore Tom's silent laughter from the backseat. "So the birders keep count?"

"Like you wouldn't believe. They come in droves, and all of them carry these little notebooks. If one of them sees a plumed whistling duck, and the next week no one sees a plumed whistling duck, they report it to the bloody government."

"Yikes."

"Yeah, the birders here are pretty serious. Competitive as hell, too."

"Birders are competitive?"

"Yeah, they go against each other, trying to spot the most unique species in a single year. This place is a jackpot for them, though they drive the tour operators bonkers. The last time I was here, we got three search and rescue calls for tour boats run aground on the Yellow River. The passengers had all full-on insisted on moving closer to the shoreline so they could identify a tiny bird."

Andrew braked hard without warning. The Jeep skidded to a halt. We'd come around a sharp corner and there were animals in the road. It took me a second to realize they were some kind of bird. *Well, speak of the Devil.* Their dun-brown bodies looked furry rather than feathery, and moved on long legs that looked too skinny to support their weight. They had long necks, too, and bobbed their heads back and forth to get a look at us.

"Are those... ostriches?" I asked.

"Emus," Andrew said. "Mean buggers. They're hell on the vegetation, and as you can see, they like to clog up the roads."

Just as he said, the emus were walking slowly away from us, quite unperturbed at the loud rumble of the engine. Andrew honked, which was what I wanted to do, and they didn't so much as flinch.

"Yeah, I was afraid of that," he said. "They've seen humans and cars before."

"Can you sort of... nudge them out of the way?"

He shook his head. "Never works."

I turned around to look at Tom. "Any suggestions?"

He glanced up from his field guide on Australian reptiles, as if surprised. "Who, me?"

"Yes, does the world-renowned nature expert know how to get these big-ass birds out of our way?"

He resumed reading. "Seems to me that whoever calls shotgun volunteers to handle any navigation issues that come up."

"That's how you're going to play this, huh?"

"Yes, that's how I'm going to play it."

I groaned and looked at Andrew. "I guess I'm the only help you've got. What do you want to do?"

"Let's try it on foot." He unfastened his seatbelt and climbed out. I did the same, and we moved to the front of the Jeep. He took a quick survey around and pointed. "Grab some of those branches there. We can try to herd them with that while keeping a little distance, you know?"

I'd been planning to jog at the birds and wave my arms, but his remark gave me cause for concern. "Are they dangerous?"

"It's good to keep something between you and them, mate. Good rule for Australia in general."

"Great." I climbed down in the ditch and found a good-sized branch; it still had limp leaves attached. This one I handed to Andrew. I found another one like it. We brandished these and advanced on the emus, which had stopped walking the moment we got out of the car and now stood staring at us. There were five of them, all apparently full-sized adults. They stared with unblinking eyes, moving their heads back and forth kind of like a turkey would. Seeing a distinctly birdlike trait on these giants was a little unnerving.

We approached and shook the branches at them. This seemed to have little effect. The big one nearest me actually pecked at my branch, catching it with its beak. We had a quick tug-of-war, which I barely won. It still wouldn't move, though. Andrew was swinging his branch toward a couple of emus and failing to hit any of them. They were too nimble. We tried for another minute or so, but had to call a retreat and move back to the Jeep. I'd started to notice how low the sun was in the sky, and I didn't love the idea of being out here on this crappy road at night. *We need to get this moving.* I didn't have any bright ideas, though. This was my first large stubborn-bird encounter.

"So," asked Tom from the backseat. "How did it go?"

"You're a lot of help, you know that?"

"We couldn't scoot them away, and technically I'm not allowed to ram them with the Jeep. Which might not work anyway," Andrew said.

Tom flipped a page. "Well, if scaring them out of the road didn't work, maybe you should try *enticing* them instead."

"With what?" I demanded. *If this leads to me dressing up as a female emu and imitating a mating ritual, I'll just get out and walk.*

Tom leaned down and picked up a box at his feet. Chewy oat granola bars with dried cherries. "How about this?"

"That's my stash, mate," Andrew said. "For emergencies only."

"I think this qualifies," I said sourly.

We unwrapped several granola bars and took them back toward

the emus. They looked more alert this time, and certainly more interested in us. Andrew had brought one of the wrappers and crinkled it loudly. "You want some of this, eh?"

They shifted toward us, then started moving on their long spindly legs. The way they walked was hilarious. We took the five or six bars we'd brought, waved them in the air, and then tossed them to the side of the road. The emus followed, dipping their sinuous necks to sniff at the food.

"Move!" Andrew jogged back to the car.

I threw one more granola bar and tossed it even farther off the road. The emus skittered after it, competing with one another. Then I ran back and jumped into my seat. Andrew hit the gas and we shot past them.

"I can't believe that worked!" I said, breathless but exhilarated.

Andrew tugged his hat down further on his head. "Yeah, should have thought of it sooner. Emus are notorious food stealers."

We made a few more turns down the road. Then there was a sign and the roof of a large building ahead.

"Here we are," Andrew said. "Welcome to Cooinda Lodge."

I had trouble sleeping that night. The lodge was quiet and clean, and for once we each had our own room. But the place was crowded, too, the main demographic being older ladies wearing hats and little pairs of binoculars around their necks. *Birdwatchers.* They were all loud, whether it was in the great room of the lodge or the hallway or even the room adjacent to mine. The real thing that messed with me was the time difference. We'd gained too many hours flying east from Antarctica to here, and now my body didn't think it was time for bed.

Worse than that, I hadn't been able to reach Summer since leaving Antarctica. I sent her a message about the Queensland contract and the Australian opportunity. I didn't so much put it as a choice about going to Australia, though technically it was. I told her the company wanted me to go and we were already down here and that it was important to strike while the iron was hot. Cooinda had a reliable network, so when I got here I checked my phone first thing. Nothing from Summer, but I had eight messages from my brother and two from my mom. All of them pretty much said I had to call home. I couldn't when we arrived, though—it was the middle of the night. I set my alarm for 7:00 AM, which would be about 2:00 in the afternoon the previous day in Phoenix. Yeah, the seventeen-hour time difference really broke my brain.

I woke up groggy to the sound of my alarm and threw open the curtains. The bright sunlight jabbed at my eyes and gave me a near-instant headache. I caught a glimpse in the mirror and confirmed that I did not look the greatest—my eyes had bags under them, and my hair was a disheveled mess. But my brother Connor had sent yet another message, so I logged in and initiated a call.

He answered on the first ring. "Well, well, well. N-tropy."

"C-lane," I said. It was early and I couldn't think of anything more creative for his first initial.

His video feed came in—and, as usual, the first thing I noticed was how much he looked like me. Same dark hair, same thin build, same nose and facial features. If we were the same age, we could have been twins. If it hadn't been for a single genetic difference that changed his life, at least. He'd been born with a rare mutation in a gene called bicaudal D-2—commonly known as BICD2—one that caused a progressive loss of muscle function. A few years ago he was on a major decline. Mom and I were talking about long-term care, and carefully avoiding the word *hospice*. It was only luck, timing, and a fair amount of subterfuge on my part that helped him qualify for a gene therapy trial. Now he was largely healthy, got around on his own, and was doing most of the things young men should. As best I could tell, back to normal. The last time I'd asked him about his muscle function, he'd told me to stop asking unless I wanted to get punched.

"Good to see you," I said.

"Where are you?"

"Queensland, Australia."

I didn't have to ask where he was; I knew the look of his home office. The steel desk was massive, and the ergonomic chair had cost a small fortune. Everything else was artfully blurred with a virtual background that flickered constantly, as if things were moving all around him. He wore a button-down shirt but I could only see him from the waist up and knew for an absolute fact that he had no pants on. *The endless benefits of working from home full-time.* He'd taken a gig with a civil engineering firm. The money was great and he worked in his pajamas. He was really living the dream.

"Dude, you look like hell."

I grimaced. "Give me a break, it's seven in the morning here."

"Where the hell have you been?"

"Several islands in Antarctica and then the outback. Connections here are crap," I said. "What's going on? Is Mom all right?"

"Yeah, she's fine as she can be. But we have a bit of a situation here."

"What is it?"

"Here, let me turn off the virtual background." He did so, and the visual of the clean spaceship cockpit disappeared to be replaced with his messy office. Which was, quite literally, *crawling* with dragons. Nero was perched on a shelf, chewing an athletic sock. Octavius had the other end and was trying to tug it free. A little scaly bundle that could only be Marcus Aurelius was curled up in a ball, sleeping on the corner of Connor's desk.

"What are my dragons doing there?"

"Summer dropped them off at Mom's house."

"What?"

"Yesterday morning. Mom called me right after because they started destroying the house." He glanced behind him as Octavius and Nero lost their balance and fell, dislodging several books as they fought on the way down. "I guess she thought they'd be better behaved here or something."

"How was she? Did Mom say?" I dreaded the answer.

"I don't know, pissed? Mom said she didn't say much."

"Oh, God." I rubbed my eyes, willing this to be a bad dream from which I'd wake up. Even if that meant I'd be on the goddamn boat again. "This is not good."

"No, it's not. What the hell is going on?"

I explained about our arguments before the trip, and then our fight, and then the radio silence. "I knew this extra trip was pushing it. But it's Australia, man. I had to take the chance."

He shrugged, as if to say *You made your choice, man*. "I'm not an expert but when your girlfriend won't answer your calls and dumps your pets off at your mom's house, that's a pretty clear message."

"Ugh." Part of me wanted to say *she's crazy* but that was ungenerous and also not true. She'd only agreed to look after the dragons for two weeks. She never signed on to be their permanent guardians or anything. *I should have thought of this and asked Connor to take them a week ago.* It was a simple, stupid missed opportunity. And it was way too late for that now. My head was pounding and now my stomach hurt. "I don't know what to do."

"Dude, *come home.*"

"I can't leave right away. We just got here, and we have to—"

"Yeah, yeah. You have to do something dragon-related for your dragon company or else dragons will cease to exist. I know, man."

I sighed. "Okay, you made your point. Do you think you can look after the dragons for a while?"

Connor had a resigned look on his face. "Sure. But seriously man, come home."

Marcus Aurelius had roused at the sound of my voice and now ventured forward to poke at Connor's screen with his claws.

"Marcus Aurelius!" I said in my firm dad-disciplinary tone.

He jumped back, hissing. Then he turned around like a dog would before sleeping, put his back to me, and went to sleep again.

"Where's Timur?" That was his dragon, the one I'd given him after the gene therapy trial.

"Hiding. He didn't get a lot of sleep last night, and his cousins are...a lot."

"I'll be home as soon as I can. Tell Mom, will you?"

"She wants you to call her."

"Tell her my tablet died."

"*You* tell her."

"Fine. But you owe me."

"I know." I disconnected. *What a disaster.* Well, I couldn't fix any of that until we got the job done here. I got dressed and found Tom in the huge two-story, wood-paneled dining room. They'd really gone for the lodge experience, complete with dark wood furnishings and various taxidermy-preserved animals decorating the walls. There were antlered deer, wild cats, and some kind of massive buffalo, all similar to North American species but somehow different at the same time. They had birds, too, preserved in flight positions and dangling fancifully from thin wires that ran down from the ceiling. A large group of birdwatchers in bright clothing occupied a table on the far side of the dining room, their boisterous conversation carrying across to us. Tom sat as far away from them as possible, against the near wall. He was eating a massive bowl of hot oatmeal.

"Hey," I told him.

He glanced up at me. "Rough night?"

"Yeah. Couldn't fall asleep to save my life."

"Bummer. I nodded off but woke up two hours ago, raring to go."

"How's the oatmeal?"

"Really good. You'd like it." He caught the attention of a waiter who'd fled from the birdwatcher table, and signaled at him to bring another bowl of oatmeal. I was glad for that. After the long restless night, I didn't have a lot of energy for forced cheerful conversations with strangers.

"Glad you're up, though. Andrew's already on his way over."

"Over from where?" I asked.

Tom grinned. "You know where."

I pointed at him. "Don't say it. Do *not* say it."

"From the marina!"

I groaned.

The boat was twenty feet long and metal, with open sides. Andrew insisted that this was the best way to scout the park for signs of dragon activity.

"It's also the best way—" I caught myself ahead of a snippy remark, and didn't finish. Andrew was excited about our little mission, and he'd brought a thermos of coffee. I couldn't fault the guy. He'd changed into tan khakis and a button-down shirt, but kept the same wide-brimmed hat. At any minute I expected him to start pretending to shave with a large boot knife.

It had rained overnight but the sky was mostly clear now, with most clouds pushing off to the west. The sun was halfway above the horizon and painted half the sky in pink and red. It was a beautiful morning. I just wished I wasn't so damn tired.

Once Tom and I were settled, Andrew nosed the boat away from the lodge's private pier and pushed us out into the river. The motor hummed quietly. It must be electric. The water was smooth as glass. If the conditions stayed like this, I might keep my oatmeal down.

Tom and I had binoculars, and swept the shoreline while Andrew drove. He was giving us the tour guide experience, explaining the history of the park while he piloted upstream.

"We're in the middle of the wet season now, which is the best time to visit," he said. "This park draws migratory birds from all over the southern hemisphere."

"Are we in cane-toad territory now?" I asked.

"Should be. This time of morning, we might hear them calling one another. It's mating season, after all."

A massive cigar-shaped fish leapt and splashed loudly near the boat, startling me.

"Big one," Andrew remarked. He steered us closer to the shore.

The birds were hard to miss. We saw egrets wading the shoreline, hunting for their breakfast. There was a heron with gray wings and a white head stalking nearby as well. A few minutes later we disturbed a small flock of red-faced geese of some kind. They honked their annoyance and pushed out into the current to move away from us. Andrew slowed the boat to point out a royal spoonbill, which had a white body and a comically long black beak. We watched it catch a fish from the reeds. It seemed to sense the attention and flew away downstream, the fish still struggling in its mouth.

I saw something with my binoculars along the shoreline. It was mostly in the water but not moving, its scales gray and tan. That matched the description Evelyn had given us. I grabbed Tom's shoulder and pointed.

"I see it," he said grimly. "Andrew, can you take us over there?"

"Sure thing, mate." He slowed the motor as we neared the shoreline. Tom found a wooden paddle beneath the ship's gunwale and positioned himself along the nearside hull. We drifted up alongside it. The boat was a little unsteady so I had to stay on the far side to balance Tom's weight. That's what I told myself, anyway. He reached out with the paddle and lifted the thing up out of the water. It hadn't moved, and it was floating.

"Poor bugger," Andrew said.

I couldn't take the suspense anymore. "Well?"

Tom moved his body and lifted the paddle higher so I could see the limp creature draped across it. It had a long head, lizard-like body, and long slender tail. The color was right but the body shape looked wrong. It was smaller than it should have been, too.

"It's a Mitchell's water monitor," Tom said. He brought the paddle closer and inspected the limp body from multiple sides. I could see now that it looked more like a lizard than a dragon, and had a little round black spot on the side of its head. It should have relieved me that this wasn't a dead dragon.

"How did it die?" I asked.

"No signs of external trauma," Tom said. "Based on the stomach girth, it ate recently."

"I can tell you what it ate," Andrew said.

"Cane toad?" Tom asked.

"S'right."

Tom set the thing back in the water gently and stowed his paddle again. "Let's keep going."

We rounded another bend in the river. I'd caught a flash of movement on the shore behind us and tried to find the source, but it was another bird of some kind, a bright blue little guy with an orange belly and a long curved beak. I was about to ask Andrew what kind of bird it was when Tom spoke softly. "There."

I looked at him and saw the way he was pointing. Ahead on the shoreline. I pulled up my binoculars and there they were. Two large reptiles. Bigger than the monitor had been, and stockier of build. They were built like lizards but moved with a sinuous grace, almost like serpents. Andrew slowed down to match their pace as they stalked upstream.

"Is that them? The dragons?" he whispered, his tone almost reverent.

"Yes."

"They're beautiful."

I don't know why, but that made me well with pride. "They sure are."

The dragons had light brown coloring with black spots. They moved in tandem along the sandy shoreline, their snouts low to the water. Pink tongues flicked in and out.

"They look healthy," Tom said, his eyes glued to his binoculars. "Definitely been getting their calories."

The dragons froze in place, almost as if they'd heard this remark and taken offense to it. The one in front scampered up higher on to the shoreline. It was after something. It pounced and covered something with its front claws. Then the snout lowered, teeth flashed.

"That was a toad!" Tom said.

It had all happened so fast. "Are you sure?"

"Definitely. Round amphibian, short hop, and the coloring was right."

A moment later, the dragons caught another toad. This one we got a better look at. The dragon pounced with its claws again, then clamped the prey in its teeth and swung its head back, flipping the hapless creature over its shoulder. The second dragon lunged and caught it before it hit the water.

"That was a cane toad for sure. A fat one," Tom said.

"Did you see that, how it shared with the second dragon?" Andrew asked.

"Yeah," I said.

"Cooperative hunting," Tom said. "It's a pack instinct in some animals, but seems to have come out with our pest control models."

Andrew shook his head. "What'll they think of next?"

We shadowed the dragons as they continued their hunt. They caught something else that looked more like a frog to Tom. They rooted something out of a log that proved to be a long black snake with a red underside. The dragons were curious about it, but let it slither away.

"Red-bellied blacksnake," Tom said.

"Good thing they let it go, then," Andrew said.

"Are they venomous?" I asked.

"Yes, but they don't attack unless provoked." Tom put down his binoculars and looked at me. "If you provoke one, you'll know. They rear up and flatten their necks like cobras." He delivered this as if it were a fun fact rather than something that would haunt my dreams.

We followed the dragons for over an hour. They caught at least four more things that Tom confirmed as the target species. The best part was when we came upon one of the tour boats filled with birdwatchers. It was heading downstream and loaded with older couples, most of whom were using binoculars. They all seemed to catch sight of the dragons at the same time, and several of them actually screamed. Tom and I about died laughing.

This was right around when the dragons took notice of us following them. Their pace increased. They clocked us over their shoulders a few times, and seemed hesitant to stop, even to pursue prey. Eventually they broke away from the river and disappeared into the forest. I was sad to see them go, but I'd gotten some excellent photos and videos on my phone. *My friends at Build-A-Dragon will want to see those.* The best part was that we might even be back near some high-speed internet soon. I could think about sending media files without spending a fortune.

"How fast do the toxins in cane toads work?" I asked, as Andrew drove us back downstream.

"Quick," Tom said. "Usually less than an hour."

"I'm not the expert, but those dragons looked pretty good to me."

Tom gave a nod. "They were." He grinned. "And I *am* the expert."

"Evelyn will be thrilled."

"So will the Australian government," Andrew said.

"Has your group come up with a name for this model yet?" Tom asked me.

"They floated one possibility," I said, fighting to keep my face neutral. "The *Toad-wong*."

Tom laughed. "That does not surprise me."

CHAPTER THIRTY
The Birder

We got back to Coiinda Lodge and I was glad to have a private room with an actual shower. Andrew had advised us not only to wash off but to check ourselves for leeches and "bite-me" bugs. I didn't know what those were but said I'd look. As best I could tell, I was parasite free. I was also thinner and more tan, which was weird to notice. I'd charged all of my devices while I was gone—electricity was free here and it wasn't like I could use them out in the bush—and my tablet showed a new message.

I saw Summer's name and my heart skipped a beat. I pawed at the screen but couldn't get it to unlock. The biometric unlock kept telling me it was NOT RECOGNIZED. I tried repositioning my thumb two different ways. Then it informed me there was a "cooldown period" before I could try again.

"Open up, you son of a bitch!" I shouted.

A green check mark appeared, along with the message VOICE RECOGNIZED. It unlocked and I pulled up my messages.

Summer had sent it two hours ago, 4:00 PM local time, 11:00 PM the previous night back in Phoenix. There was no subject line, and the message was short.

I'm taking the job in San Francisco.
~Summer

Oh God, no. I sank onto my bed, clutching the tablet with white knuckles. Connor was right. Hell, maybe Summer had said something to Mom and he didn't want to be the one to tell me. This was a breakup. No, it was worse. She was leaving me *and* Phoenix. I really wanted to call her, but it was the middle of the night in Phoenix. Besides, what was I going to say? *No, don't leave, and also don't break up with me?* I knew she was mad at me, but I never thought it would go this far. Connor was right about another thing. I'd been away from home too long.

I hurried downstairs to the great room. To my surprise, I found Tom ensconced in a large group of ten or twelve birdwatchers. All were women, and not one was under sixty years old.

"So I woke up in the middle of the night, and I could *hear* it."

"No!" a woman said.

"Yes, plain as day."

"Was it a male or a female?"

Tom smiled. "You tell me. It sounded like this." He made a high-pitched, trilling whistle.

The birdwatchers squealed in delight and then applauded. "Female! Female!" they shouted.

I knew I was staring, but I couldn't help it. I couldn't recall Tom ever speaking to more than three people at a time, let alone a table full of old ladies. They were sitting around him, too, as if he were a game show host and they the hopeful contestants.

"Well, I couldn't go back to sleep," Tom said. "For all I knew, it would continue its migration in the morning. Luckily, I still had my infrared lens and my camera in the tent. There was only one problem." He leaned back in his chair, drawing out the suspense. "I didn't have any clothes on."

The ladies roared with laughter. I chuckled myself.

"What did you do? Did you get it?" A woman asked.

"You can bet your ass I got it!" Tom held up his phone and showed them the photo of what, to me, looked like a pretty standard bird. Everyone cheered. He handed his phone to the woman on his right. They passed it around, murmuring appreciatively. That seemed like a good opportunity for me to slide in.

"Morning, Tom," I said. "Sorry to interrupt."

"It's fine," he said. "I was just telling these fine ladies about my trip to Burma a few years ago."

"Can I have a word?"

"Sure. Let's get some chow."

The ache in my belly made the idea of eating seem impossible, but I nodded and followed him over to the buffet area. The spread here was impressive—at least eight or nine wide metal chargers piled high with eggs, bacon, sausage, biscuits, and pancakes, covered in metal cloches to keep the foot piping hot. The mixed aroma of savory meats and maple syrup reached outside. Beyond that was the mango bar. It had bananas and pears and several fruits I didn't recognize, but everyone called it the mango bar. After that came the pastry table, and then the tea table. There was coffee as well, brewed strong and served practically boiling. My stomach rolled at the thought of that, so I went for English breakfast tea instead.

The teacups were made of a pale blue unglazed stoneware decorated with bright white flowers and trees. They looked like something out of *Antiques Road Show*. I was hesitant to use one but it was the only teacup offered, and everyone else with tea was using them. *If I break this it's going to cost a fortune*, I thought, but when I picked one up it felt solid. Not heavy, but strong. The bottom was imprinted in block letters: WEDGWOOD. MADE IN ENGLAND.

I found a small table and sat down to let it steep. Tom joined a moment later, his plate piled high with bacon and eggs.

He took note of my teacup and saucer, which was the only thing I'd taken. "You're not eating?"

I glanced at his food, suppressed a wave of nausea, and shook my head. "Not hungry."

"You look like you went on a bender last night."

"Thanks," I said dryly. The tea was too hot to drink, but I held it underneath my face and inhaled. The warm, rough porcelain felt reassuring. I blew on it.

"Andrew has a morning gig, but I asked if he can get us a seaplane for later." Tom bit into a round sausage, chewed, and took a swig of coffee. "Thought I'd show you some of the outback. We can fly out to one of the billabongs deep in the park. See if any dragons are hanging out with the crocs."

It sounded like a kick-ass adventure, but I'd already made up my mind. "I have to go back to Phoenix."

"When?"

"Right away. Now, if I can. There's an afternoon flight out of Darwin International."

"Did something happen?"

I sighed. "It's a long story. But I gotta get back." I had no idea how I'd get from the lodge to the nearest town, or from there to Darwin. But I had to leave soon if I was going to make it.

He looked at my face and seemed to understand. "Give me a sec." He got up and retrieved his phone from the birdwatchers, who were still fawning over it. By the time he got back to the table, he was already dialing.

"Andrew. Tom. Yeah, good. Change of plans. Parker has to shoot through. Can we borrow the rumbler?" He listened for a moment. "Bonzer. Thanks, mate. Hooroo."

I had no idea what most of it meant. He might as well have been talking in Swahili.

He hung up and grabbed a fistful of bacon from his plate. "Get your gear. I'll drive you to Darwin."

In less than ten minutes, we were rumbling east on Highway 21 in Andrew's truck. He'd left it in the car park of the lodge. By the time I got back downstairs, Tom already had the keys. I'd managed to slurp down half of my tea. The woman at the front desk was incredibly friendly, didn't mind the early checkout, and insisted that I take some mangoes for the road.

We were driving on the left side of the highway, which was more than a little unnerving. Even with Tom on the side closest to the center line. *Thank God I didn't try to rent a car.* Almost everything was a two-lane road with no shoulder. I knew I should eat something even though I wasn't hungry. I opened the glove box and almost wasn't surprised to find several well-used knives in leather sheaths. *Straight out of the movie.* I used the cleanest-looking one to slice a mango in half. It was perfectly ripe and surprisingly sweet, with a flavor like a zesty peach.

"You've got to try one of these."

He took the other half and bit into it. "Damn, that's good."

We split two more. They left my hands and lips sticky, but were hands-down some of the best fruits I'd ever eaten. I cleaned the knife and stowed it away in the glove box.

Tom glanced sidelong at me. "You've got a bit more color in your cheeks. Feel better?"

My stomach had settled down, the sharp ache giving way to a vague unease. "Yeah. A little."

He drove on in silence for a minute. There was virtually no traffic. A canopy of trees scrolled by on both sides, broken occasionally by rocky, grass-covered ridges.

"Are you married?" I asked.

He shook his head. "Used to be, a while back."

"Any kids?"

"No. I was traveling three hundred and fifty days a year. We didn't last too long."

"Oh," I said. That meant it had been some time. "Sorry."

He nodded and glanced at me. "Girl troubles?"

I laughed but without humor. "How did you know?"

"You don't have much of a poker face."

"Trust me, I know."

"So, what happened?"

I sighed and looked out the window. "My girlfriend told me she's moving to take another job."

"Far away?" he asked.

"San Francisco."

"She want you to go with her?"

"I don't think so. She dropped off all my dr—" I caught myself. "Er, my stuff, at my mom's place."

"Ouch."

"Yeah."

"How long were you seeing her?"

"Over a year, but I knew her back when we were in college. We used to hate each other back then."

"Yeah?"

"I was dating her roommate, Jane. It was...sort of a toxic relationship. Summer and I clashed constantly."

"Summer's her name, eh? I like that," he said.

"Oh, it fits her so well."

"Go on."

"We were like oil and water back then." I remembered some of those interactions. The face she used to make when I'd show up at the door used to bring me to an instant boil. I'd been under so much stress then, too. That's what I told myself. In retrospect, it was small-time stress. Grad school stuff. I shook my head. "I said the meanest things about her. And to her."

"What did Jane think of all this?"

"I don't know. She was a little chemically imbalanced." She never defended Summer, now that I thought about it. She always had this little smile. "She might have even encouraged it."

"An insecure female will encourage hostility between her mate and a possible rival," Tom said in his nature-show voice.

"Heh. Maybe that was the problem," I said.

"Not entirely your fault."

I heard the way he hit the word *entirely*. "True, but I was kind of an ass back then."

He grinned. "Yeah, back then."

I had to laugh. "Hey, man, screw you."

"So you pulled a roommate switch?"

"Oh, no. It wasn't really like that. We all went our separate ways. Around the time I got the job at Reptilian, I met her when I was out geocaching."

"Oh yeah, your little hobby. I remember."

"I didn't know it then but she was my rival on the scoreboards." I told him about the real-time scoring system where I'd jostled for the top spot against her nerdy username, SumNumberOne.

"Sort of a ranking system for nerds," he said.

"Hey! It's not nerdy. It's usually outdoors."

"And what was your username?"

"NPdesign."

"I see." He nodded with mock seriousness. "My mistake."

"It was going really good. We were sharing time with the, er... between our condos."

"You don't live together, then."

"Almost. I mean, we both have places in Scottsdale. Different buildings. Her firm designed both of them, though."

"Sure. That counts as living together."

I ignored his sarcastic tone. "I get busy a lot, and so does she. Sometimes we'd go four or five days without seeing each other. She said I wasn't making an effort."

"Sounds like she was right."

Whose side are you on? It might be the truth but I didn't need it thrown in my face. "*Anyway*, she had this big successful project at work and got a call from a recruiter."

He made a face like he'd tasted something bitter. "I hate those guys."

"Me too."

"They're always trying to corner you on the phone and explain how tagging hippos in the wild would be 'good for your career.'" He snorted. "I'd like to see them try to poking fifteen-hundred-kilo breeding males with sharp objects. Sure, bud. Let me know how *that* goes."

"Uh, wow." *We seem to have stuck a nerve here.*

"Then there's the ones who try to get you to trap exotic animals. Not for science, but for fat old millionaires to shoot at with high-powered rifles." He rubbed the back of his neck as if this topic had given him a tension headache. "Sorry, go on."

"Okay, but let's come back to that. Anyway, we had a fight about the recruiter." I remembered our talk about that, which had become a tangent of how recruiters were such bottom-feeders. "I guess I was kind of negative about it. And I didn't even know the job was in San Francisco."

"When was this?"

"I don't know, a month ago? Before we left. I didn't like the thought of her changing jobs, and she didn't want me going to Antarctica."

"Ah."

"She said I could die."

"In fairness, you almost did."

"You're a great listener, you know that?"

He held up his hand and clamped his mouth shut.

"When we extended to go to Australia she went radio silent."

He frowned. "You didn't have to go."

"I know, but it was Australia. Once in a lifetime, you know?"

"Parker, I've been down under more times than I can count."

I rolled my eyes. "Okay, fine, it's once in a lifetime for *normal* people."

"I'm perfectly normal. Just an ordinary guy."

What happened next could not have had better timing if we planned it. As we approached a digital billboard, its display changed to an ad for *Tom's Wild World* with a huge photo of Tom Johnson grinning and giving the camera a thumbs-up. The sign informed us in huge red letters that It's Dingo Season!

I laughed so, so hard. It took me a while to catch my breath. "You know what? You're right. You are *perfectly* ordinary."

"That was unfortunate timing," Tom admitted.

"It *was* a big deal for me to come here, even though I have to leave. But I think it was the final straw. The thing is, I don't know if our fight was about the travel, the dragons, the lack of communication—"

"What dragons?"

Whoops. "Oh, you know, the designs we had to do for the locusts and then the Antarctica model. They gave me some late nights. It could be one of those things or any of them."

"I've studied animals of every shape and size, all over the world," Tom said. "Not one of them is as hard to understand as a woman."

Well, that's reassuring. "I thought I did. At least, I thought we were happy with things."

"You ever see a California newt?"

This question seemed to come out of nowhere. "A what?"

"California newt. Reddish brown amphibian, looks a lot like a salamander."

"No... though I'm not sure I'd recognize one even if I saw it."

"They're shy. You wouldn't just bump into one unless you went looking. They always return to the place they were born to breed. Even if they get swept ten miles down a river, or carried across state lines with a load of lumber. After a lot of research, herpetologists determined that they achieve it by celestial navigation."

"Wow, that's cool." Amphibians using the stars to get around was my new favorite thing I wanted to see on one of Tom's nature shows.

"It is, isn't it? And it fit what we knew already, that the newts were nocturnal, they preferred open areas, and they had an outstanding sense of direction."

"You convinced me," I said.

"Exactly. But here's the problem. Some California newts go blind. It's a retinal degeneration thing, don't ask me the specifics. But those blind newts found their breeding grounds, too. So did newts that were confined during the night and not allowed to travel during the day."

"How did they find their way, then?"

"Magnetic fields, but that isn't the point," he said.

"All right, what *is* the point?"

"Just that even smart people who think they have the answers can be mistaken. We're wired to find patterns in a chaotic world. Sometimes we see a pattern that fits the available data, and we get to the wrong conclusion. Because we're missing something. Sometimes that's a subtle detail, but I've found that when we jumped to the wrong answer at times, we'd overlooked some fundamental principle."

Maybe I was missing something. I played back the recent fights Summer and I had had. They were all different, but I supposed there were common threads. A lot of the hot-button topics were indirectly about the future. Or, more accurately, my apparent disregard for the future. I couldn't quite put my finger on what that meant, but it was clear that I was playing the cards I held—my job, my interests, my long term goals—and I hadn't given much thought to the cards Summer was holding. Yes, this was something, but thinking along those lines hurt. "It doesn't matter anyway. I made my choices, and she made hers. Understanding is useful, I guess, but it doesn't change the crappy situation." And it *was* a crappy situation. I should have been rushing home to hug her and pet our dragonets and enjoy some time telling the stories to my family. Instead they were all pissed and the dragons were homeless. All because I was selfish, and didn't really think two moves ahead for the people that mattered to me.

Tom drove on and seemed to be pondering something. "I'm going to tell you another story."

Oh God, another *story*. I didn't mind the entertainment but he'd made his goddamn point. "If this is about some turtle that got hit by a car, and managed to survive or something—"

He waved me off. "It's not about an animal. You have my word."

"Fine." *This ought to be good.*

"About twenty years ago, I knew this kid. Young guy, smart and ambitious, like you. Lucky, too, because he met a girl. A great girl. They fell in love and got married pretty young. They were pretty much broke, but they were on cloud nine anyway. They spent every minute together they could. They're talking about starting a family. Then his career starts to take off, which means he's got to travel."

"Sounds vaguely familiar," I said.

"Then you can probably guess where it goes. They put the family plans on hold. Whenever she brings it up, he tells her they'll talk about it after his next trip. They start having rows about little things. Like the family events he misses when he's away, and how he always comes back with a month's worth of dirty laundry. He thinks these little things are what bother her. That they still see eye to eye on waiting before they put down roots. When she keeps bringing it up, he thinks it's because she doesn't support him or his career. Which means it's all on him, so he doubles down on the trips and the risks. But guess what?"

"He was wrong about something?" I asked.

He snorted. "Well, yeah, or it wouldn't make a cautionary tale. See, his wife's mother died young. He knew that worried her, but he didn't realize that she was expecting to die young as well. So he thinks they have ten, fifteen years to have kids and a lifetime to raise them. But she doesn't. She's a planner, and the way she sees it, waiting ten years means that she'll leave him a widower with little kids to raise on his own. So she ends it. She tells him they aren't meant to be. That she met someone else, a guy who wants kids right now. It crushes him. He blames her for finding someone else, and he blames himself for not seeing this coming. But he knows the ship has sailed, so it doesn't matter."

I felt for him, because it was a sad story. Sure, his career had worked out—and maybe doing what he'd done was the only way to make that happen—but it came with a cost. And I could tell the debt of it still weighed on him. "That's too bad, man. Seriously."

"Wrong."

"What?" Now I was confused.

"He was wrong *again*."

"How? They split up and she moved on. It happens."

"He *thought* she moved on because that's what she said. So, he threw in the towel and said screw it, at least now I can focus on my career. He signed the papers and cut off all contact. Didn't try to reconcile. Thought it would only make things harder for both of them. But here's the kicker: she hadn't met someone else. All she wanted was for him to come home, and stay for a little while, so they could try to have a baby and *start* that part of their lives. She thought filing for divorce was the only way to get him to be serious and follow her timeline."

"That's terrible," I said.

He nodded. "She waited for him, too. Longer than she had to, longer than she'd promised herself she could afford to wait. If he had gone to her and said *Look, let's try to work this out*... they probably would have found a way to. But he cut his losses and moved on."

"Did she?" I knew I shouldn't ask, but I had to. And I knew he'd know.

"Eventually. Five years later, she met a guy. An accountant with a good job, a nine-to-fiver, and they got married. They had a couple of little girls, I think."

I took a breath. "So she got her happy ending, at least. She was wrong about thinking she'd die young."

"Nah, she wasn't. When her oldest was in kindergarten, she found a lump. Breast cancer, just like her mom had. Stage four. She died a couple of years later, on her mom's birthday."

"What the *hell*, Tom?" I shouted.

He glanced at me, alarmed. "What's wrong?"

"This is a terrible story!" My mind was reeling with the chilling end to it, the thought of those two little girls growing up with just their dad. *Oh, hell no.*

He only shrugged. "I never said there was a happy ending."

"I'm sorry, but that's messed up. This is, like, the worst inspirational talk in the history of time."

"I'm just making conversation."

"Sheesh." I shook my head. "Now I feel even worse."

"Look. Noah. You care about this girl, right?"

He called me Noah. For the first time that I could remember. "I do."

"Are you willing to get off your ass and try to make amends?"

"Like I said, I would except—"

He held up his hand. "Are you willing to try?"

I bit my lip. "Yeah. Of course."

"Then you gotta see this through. Don't make the mistake I did. Don't go quietly."

"I will." I didn't know how, nor could I so much as guess what her reaction would be. "It's a little terrifying, but I will."

He gave me a sympathetic smile. "There's a lot of scary things in this world. Not all of 'em have scales."

Soon after we pulled into the Darwin International Airport and the drop-off area. Thanks to Tom's quick thinking and heavy foot, I had an hour and forty-five minutes before my flight left. He found a parking spot and got out to help me retrieve my bag. I'd thrown everything into my duffel with zero organization, which was going to be fun when it came time to go through security.

"Thanks for the ride, Tom."

"You bet." He offered his hand, which I shook. His grip was strong, and his hand calloused like a carpenter's. "I don't mind telling you, you did all right on this trip. For an egghead."

I laughed. "You know what? I'll take it. This was a hell of an adventure."

"Listen up. This is important," Tom said. "Do you know how to drive a manual transmission?"

"Of course," I said. Summer's Jeep had one and she let me drive it sometimes. *Used to let me,* I corrected myself.

"Good. Take this." He fished something out of his pocket and handed it to me. It was a key fob with an actual metal key attached. A machine-cut key, no less. "Bessie will get you home."

"Who's Bessie?"

"My truck."

He climbed back into the driver's seat, then turned back to look at me. "I'll be back myself in ten days. I expect you'll treat her like the queen she is."

I didn't know if he meant the truck or Summer, but the answer was the same. I saluted. "Yes, sir."

CHAPTER THIRTY-ONE
The Homecoming

Twenty-four hours. That was how long it took to get from Darwin back to Phoenix, thanks to stops at Brisbane and Los Angeles. Twenty-seven if you counted the amount of time I spent going through customs, where I was "randomly selected" for additional screening and invited to a small, windowless room. There, I had to answer questions about how and why I'd gone to Antarctica, why I'd visited Australia for such a short time, and what I was planning to do with the strange metal weapon that they'd found in my duffel bag.

"What weapon?" I had asked, wondering if I'd somehow ended up with one of Tom's knives in my bag. Or one of Andrew's. It was like they were in some unspoken contest to see who could carry the most large blades.

The customs agent was a big black guy who introduced himself as Carl and shook my hand. He had a super-deep voice and the *I'm-your-friend-here* tone that told me I was possibly in serious trouble. "I don't know, man. You tell me." He leaned forward and put his elbows on the table. "Let's just run through the list of all the weapons you've got."

Nice try. I'd seen way too many police procedurals to fall for an open-ended question. "I don't have any."

"You don't have any?"

"Not that I know of."

He looked down at the table and shook his head, as if in disbelief. "I'm trying to help you here. But I can't help you if you're not honest with me."

I rubbed my eyes, which hurt like hell and were probably bloodshot. *Not helping my case, that's for sure.* "I didn't bring any weapons, so let's just fast-forward to the part where you tell me what this is about."

He got up and knocked on the door, which opened wide enough for someone to hand him a large bundle that I recognized as my snowsuit. He brought it to the table, unrolled it, and Rousseau's ice axe clanged to the tabletop. "*This* is what it's about."

I sagged with relief. "That's an ice axe." I'd totally forgotten about it since Australia.

"So you admit that it's an axe."

"Yeah, but it's a tool for mountain climbing. Kind of like an ice pick, but bigger?" I touched the end of the spike, which caused him to clamp a hand down on the shaft of the axe. I guess to make sure that I didn't use it to murder him. *No sudden moves,* I told myself. "You swing this end into the ice. You hold it by the handle, and you can also hold on to the shaft like you're doing if you're going to slip." I leaned back away from the table and looked him in the eye. "That thing saved my life."

"How?"

I told him the story of the glacier climb and the crevasse that had almost swallowed us.

"That's a wild story, Mr. Parker. But it doesn't change the fact that this *looks* dangerous."

"No more than a shovel." A flash of inspiration came. "And I can prove it. Look at the inside of the shaft under your hand. There's some etched lettering."

He looked dubious but lifted the axe and squinted. "Made in... France."

I smiled. "When's the last time the French made a dangerous weapon?"

I cleared customs ten minutes later.

Driving Tom's truck was an adventure. The clutch was heavy and the gears groaned any time I shifted, but I eventually learned to ignore that. It felt like I was driving a big rig, so I took it extra slow. By the time I reached my condo, it was almost midnight, but somehow the same day I'd left. Thursday. I was too tired to do the math. I'd hardly slept at all on the planes—I was too busy figuring out my next moves.

I set my alarm to get up early. I was going to work tomorrow to put my plans in action.

I dragged myself out of bed and managed to get into work a few minutes early like I'd hoped. I wasn't brave enough to navigate Build-A-Dragon's narrow parking garage in Tom's massive truck, so I took my own car. It was much less stressful but also felt strange. I hadn't driven anything the whole time we were gone.

The entrance to Build-A-Dragon HQ had started to lose its mystique the longer I worked there, but I forced myself to enjoy the moment of hauling the heavy door open. The wash of cool air carried the faint smell of metal and silicon. I stepped inside and glanced at the murals that decorated the ceiling. They were the thing that first struck me when I'd come to interview here, the vividly painted scenes of our dragon in the wild. There was only one back then. Gradually, the murals changed along with our business, the single model making room for the Rover, the Harrier, and all of our various pet lines. More recently, a new mural on the south part of the ceiling showed our dragons running beside soldiers in fatigues. It had taken forever to get that done—probably because Evelyn had asked her DOD contacts for their blessing. So I was surprised to see yet another addition to the ceiling. The color contrast drew my eye to it: dark gray mountains capped with pure white snow. Then white again, the glacier, and the black forms of hundreds of penguins. They were all clumped together, the way we'd seen them in the big colony off of Deception Island. All that was background. In the foreground, two of our ice dragons crouched in a defensive stance, their knees bent, wings spread wide. They bared their teeth at a handful of rats. Behind them were the penguins on their nests, looking appropriately fearful. A third dragon was off to the side, clutching a dead rat in its jaws. The scene was so vivid, for a moment I felt like I was back there. They must have had Tom's camera footage or something.

I took the elevator to the seventh floor, Design & Hatchery, and took the shortcut though the latter to our area. Bright sunlight shone through the window of every single incubator pod. They were all active, their status screens indicating full capacity. It gave me a thrill to see that. *Business is up again.*

Korrapati and Dave stood by Wong's desk in the design lab, either waiting for me or taking part in some kind of morning ritual. They lit up when I came in.

"Noah!" Korrapati hugged me.

"Hey, guys!" I shook Dave's hand as well as Wong's. "God, it's good to see you." I hadn't realized how much I missed these interactions every day.

"We didn't know if you'd be in today," Korrapati said.

"Yes, we think Noah Parker sleeps five, seven days after so many travels," Wong said.

"Some of us were betting you wouldn't be in until Monday." Dave smiled at me, then looked at Korrapati.

"That's right, somebody owes me five bucks," she told him. "Well, I'll add it to your tab."

Something is going on there, I thought, but decided it wasn't my business. "Yeah, I'm jet-lagged as hell but I had to come. Guys, outstanding work on the cane-toad dragon."

"Oh, you got there in time?" Korrapati asked.

"Not for the hatching, but Tom and I saw them in action." I found my phone and played the video I'd taken of the dragons prowling the river bank hunting toads. Dave and Korrapati crowded closer.

"Ohhh," she said.

Even Wong rolled out his chair for a closer view. "Movement is good. Very good."

Dave watched with too-wide eyes, his mouth open. "It's one thing to see them in the simulator." He glanced at me. "No offense. But the real thing is just... incredible. Look!" He nudged Korrapati, pointing. "The tail's just right."

"I told you it would be."

"And the sinuous movement. Look at that!" Dave gushed.

Korrapati giggled. "I can see. I'm right here, too, you know."

"For what it's worth, Tom was impressed with their hunting tactics," I said.

"Tom? You were with Tom Johnson?" Dave asked.

"Yep. He was on the trip, too."

He grabbed my arm. "You were with him the whole time? How did I not know this?"

"He let me borrow his truck to drive home. It's hilarious. From another century."

"I haven't met him yet, and you're driving his truck." He sighed. "I'm such a fanboy of his animal shows."

"Oh my God, so is everyone, let me tell you." I regaled all of them with some of the adventures of traveling in the company of a world-famous herpetologist. They ate it up, of course. Then I asked how things had gone around the company while I was away, because I hadn't been keeping up. What they shared sounded good. Evelyn had landed two more contracts, one of which was from the state of Hawaii for an order of dragons for cane toads. The other was a new custom design request from, of all places, the Galápagos Islands. Apparently they had a feral cat problem. It sounded like we had enough design work and egg-printing orders to keep us busy for a while. All of it sounded good. *Apparently I help this place best by leaving.* I congratulated them all, then looked at Dave. "You have a minute? I want to ask you something."

"Sure."

He followed me down the hall. We made a pit stop at the coffee bar. The free, customizeable premium coffees were one of the best perks at Build-A-Dragon. I put in my order for a sugar-free vanilla latte. I'd forgotten my mug, so it 3D-printed one before brewing. The side had a gentle reminder to recycle the thing when I was done. Dave got a chai tea. They were both too hot to drink right away so we blew on them as we walked to my office. I took my chair and gestured for him to take the one across from it.

"So, how's it going?" I asked. "Regretting any of your life choices?"

He chuckled. "Nah, it's been great. Everyone around here is so talented. It's going well, I think."

"You can't argue with the results. The cane-toad dragon is a natural-born killer."

"I know." He furrowed his brow. "It's too soon to really evaluate the impact on the ecosystems, though. Last we heard, the dragons on King George Island were still colony-hopping along the coasts. Plenty of rats to go."

"Ugh." I remembered the smell of rat meat and shivered. "The sooner the better. Those rats are nasty."

"It sounds like Queensland is working out nicely," he said.

"Yeah, maybe. It'll take a while before we really know if the dragons make a difference. It's only a success if the predators that died off from bufotoxin poisoning can rebuild their populations."

He smiled, clearly amused, and looked down.

"What?" I didn't think I'd said anything funny.

"It's amazing how much you've changed, that's all. Once upon a time, Noah Parker would declare that the dragon got the job done and that's all that mattered."

That made me laugh. "Touché."

"I'm serious, though. You've grown so much from the old days. When we were forged together in the fires of grad school misery."

"Fires that could only be doused with a lot of alcohol," I mused.

"For what it's worth, I like Noah 2.0."

The compliment warmed me. "Well, as you might guess I wasn't exactly thrilled when the government insisted on so much scrutiny. But going on this trip and seeing the pristine environments where we wanted to release them ... I understand the reasoning now. We don't want to repeat the mistakes of the past generations."

"Like the cane-toad mistake," Dave said.

"Exactly. They saw a problem and they thought they knew what to do. Just throw another animal at the problem and don't worry about the risks." Which were many, of course, when you introduced an invasive species that produced a deadly poison. "It's good that we can help correct some of those mistakes."

"Well, since we're sharing, I didn't think creating customized dragons with genetic engineering would be so much fun."

"See, that's funny to me. I always assume people think my job is, like, the best job ever."

"I didn't before, but I get it now."

"So, you like it," I said.

He nodded. "So much."

"Do you think you'd like to stay? You know, longer term?"

"Well, I'm not sure." He took a sip of his tea, and I sensed he was choosing his words carefully. "I like the company and the day-to-day. I just didn't know how well you and I would work together."

"Because it feels a little awkward."

"Yes!" He looked immensely relieved. "I got this vibe like maybe you didn't want me here." He dropped his gaze to his feet. "Or, I don't know, that you didn't like me."

"Dude, of course I like you. Everyone likes Dave."

He shook his head. "Not true, man."

I tried my own coffee, mainly to figure out how to put my feeling into words. "Look, I know we talk about Dr. Sato's lab like it was mostly a positive experience, but that was a hard time for me. Emotionally, you know? I worked so hard to get a spot in his lab. So, once I was in there, I set unrealistically high standards for other lab candidates."

He nodded, still not looking at me.

"So, when we interviewed you, I thought you didn't have the right experience and I said so. Dr. Sato hired you, of course, and he was right to. But it made me feel like I had less value. But I figured I still had my skill sets and the benefit of more time in his lab. Then the next thing I know, you're my supervisor and I have to run things by you."

"That was just a formality. We all knew who was in charge."

I nodded. "Still, it was hard for me."

"It was hard for me, too," Dave said. "I was as surprised as anyone to get hired into the lab. And later, when Dr. Sato asked me to be the supervisor, I told him it was a terrible idea. I was too new and everyone would hate me. I said if he was going to put anyone in that position, it should be you."

For a second I didn't know what to say. "I... didn't know that." It wouldn't have mattered because once Dr. Sato made up his mind, he rarely changed it. But it gratified me a tiny bit. "You know, I think that my great struggle in life is I always think I deserve more than I probably do."

"It's not the worst flaw. The only other option is imposter syndrome, which is no joy, either."

"I've also been told that I focus more time on technical skills and not enough on people skills."

"You're kidding," he deadpanned.

"I know, hard to believe, right?" I made myself smile. "But on this trip, incredibly, none of my hard skills were very useful. Honestly, neither were Tom's. Yes, he stopped me from touching several venomous animals, but we had to do a lot of things outside our wheelhouse. When it came to that, he carried us both. Mostly because of his soft skills." I shook my head, still trying to grasp everything that had gained for us. "It's why we managed to deploy at three sites in as many weeks. He got help everywhere he went just by being good with people. It was so effective, I tried to do a bit of it myself." With much more limited results, but that was to be expected.

"It's not exactly a fair comparison. He's a celebrity," Dave said.

"Skills are skills. And I'm coming to appreciate the value of all types. I guess what I'm trying to say is that I'm sorry for not realizing that until now."

He smiled. "Apology accepted."

"And listen, I'm probably going to have to change some things. Take a step back from the trips to deploy the eggs, at the very least."

"For real? No more adventures."

"For a while. I hate to do it, but it's necessary. But I know Evelyn is going to want someone from Design to be there for the hatching."

"Yeah, you're probably right about that."

"I think that person should be you."

He started to protest, but I held up a hand. "No, let me finish. You've got the same training I did. The rest of it you can pick up along the way. Besides, you already have those people skills that I'm beginning to appreciate."

"I don't know, man. That has Sato lab fiasco repeat written all over it."

"You handled that well and we both know it. Besides, aren't you technically supposed to be monitoring environmental impacts as the EPA's expert?"

He groaned in a good-spirited way. "I knew that you'd find a way to use that against me."

"Come on, you like traveling, don't you?"

"Ooh, did you fly first class?"

"No, of course not."

"Oh, too bad."

"You're not really first-class material, though, are you?"

"Hey!"

"No offense, man, I'm not either. But these trips might have a perk you would enjoy. One-on-one time with Tom Johnson."

His eyes widened and he bit his lip. He forced himself to think it over, though probably not as long as he should have. "All right, I'm in."

CHAPTER THIRTY-TWO
Into the Wild

I slipped out of work early that afternoon. Everyone understood; I'd been traveling for more than a solid day with only one decent night's sleep. I didn't go home, though; I drove to Connor's house and banged on the door. After a couple of minutes, he jerked the door open.

"This better be imp—" He broke off and grinned. "N-carcerated!"

He was wearing a blue Oxford button-down shirt underneath a navy sport coat with brass buttons. And below the waist, he had on ratty green gym shorts.

I knew it. "C-me from the waist up."

"Ha! Yeah, you caught me." He leaned out and looked both up and down the street. "Matter of fact, come in quick. It's always possible a coworker will drive past."

I followed him inside to the front room, which he'd never kept particularly clean but had descended into dragonet-fueled chaos. Titus saw me first. He abandoned one of Connor's slippers, which he'd carried up to a high windowsill, and swooped down to clamp onto my shoulder.

"Hey, buddy. Ow! Watch the claws!"

Marcus Aurelius had curled up in a ball on the floor about six feet inside. It didn't make sense until Connor closed the front door, and the bright slash of sunlight from outside disappeared. Only a small rhombus appeared, from the sunlight streaming in the door's square window, and it shined right on the spot where the little dragonet was laying.

I nudged him with my foot. "You alive, little buddy?"

He snorted and rolled over like a dog trying to scratch its back, but didn't open his eyes. Still, he curled his tail around my leg. That was all I was likely to get. Marcus Aurelius was the runt, and he'd learned early that most of his brothers would leave him alone if he appeared to be asleep. The others had all swooped into the room, crawled out from under tables, or, in one case, tumbled down the stairs to land on top of Marcus Aurelius.

"They eating you out of house and home yet?"

"Um, yeah. I had to sign up for a meat delivery service. Seven days a week, man."

"Aw, you're good to your nephew-dragons."

Connor laughed. "I'm broke, that's what I am."

"Well, thanks. You seem to be taking it well."

He shrugged. "I just gave up living in anything but chaos."

"Yeah, that's what you have to do."

"Have you talked to her yet?" he asked.

I clamped my jaw shut so hard it hurt, and shook my head.

"Sorry, man, that sucks. Did you at least call Mom?"

I shook my head again.

"Man, you're behind the eight ball, aren't you?"

"Yeah, I know. That's why I'm here. I need to assemble my troops. Besides, you've done more than enough to take care of my—" I broke off because Octavius had not left his perch on the high shelf. He was quite awake but studiously not looking at me. "Octavius?"

No response.

"Hey, buddy. Down here." I snapped my fingers.

His ears twitched, but his head didn't move. Now I understood: he was mad at me for being gone so long. *Join the club, buddy.* "Octavius, I'm sorry. But I'm back now. You can come home."

He did turn his head to glance at me, but then looked away just as quickly.

"I'm here to stay now. No more long trips."

Another look and look-away.

"I have burritos in the car."

That, finally, got his attention. He took his sweet-ass time stretching slowly, but grudgingly swooped down to my other shoulder, and crooned something that sounded a lot like *let's go.*

We drove to Summer's condo. Something told me that she wouldn't answer if I called. If I managed to see her in person, maybe we'd talk. At the very least, I'd see her face when she saw me and that would probably tell me what I needed to know. Like me, Summer had no poker face. Plus, if it was really bad, she probably wouldn't kill me in front of the dragonets. They were all piled in the backseat, having gorged on burritos and then fallen asleep while I drove. It always happened. Full stomachs and the gentle whir of the electric motor were better than sleeping pills. Which I may or may not have tried in my early days of dragon ownership.

My plans were foiled when I reached Summer's condo. The first thing I saw was the FOR SALE sign outside her unit. I'd hoped it was a bluff, that maybe this was an elaborate trick to lure me home sooner than I might otherwise have come. The sign was bad enough, but the placard underneath it was worse. SOLD, it said.

How the hell is her condo sold already? I wondered, though in the back of my mind, I already knew. This was Scottsdale, the market was white-hot, and Summer lived in one of the most coveted buildings. I did, too, but hers was prime. It was a running joke in the northern 'burbs of Phoenix that you could always sell your house for a huge profit, but then you'd have to blow it by buying a new place.

My phone dinged with an update, and I checked it by instinct. It was an alert I usually ignored, a change in the geocache ranking. *Oh, please tell me.* It was Friday afternoon. I'd forgotten that before we got together, that had always been her favorite time to go for a cache. Sure enough, the rankings had changed for SumNumberOne. She logged a find, and it was a place I knew. Big Mesa. A bit of a drive, but it was big enough that she might still be there when I arrived. I backed out of her complex's parking lot and hit the gas.

Big Mesa was a wildlife preserve in the Sonoran Desert. It was a sprawling preserve with dozens of trails through its high plateaus, low valleys, and rolling hills in between. The hiking could be intense, especially during the heat of midday. Now, in the early evening, it was perfect. There was a single, very ambitious multiday geocache running through a large swath of the park, but there were smaller ones, too. You could do several in a day if you wanted. In the time it me took arrive, Summer had logged a second one. That told me what she was up to, but not where she'd go next. You could tackle any cache you wanted in any order. Summer's Jeep was a modified 4×4 that could park almost anywhere.

"All right, listen up," I told the dragonets when we arrived. They were waking up now, most of them, even Marcus Aurelius. "We're here to find Summer. You know Summer, right?"

Octavius chirped, and they all answered in what sounded affirmative.

"Good. Spread out, but I want you to stay in small groups. Two or three of you. Search around and come back when you find her."

I started hiking the main trail and the dragons took to wing around me. They were a little unfocused at first, playing hide-and-seek among the cacti and chasing each other in the air. I yelled, and eventually they got to work. They swung out over the hills and valleys. Most of the time I couldn't see them, and I wished I'd thought to bring GPS tracking. But the batteries weren't charged on their collars anyway. Besides, it felt wrong to go high tech on this. Just as it felt wrong to wait and ambush her at her condo.

At last, two dragons came wheeling back, crooning for me. Octavius and Marcus Aurelius. The biggest brother and the runt. They spotted me, circling, and calling down, then clearly indicated a direction. North.

Naturally, the trail I was on ran east-west, and the way north lay over a steep ridge riddled with loose rock and sharp cacti. I had my hiking boots on, but was wearing shorts. This could be miserable. Still, the clock was ticking and if I missed this chance I might not get another. I marched uphill, trying to skirt the cacti. It almost worked, but I slid on the loose rock and jammed into sharp spines two different times. I gritted my teeth and kept going. The ridgetop was a plateau and the dragonets, now joined by at least two others, were directing me across it.

I found her on the far side, checking her GPS watch as she hiked uphill. She wore olive green shorts, hiking boots, and a white tank top. She'd pulled her hair back in a ponytail, but I could tell she'd had it cut much shorter. And had a streak of it colored pink. *God, she's gorgeous.* She wore sunglasses, of course. Which made it hard to read the expression on her face when she saw me and stopped.

"Um, hi," I said, in the world's least ambitious opening. "I'm back."

"I can see that," she said. "What do you want?"

"To see you and talk to you." I started down the slope toward her, sliding more than stepping in the lose scree.

"Why?"

I gained the bottom. From her stance—hands on her hips, frowning at me, eyes inscrutable behind her sunglasses—I didn't dare go any closer. "Well, I missed you."

She made a scoffing noise. "Right."

"I did!"

"It doesn't matter," she said. "I'm done. *We're* done." She waved me off and started to turn away.

"I don't want this to be over."

"Then you shouldn't have gone to Antarctica. And Australia."

"I know."

"You never called. You hardly ever texted. It was like I didn't exist, except to stay here and look after *your* dragons."

"I'm sorry. I wasn't thinking about you and what you were going through."

"No, and that's the problem. You never do, Noah."

I thought that was unfair. I thought about her all the time. But arguing for the sake of truth wouldn't help here. "I said I was sorry."

"I have my own life, you know. I have dreams and responsibilities."

"I know, I was being selfish. An—"

"Yes, you were."

I inhaled slowly, trying to keep myself calm. If she turned away and left, I knew I'd never have another chance with her. Right there, in that moment, that was all I really wanted. "I was going to say that I'm working on it. I want to be better."

"Right."

"I already told Evelyn no more travel."

She scoffed and dropped her arms. "So what? There'll be some new emergency somewhere, an infestation of fat guinea pigs on a tropical paradise. You'll dump the dragons at my condo and take off again."

"No." Firstly because that was a ridiculous scenario. "I talked to my group, too. Dave is going to step up and handle the deployments from now on."

"Dave, your old rival who you didn't even want in the building," she said flatly.

"I was wrong about that, too." I risked a tiny step closer to her. My ankles stung from the cactus spines. "He's the right person for it. One of three things I realized while I was away. The second one is that I'm going to stay here, and be here, and leave work at work."

"Good for you. But I'm not going to be here. I'll be in San Francisco."

I despised San Francisco with every fiber of my being but I couldn't say that. "Do you really want to leave Phoenix? Leave the company where you've done so much? Just for more money?"

She looked away from me. "Actually my company countered. They matched the offer."

Oh, my God. "Then why the hell are you leaving?"

"It's a good job."

"You already had a good job," I said.

"Well, I wanted a fresh start."

I took another step. "Don't run away because of me. Seriously. I'm a dumbass. I almost died several times over the last two weeks."

"You almost *died*?"

"Yeah. Nearly fell in a crevasse in Antarctica, and threw up my insides on the way to and from."

"I told you to be careful. That's literally the last thing I told you."

So you do care a little. "I also tried to hug several poisonous reptiles in Australia."

"I think you mean *venomous* reptiles."

"Oh, not you, too!"

She started to smile, but it disappeared just as fast. "Well, you made your choices. And I made mine. I'm not going to sit around with dragons tearing up my condo because you want to play hero. What if it was..." She trailed off and looked away.

"What?"

"Nothing."

I really wanted to know, but I didn't want to risk pressing her. "Look, if San Francisco is what you want, that's okay. But it doesn't have to mean *we* are over."

She shook her head. "I'm not doing the long-distance thing."

"I'm not asking that. I'm asking to come with you." Even as the words tumbled out, I kind of didn't believe I'd said them. But I'd pay any price if she wouldn't walk way. That was the only thing that mattered.

It caught her by surprise, and she finally looked at me. "What about your job?"

I shrugged. "They'll understand. Maybe I can work remotely, but if not, I can always find a different one."

"You'd leave Build-A-Dragon?"

"If you let me go with you, I will."

She made a *psh* sound and shook her head. "You're just saying that."

"I'm serious." It felt safe enough for me to move closer to her. "I love you. My trips are over, and you get to say where we go. Just let me come, please. I'm really sorry, and I want to come."

"To San Francisco?"

This was it. If I agreed, I committed, and I couldn't back down from that. *Go big or go home.* "Yes."

She stared at me, her eyes unreadable behind the sunglasses. A rising terror stabbed into my gut. I'd put it all on the line and it still wasn't going to be enough. *God, why did I screw up so badly?*

At last, she sighed. And gave a hint of a smile. "Why do you have to make my life so complicated?"

"Apparently it's what I'm good at."

She smiled, almost a laugh. "Better than you know."

I held my breath but said nothing. I just stood there.

"I love you, too," she said. "I guess."

I will take that. I moved in and put my arms around her. She let me pull her close. I'd forgotten how soft her skin was. Her hair smelled faintly of wildflowers. Familiar and wonderful. The streak of pink was definitely new and not a trick of the light. "What's with the hair?"

Now she did laugh, and she leaned in to me. It was the most incredible feeling in the world. "I said I wanted a change, didn't I?"

"It's, um ... kind of hot."

She smacked my chest, but gently. "Stop it."

I let her go, but kept my hands on her. "So, what do you want to do?"

"What do *you* want to do?"

"Whatever makes you happy. If that's the Rice-A-Roni capital, I'm in." Inwardly I was trying not to vomit at the thought of the city and the food. I said I was all in, and somehow that was freeing. She got to call the shots now. And I was fine with that.

She chewed on her lip. "I guess I could take my firm's counter. It was nice. But I already sold my condo."

"That's not a problem."

"Um, yeah, it is. I have to be out in three weeks."

I waved this off. "That's plenty of time."

"To do what? Have you *seen* the real estate market? I got, like, three offers in six hours."

"No, silly. To move in with me."

She put her hands on top of mine. "What?"

"I want you to move in with me. I know, it's not quite as fancy as your building with the premium shower installation and—"

She threw her arms around me, stood on her toes, and kissed me. *Hard.* I absolutely let her, and rejoiced in how good it felt. She pulled back. "I was beginning to think you'd never ask."

I was aghast. "You've thought about this?"

"Of course." She cleared her throat. "I *will* be making a few changes."

God help me. "I can't wait."

We walked back, holding hands, to where she had parked her Jeep on a thirty-degree slope. The dragons were playing a game of tag in midair, chirping and squealing at one another.

"It's going to be a little crowded with all of us sharing the same condo," Summer said.

"Only for a little bit," I said. "That's the other thing I wanted to run by you."

Four weeks later, we returned to Big Mesa. After hours spent poring over the hills and valleys on the topographic map, I found a place that looked just right. Summer drove us out in the Jeep so we could get close. I brought burritos and made sure the dragonets all ate their fill. I'd laced them with vitamins to give them an extra boost.

"Are you sure about this?" Summer asked.

"Don't ask me that."

"But what if something happens?"

"We have to hope it won't. But you can't dwell on the unpredictable."

"I guess."

It was a good hour's hike to the place I'd wanted to reach. The vegetation was thicker here and the trails smaller. It was remote, but the terrain showed promise. This part of Big Mesa actually had a shallow river running through a gorge. Frogs sang from the reed-lined banks. There were berry bushes on the hillsides closest to us. The rocks on top of the ridges were flat and angular, creating all kinds of nooks and crannies that made good shelters. I called the dragons down to me and made them land, so I knew they were listening.

"You guys like it here?" I asked.

They chirped in agreement.

"Good. This is going to be your new home. Do you understand that, *home*?"

They looked at me, a little confused, maybe a little scared. I felt the same way, too.

I pointed down at the valley. "There's water down there, and things you can hunt for food. No more human food, okay?"

Marcus Aurelius seemed to deflate at this.

"You guys can hunt your own food. You're dragons, remember? Clever little dragons, and you'll—" I sort of choked up there. It took me a second to talk again. "You'll be happier out here. You can stay as a pack and look after each other."

"Be smart and be safe," Summer told them. "There are caves to hide in at night. It gets cold out in the desert, so stay together to keep warm."

I sure as hell hope they understand all of this. That was the truly terrifying part. I thought they did, I hoped they would, but I didn't know for sure. The only certainty was that they were dragons, and they belonged in a place where they could fly free.

"We'll come to visit as often as we can, okay? Starting tomorrow. You guys be good."

Most of the dragons took off. They swooped down to the water, landing and splashing in the shallows. One of them, Nero I think, saw a frog and jumped on it. The others crowded close to him, but he shouldered free and ate the thing in one bite. Then he started prowling among the reeds, looking for more. The others followed.

One dragon took off and flew back, gliding down to land on my shoulder. Octavius, of course. Summer hugged him and then walked away. I think mainly so I wouldn't see her crying.

I stroked his head and scratched him behind the ears. "You're the leader, little buddy. The other dragons will follow you. Keep them safe, all right? I know you can do it." He nuzzled me, crooning softly in my ear.

I patted him, and pried his claws. "Go on, now."

He took off, flapping to gain height, and dove down to land among his siblings on the shoreline. They had a different look from the dragons I'd watched prowl the banks in Australia, but the instincts were there. They belonged here in the wild.

We watched them for a time. Then Summer laced her fingers in mine and tugged me gently.

"We'll come back soon," she said.

"Can I bring burritos?"

"Noah!" She shook her head. "All right, maybe the first time. But no more."

"It's a deal." I kept her hand in mine and walked back the way we'd come. I'd let my dragons go, but the wildest and best thing in my life? I was keeping her.

Acknowledgements:

It takes a community to publish a book, and there are a number of people who helped with this one. I'll start by thanking my publisher, Toni Weisskopf, for continuing to support this series. I'm grateful to my editor, Griffin Barber, for carrying on the work of my previous editors, Jim Minz and Tony Daniel. I'd also like to thank Joy Freeman, Leah Brandtner, Carol Russo, Rabbit Boyett, Steve Roman, John Watson, and the entire team at Baen Books. Dave Seeley is the incredibly talented artist behind the cover art.

Thank you also to Brady McReynolds and the entire team at JABberwocky Literary Agency. I remain indebted to Paul Stevens and Donald Maass, who first helped me fulfill my dream of writing science fiction for Baen.

Thanks to my writing community—Michael Mammay, Tim Akers, Diana Urban, and my Tavern friends—for helping me stay in the game. Thank you to my family for putting up with the late-night writing sessions and distant stares.

Finally, thank you to everyone who reads my books!